Charity and the Devil

By Emma V. Leech

****

Published by: Emma V. Leech.

Copyright (c) Emma V. Leech 2018

Cover Art: Victoria Cooper

ASIN No.: B07F2YT4QP

ISBN-13: 978-1727238440

ISBN-10: 1727238443

All rights reserved. Without limiting the rights under copyright reserved above, no part of this publication may be reproduced, stored in or introduced into a retrieval system, or transmitted, in any form, or by any means (electronic, mechanical, photocopying, recording, or otherwise) without the prior written permission of both the copyright owner and the above publisher of this book. This is a work of fiction. Names, characters, places, brands, media, and incidents are either the product of the author's imagination or are used fictitiously. The author acknowledges the trademarked status and trademark owners of various products referenced in this work of fiction, which have been used without permission. The publication/use of these trademarks is not authorized, associated with, or sponsored by the trademark owners. The ebook version and print version are licensed for your personal enjoyment only.

The ebook version may not be re-sold or given away to other people. If you would like to share the ebook with another person, please purchase an additional copy for each person you share it with. No identification with actual persons (living or deceased), places, buildings, and products is inferred.

Table of Contents

Chapter 1	1
Chapter 2	11
Chapter 3	20
Chapter 4	30
Chapter 5	41
Chapter 6	54
Chapter 7	65
Chapter 8	76
Chapter 9	87
Chapter 10	100
Chapter 11	110
Chapter 12	121
Chapter 13	132
Chapter 14	141
Chapter 15	151
Chapter 16	160
Chapter 17	168
Chapter 18	178
Chapter 19	187
Chapter 20	196
Chapter 21	206
Chapter 22	216
Chapter 23	223
Chapter 24	232
Epilogue	244
A Slight Indiscretion	252
Chapter 1	254
Want more Emma?	263
About Me!	264
Other Works by Emma V. Leech	266

Audio Books	269
To Dare a Duke	270
Dare to be Wicked	272
Dying for a Duke	274
The Key to Erebus	276
The Dark Prince	278
Acknowledgements	280

Chapter 1

"Wherein the devil is in a dark place."

Mr Phillip Ogden had served the Devlin family all his adult life. He had worked his way up to his position as steward, the pinnacle of his career. The previous viscount had been an admirable man, the kind it made you proud to work for. He'd been politically active and well respected throughout England. A voice of reason in the House of Lords.

Mr Ogden looked up to regard the current viscount and gave an inward sigh. He pasted a smile to his face and hoped his expression remained one of sympathy, though sympathy was not an emotion that came to mind.

"I understand your predicament, my lord. However, as I've explained, the Kendall family live at Brasted Farm." Mr Ogden looked down at the papers in his hand, noting the fact he had crumpled them in his agitation. "They are excellent tenants and the family have lived there for close to a century."

He remembered the lovely Miss Kendall's devastation as he'd outlined the viscount's intentions when he'd first realised them, two weeks earlier. He'd rather enjoyed being a comfort to her. It had been all he could do, though, to give them a little warning of the fate in store for them.

"They have nowhere else to go and—"

"What of it?" The words were cold, callous, devoid of interest in the plight of a family who had already experienced their fair share of suffering. "I need the funds and that fat old squire has been nosing after that farm since I was a boy. It will be a quick sale—you said so yourself—and I'll be out from Blackehart's grasp once and for all."

Until next time. Mr Ogden bit back the words with difficulty. Luke Linton, the sixth Viscount Devlin had a devil of a temper. He would not welcome such observations. Not for the first time Ogden wondered if the old viscount's wife had taken the fellow for a fool, for there were not two more different men in the whole of England than the present and the late viscount. While his father had been prudent, serious and the model of propriety, his son....

Ogden gritted his teeth. He'd worked every second of his whole damn life for what he could claim now, while circumstance had handed this man everything on a gilded plate... and he'd thrown it all in his father's face.

Devlin turned to him and Ogden had to fight to hold his gaze. It was unnerving: crystalline blue, cold, and cruel.

"They'll have a little over two months to vacate," Devlin said, the words clipped, indicating that further observations on the welfare of the inhabitants of Brasted Farm would not be met with pleasure. "I leave first thing in the morning. I'll ride the first stage and stop off with Lord Jenson, before accompanying him into town. My valet went to London this morning and you may also send my belongings direct. Jenson's man will see to me for a day or two. I'll return in eight weeks, by which time I expect this affair to be in order. Is that clear?"

Mr Ogden inclined his head to acknowledge that it was indeed clear. The less he said the better at this point. At least he could tell Miss Kendall that he had done his best to help her with a clear conscience. He hoped she'd be grateful to him for his efforts and sighed, remembering her lovely face.

The viscount had turned away to stare out of his study window, giving Mr Ogden a view of a coat from the finest tailor in the country clinging to broad shoulders and a lean, muscular frame. Jealousy stirred, and Ogden fought it back with difficulty. Lord

Devlin had everything: money, title, and looks that made women sigh with longing, and what had he done with it? The fool had run through his fortune in little more than a decade, whoring and drinking and gambling. Sometimes Ogden believed he'd done it on purpose, out of spite for the old man, knowing it would have him turning in his grave, but even Devlin wasn't that vindictive... was he?

The viscount turned back, an amused curl to his cruel mouth suggesting he knew exactly what Ogden was thinking. Ogden fought the flush that rose to his cheeks and wished that Devlin, thirteen years his junior, couldn't unnerve him with quite such ease.

"What are you waiting for?" Devlin challenged, irritation threading his precise, sharp edged voice. "You have your instructions, now get out."

Ogden swallowed his anger and his pride, bowed, and retreated to brood in private.

***

Lord Devlin snorted as Ogden closed the study door behind him. Poor Ogden, trying so hard to give good advice and wringing his hands as everything fell apart. His father's man. Loyal to his last breath and still trying to pass on the old bastard's advice from beyond the grave. Dev wondered why he kept him on. Some masochistic tendency, perhaps, or perhaps he just enjoyed watching the man's distress as he descended further into the dark. His father had missed that; he'd died just as Dev was getting into his stride, though most people had blamed his excesses for the old viscount's demise. Pity. He'd loved to have seen the horror and distress in his father's eyes as he saw what little was left of the great fortune he'd worked so hard to amass.

Dev poured himself a drink. He lifted the fine crystal to his lips and savoured the quality of the liquor. How long before he was finding oblivion in cheap liquor in some seedy gin palace He almost welcomed it. Almost. A run-in with Mr Blackehart had made him question his own quest for self-destruction. Perhaps he valued his life a little more than he'd imagined. Blackehart was not a man to be taken lightly. The truth was he'd made Dev's blood run cold, and that was no easy task, hence the sudden need to divest himself of property. The man had demanded payment in full and Dev had to make good on it, or he might fulfil his father's prophecy about his inevitable demise sooner than anyone had anticipated. The only way to meet such a sum quickly was to sell land and property, with the added advantage that his father would have despised him for it.

Brasted Farm wasn't large, but it had good soil. Good enough for growing wheat and barley, something which was rare around Dartmoor which was only fit for grazing.

Tomorrow, Dev was meeting the dreadful Blackehart himself, to show him the papers that had been drawn up between him and the squire. While the idea occurred to him, Dev removed the heavy gold signet ring which bore the Devlin seal and put it in his desk drawer. He wouldn't put it past Blackehart to have the shirt from his back in lieu of payment, but he'd not be able to take what wasn't there. He only hoped that the proof of the sale being set in motion would be enough to make the man wait a little longer, knowing payment would be made in full.

Freeing himself of the man's grasp on his throat was tantalising. He'd been looking over his shoulder for weeks now. Perhaps after this meeting he'd be able to breathe again. He snorted. Perhaps not. He wasn't fool enough to believe his debts alone had caused his misery. They were merely symptoms of it.

He still wasn't sure what he hoped to achieve, or what left the hollow ache gaping in his chest. A desire to grind his father's hopes and dreams into the dirt? Oh, yes. He wanted that. Yet it had been more than that, once at least.

A knock at the door sounded and had Dev turning on his heel. He barked at whoever was fool enough to disturb him to come in.

Charity and the Devil

To his irritation, Ogden entered once more. There was an uncharacteristic, challenging look in the fellow's eyes that Dev could almost admire.

"A letter for you, my lord," he said evenly. "I thought perhaps you should see it before you left in the morning."

"Leave it on my desk," Dev muttered, pouring himself another drink. He suspected he knew who the letter was from and he knew damn well Ogden would recognise the precise lettering of the woman in question. It wouldn't be the first he'd received. No doubt Miss Kendall had thought of another colourful stream of invective with which to assassinate his character. One had to admire her vocabulary if nothing else. She'd even come to the house herself on more than one occasion. Dev had refused to see her. The last thing he needed was some overwrought female vacillating between fury and tears. Besides, it would change nothing. Dev's heart was a dead thing, blackened and shrivelled from lack of use. No feminine tears had the power to move him, as many had discovered to their cost.

He sat brooding for hours. The tray brought to him for dinner sat untouched while the decanter at his elbow emptied. His mind turned, going over the past as it often did and fuelling his despair. By the time the first glimmers of daylight lightened the skies, his mood was as bleak and pitiless as a frozen sea.

More from boredom than interest, Dev reached for Miss Kendall's letter. The last one had made him laugh out loud at her audacity, and entertainment of any variety would be welcome at this moment. He picked up the missive, sliding his finger beneath the seal and settling down to read the dreadful creature's words. He wondered what she looked like. As Dev's experience of women was of the perfumed and pampered variety, a woman who would live in isolation and run a small farm was outside his experience. He conjured the image of a short, dumpy figure with large, capable hands, a squint, and a moustache. Mr Ogden knew her, but he'd never commented on her outside of expressing sympathy for her and her family's predicament. If she'd been pretty, the fellow would have married her himself, wouldn't he? He must be pushing forty. It wasn't as if there were many options for a fellow in this backwater, either.

Dev scanned the missive in his hand and any amusement he might have felt fell away as Miss Kendall dissected his character with a surgeon's dexterity. Something like fury fired in his blood. How dare she? How dare she write such... such....

Dev took a breath, getting himself under control. As he got to his feet, he swayed a little as the contents of the decanter made its presence known. The insolent baggage. Well, enough was enough. She'd wanted to see him, to put her case to him in person and he would damn well give her the opportunity. This time, however, he'd have a few choice words of his own.

He sent the stables into chaos, yelling with fury for someone to ready his horse even though it was not yet daylight. Men stumbled into the yard, bleary eyed as they pulled on breeches and boots and scurried to do his bidding.

Dev had not been to Brasted Farm since he was a boy, dragged about by his father to show him the responsibilities he would one day face. He had a vague recollection of a handsome stone building and thought he remembered where it was. It had been a long while, but he'd ridden the moors as a young man and had a good sense of direction. It was at least two hours ride from here, taking the road. If he cut across the wild moors, then he might do it in an hour. He'd arrive early enough to give the woman the shock of her life. She'd still be in her nightgown at such an early hour, and if she thought he'd wait for her to dress and prettify herself to face him she'd be sorely disappointed. The thought satisfied him.

With fury and indignation still burning in his blood, alongside a skin-full of cognac, Dev rode off to meet his nemesis.

***

Charity and the Devil

Charity Kendall stared at her bedroom ceiling. It was the same ceiling she'd stared at as a little girl, dreaming of all the things of which little girls dreamed. At least, she assumed she'd dreamed like that. It was hard to remember. It seemed a long time ago she'd been a girl at all. She knew she should be up and about already, but she felt worn down. The weight of her worries seemed heavier at this hour of the morning, filling the room in the hours before the daylight crept in. Worries snuck under the curtains ahead of the first fingers of daylight, stealing the air from the room, smothering her in its suffocating grasp, pressing down on her. She took a breath, forcing the air into her lungs even though her chest protested, unwilling to expand. Such wallowing was beneath her. Dramatics and hysteria had never been her style. She left that to her twin, Kit. He was the dramatic one in the family, full of romance and fire and dark musings. Charity had little enough energy to consider what they ought to have for dinner, let alone find anger enough that her 'art' was misunderstood. Not that she had any art. She hadn't a creative bone in her body.

In her spare moments, such as they were between running a farm and raising a family, she had been considering their options. There were two abandoned farms in the region. Charity had hoped to move the family to whichever one of them suited best. On visiting however they'd discovered the buildings in a state of decay, the land sick from neglect, and a raft of jobs so overwhelming it would take years to turn them around. Years and a great deal of money they didn't have.

The only solution was to go to Bristol as their Uncle implored them to do. He lived there with his own family but was fond of his nieces and nephews. The man worried for them she knew. As a doctor he could keep a closer eye on Kit's poor health too. Yet living in a city, leaving the moors and this place which had been her home since birth … it cut her heart to ribbons.

Charity's fist hit the pillow as she pummelled it into a more comfortable shape and turned onto her side with a huff. There was one thing she *could* get angry about, no matter how exhausted she was. Anger was a hopeless, fragile description for the fury which filled her veins. Far more than mere anger. It was just possible she might even do the hateful man bodily harm, should the two of them ever be in a room together. Lord Devlin must know that too, as he'd refused to see her, despite the many times she'd called.

Frustration had burned so hard that it had reduced her to writing vitriolic letters to let off steam. Her last letter was keeping her awake. She suspected she may have gone a little too far.

Just a little.

She swallowed, unable to move the heavy bricklike sensation that seemed to lie somewhere in her throat. Well, all right then, more than a little. She pressed her hands to her cheeks. They were scalding beneath her rather sweaty palms. Oh, dear Lord. What had she done? It wasn't as if the wretched man cared a jot for what happened to her and those she loved. No amount of rage or tears or begging or screaming would have changed his mind. She'd known that, yet the impotence of being able to do nothing as he tossed her family onto the street like rubbish… well, it had unbalanced her mind. Temporarily of course, Charity added, imagining putting her case before a magistrate. Which was all too likely if Devlin ever saw that letter. Nausea roiled as her stomach clenched and twisted, but before she could indulge in a rare display of self-pity and bawl her eyes out, her bedroom door flew open.

"Charity, oh, Charity!"

Charity started and flung back the covers as her seven-year-old sister flew into her arms, clutching her about the waist. Their brother, John, three years' Jane's senior, hung back, white faced and solemn as the little girl sobbed her heart out.

"Whatever is all this?" Charity demanded "What's happened?"

"Oh, oh, don't let them take him away, Charity," Jane pleaded, fisting Charity's nightdress in her hands. "It was an accident! He didn't mean to kill him."

Charity and the Devil

"What?" Charity gasped, noting with horror that John just swallowed instead of leaping in and telling Jane not to be such a silly goose as she might have expected. "Killed who? Whatever has happened?"

"It was an accident, Charity," John said, his voice trembling with the effort of keeping calm. "I swear it."

"Well, of course it was," Charity murmured. "There's no question of that."

She sat up, her mind working overtime as she swung her legs out of bed and grabbed a faded pelisse to pull on over her night rail.

"What were you doing out at this time Wait… no. Don't tell me."

She lifted her hand to halt his reply and groaned. She could see it now. John was determined to be the man of the family as Kit spent most of his time with his head in the clouds and his mind on poetry. She could see it now. The boy had crept out to go hunting rabbits and his devoted little sister had foisted her company upon him despite his protests.

"I got two," John replied, a little defiant despite the circumstances and the fact that she had expressly forbidden him to leave the farm before daylight and never, ever, alone.

Charity sighed and sat down again as Jane returned her arms to her waist, clinging like a limpet and sobbing. She stroked her little sister's hair. "You'd best tell me, and quick."

"He came out of nowhere," John said, looking like he might be sick at any moment. "I was just lining up a shot and suddenly this huge horse came out from behind the tor. It gave us such a fright that my finger squeezed the trigger."

Jane sobbed harder as John recounted the sorry tale. "The horse reared up, screaming and the fellow tried to hold him, but he couldn't. He fell a-and h-h-hit his head on a rock and there was blood everywhere and h-he was s-s-so still, Charity." John swallowed, tears in his eyes, his narrow chest heaving.

Charity got to her feet and gave John a reassuring hug, her expression calm. "Don't fret. Head wounds can bleed prodigiously, it doesn't mean the fellow is dead. Jane, fetch Kit, tell him to get Mr Baxter and bring the cart, and then go finish your chores, everything will be all right. John, you'd best show me."

John nodded, looking a little braver as he led her out of the room and down the stairs.

Chapter 2

"Wherein a body lies alone on the moor."

Charity was not a fanciful girl. Legends abounded on this part of Dartmoor, full of ghosts, fairies, and spirits, but none of them had ever stirred her imagination. She'd been too busy trying to keep her family fed and the farm running to have time for a fit of the vapours or indulge in flights of fantasy. As she walked the moor now, however, looking for a possibly dead body as the mists rose in the early morning sunlight, her flesh prickled with foreboding. There was some sixth sense tugging at her conscience, warning her that what happened today would have consequences beyond anything she could imagine.

She shivered, though it wasn't cold, and clutched her coat around her. As John gave a shout, Charity turned and gestured to Kit who was following behind with the cart. Her twin ought not be out in the damp of the morning, his health was too frail, but there was nothing to be done. If there was a body she'd not get it in the cart with just Mr Baxter their handyman to help.

To her dismay, as she hurried towards her little brother, she discovered his words were not those of a hysterical boy, frightened by the dark and an overactive imagination.

He was a big man, handsome too, despite the blood and his dishevelled appearance. His hair was black, his skin a rather olive complexion that was striking despite his current pallor. With relief, Charity found his heart beating strong and regular beneath his broad chest.

"He's far from dead, John," she said, casting her brother a reassuring smile.

John sat down on the damp ground with a thud and put his head in his hands. Charity ruffled his hair but said nothing, giving the young man a moment to gather himself.

"Knocked out cold, eh?" Kit said, observing the body as he strode nearer.

Charity nodded as Kit and Mr Baxter got closer. Ralph Baxter and his wife Beryl had been at Brasted Farm since before Charity was born and had worked for both her grandparents and parents. The farm was all they knew. Mr Baxter was as skinny and spare as his wife was round, and the dark cloud to her sunshine. They were an odd couple but as much a part of Charity's life and the farm as the ancient stones of the building itself. She wondered what would happen to them now but shook the maudlin thoughts away and returned her attention to the problem at hand.

"Mr Baxter, you take his shoulders, Kit and I will take a leg."

Baxter glowered at the body. "Fellow will cause trouble, mark my words," he said, his voice heavy with foreboding as he spat on the ground at his feet. "There was a dead crow in the courtyard last night. 'Tis an ill omen."

Charity held back the desire to roll her eyes and curse with difficulty. She looked up to see Kit's lips twitch with amusement. Her brother knew of her scepticism for anything she couldn't see with her own eyes. "Jolly good," she said briskly. "Now, let's get him home and see if we can't patch him up."

They had the devil's own job getting him into the cart they used to go to market. The fellow weighed a ton and between Charity, Baxter's skinny frame, and Kit's poor health. they made a wretched mess of it. With chagrin, Charity observed that if the man hadn't had a concussion before they'd got him in the cart, he damn well would have after.

"Charity," Kit said, staring at the stranger at their feet as they jolted back to the farm, "look at his clothes."

Charity and the Devil

Charity nodded. The fine silk waistcoat and beautifully tailored coat the man wore hadn't escaped her. She'd noted his hands, too: softer than hers despite the bulk of him. Not a man who laboured for a living. He was a fine gent, whoever he was. She hoped he wasn't the vindictive kind, hell bent on causing trouble.

"What on earth was he doing out here at this hour of the morning?" she wondered.

An isolated place, Brasted Farm was the only dwelling in the area and on the road to nowhere, the nearest village being an hour away. They'd had neighbours a scant half hour's ride away until two years ago, when the old couple had given up and moved to be closer to their children and civilisation. Life on Dartmoor was harsh and unforgiving, and the winters were cruel. You had to be tough to survive here. Tough, stubborn, and stupid, Kit would say with his crooked smile.

"Lost more than likely," Kit said, his expression thoughtful. "Did you catch a whiff of his breath? The fellow was drunk as a wheelbarrow, likely why he couldn't control that flashy mount of his." He cast a rather covetous look at the huge black horse tied to the back of the old cart. It was no wonder it had startled John, appearing out of the mists like an ebony monster. "Prettiest piece of horseflesh I've ever seen," Kit added with a sigh. "Must have cost an arm and a leg."

"You'll be able to afford such things too, when you're a famous poet," Charity said, solemnly.

Kit grinned at her, his handsome face lighting up at the familiar joke, and her heart ached for him. Poets spent their lives starving in garrets and they both knew it all too well—that and dying young. That Kit was probably doomed to do exactly that was something Charity refused to contemplate, hence the jokes about him being wealthy and successful. Kit would be different. He had to be.

As Brasted Farm came into view, for once the skies showed a glorious blue. The high moor was a dramatic landscape, with far-reaching views, and the farmhouse was a large determined granite building with a grey slate roof. It huddled into the countryside, stubborn and a little grim, presiding over a cluster of outbuildings, daring the moors to do their worst. A few stunted firs clustered in the meagre shelter of the low, gnarly, grey stone wall that surrounded the farm, facing the north wind.

Charity loved it.

"Look!" John cried out from his position at the front of the cart beside Mr Baxter. "There's someone at the farm."

Charity angled her neck to look and gave an exclamation of joy. "Uncle Edward!"

"It never is?" Kit questioned, standing up in the back of the cart to get a better look. "Well, I'll be damned."

Mr Baxter snorted, turning his head to give the still unconscious body in the cart a look of deep distrust. "Aye, we'll all be damned I reckon. Whoever that fellow is… he's got the luck of the devil."

***

Once his patient had been seen to, Uncle Edward—who by happy circumstance was a doctor—settled down to a jovial breakfast with his nephews and nieces.

"Well, well, isn't this a welcome sight," he said, the white whiskers at his cheeks bristling as he beamed at the laden plate of bacon, eggs and fried bread that Mrs Baxter set before him.

"No one makes breakfast like old Batty," Kit agreed, stuffing his mouth with bacon as the lady herself clouted him about the ear.

"Mind your tongue, you dreadful young scape grace," she scolded, though there was amusement in her eyes and no heat behind the words.

"Sorry, Batty," Kit mumbled through his bacon, his brown eyes glinting with mirth.

Mrs Baxter snorted and returned her attention to frying more bacon as Charity filled her uncle's cup with tea.

"You really think he'll be all right?" she asked, still anxious that their guest had not yet awoken.

Edward cast her a sympathetic glance before reaching for his tea. "Head wounds are tricky things," he said, repeating his words from earlier that morning. "They can do odd things to a fellow, but he's young and fit and strong. As I said, he badly bruised his arm and shoulder in the fall. Nothing was broken, from what I can tell, but he'll be feeling pretty sorry for himself when he comes to. I've left laudanum for the pain and you've got the other instructions written for his care." He set down his teacup and picked up his knife and fork again, spearing another piece of bacon. "I'm afraid you have a house guest for a good few days, though, depending on how he recovers."

Charity nodded, biting her lip. They had been fortunate that the man had landed in their midst during one of their uncle's visits. It was a long journey from Bristol for their closest relative, who was not as young as he once was. He was a kindly man though and he worried for Kit, placing about as much faith as they did in the local doctor.

"And how are you, Kit?" Edward asked, striving for nonchalance. "I'll have to be off again tomorrow, but I'll give you a once over before I go."

There was a flash of irritation in Kit's dark eyes before he pasted a smile to his face.

"I'm in fighting form, Uncle," he replied, his smile stretching into a grimace. "You know the summer is always better for me."

"Hmph," Edward replied, his voice noncommittal. "Until it rains."

Kit sighed and gestured to the cloudless skies beyond the window. "I have it on good authority it will be a long, hot summer," he said, winking at Charity.

Another of Mr Baxter's predictions, though he'd said it would be too hot and too dry, the fruit would be no more than little bullets, and their garden would die of thirst. Ever a shining light in the darkness was Ralph Baxter.

"There's a first time for everything I suppose," Edward said, chuckling as he returned his attention to his breakfast with gusto.

***

The sound of conversation and laughter filtering through his clouded mind was the first inkling Dev had that he wasn't at home. *Laughter* and *home* were words that did not go together. Pain seared through his tender brain as he tried to open his eyes and an unfamiliar room swam into view: white painted, with heavy oak beams. He hissed at the sunlight that flooded through a small leaded window and shielded his eyes with his arm.

"Oh, I'm so sorry!"

A feminine voice made him start with surprise and he tried to focus his gaze on the blurry figure that hurried to the window. Whoever she was, she tugged the curtains across, blocking out the daylight.

"I just came up to check on you. I had no idea you were awake."

Dev swallowed and tried to sit up, but his head swam, and pain lanced through his arm, which felt heavy and peculiar.

"Oh, don't do that," the woman admonished him, her voice rather stern. "Here, you must be thirsty."

A slender but surprisingly strong arm slipped behind his neck. She supported his throbbing head and brought a glass of water to his parched lips. Dev drank deeply, grateful despite the indignity of being at some strange woman's mercy. What the devil had happened to him?

"Forgive me," the voice said, becoming increasingly disembodied. "I'm afraid there was a little laudanum in that. My uncle is a doctor, you see, and he said you must rest as much as possible for the moment. I'm Miss Charity Kendall, by the way," she added. "What's your name, sir?"

Dev blinked, confusion flooding his tired mind. Where was he?

"I'm...." He paused, feeling daunted, and shocked at the roughness of his voice. A name lingered, just out of reach on the tip of his tongue. It was an important name but....

Damn it. Who was Charity Kendall?

He found a pair of wide brown eyes watching him, filled with concern. Well, he could sleep a little if those eyes were watching over him. The perplexing question of why he of all people needed charity circled his brain with no clear answer until sleep, and the laudanum, pulled him under.

***

"Anything?"

Charity raised her head as Kit poked his head around the door.

"No. He awoke for a moment, but he seemed rather disorientated. I put a drop of laudanum in his water, so he'll sleep awhile now." She bit her lip, looking at the big figure with some misgiving and no little curiosity.

Kit stepped into the room and gave the fellow a dark look before putting his hands on Charity's shoulders. Turning her around he guided her out of the room.

"He's not a motherless lamb that needs feeding, nor the runt of the litter, nor a lame duck," he said, as he closed the door on the sleeping figure. "So don't go trying to fix him. Uncle Edward has done that and, as soon as he's fit enough, he's on his way."

"Kit," Charity began, folding her arms and turning to face him. "I have no intention—"

"Of course you do," Kit said, a pitying look in his eyes. "You can't help yourself. You've made it your life's work to look after this farm, Mr and Mrs Baxter, me, John and Jane, and whatever else lands in your lap. For heaven's sake, Charity, what about you?"

Charity glowered at him, the familiar argument poking at fears and uncertainties she did not wish to face.

"You know being thrown out of this place might be the best thing that ever happened to you," Kit continued, relentless now. "You might actually be forced out into the real world, you might even begin to live for yourself, instead of hiding yourself away here, buried alive."

"Oh, don't give me your dramatics, Kit," Charity hissed, turning in the narrow corridor to scowl at him. "I've neither the patience nor the stomach for it." She tutted and shook her head. "Buried alive indeed," she muttered, rolling her eyes at him before stomping down the stairs. Kit might have longed for London, for fame and notoriety, for the society of fellow artists but not her. She had given up on any fanciful notions of marrying and raising a family of her own. At twenty-five and with a farm and two young children to support, she had family enough and no time for day-dreaming. "Now if you'll excuse me," she added tartly, "I have work to do."

She didn't see the glimmer of concern in her brother's eyes as she closed the door on him, but she didn't need to see it. It was always there; the worry about how she would manage without the money he provided from his writing, meagre as it was. He seemed well enough now, and she prayed it might continue, but they were neither of them as romantic as all that. Consumption, or tuberculosis as her uncle referred to it, was a wicked hereditary disease and one that life here at Brasted Farm did nothing to hinder. It had killed their parents and Kit believed he'd not make old bones. Little they'd experienced in the past contradicted that assumption.

So, he wanted her to go out into the world, to find herself a husband who would support her and be kind to John and Jane. How in the world he supposed she could accomplish that without leaving them all to fend for themselves ...? She snorted at the idea. They wouldn't survive till the end of the week without her. The thought was reassuring, vindicating her lack of enthusiasm to face the real world. The world here was quite real enough for her, thank you very much.

With that argument settled, in her mind at least, Charity rolled up her sleeves and headed to the kitchen.

Chapter 3

"Wherein you should let sleeping devils lie."

Charity pressed the cool cloth to the stranger's forehead and he sighed, restless. Pain contorted his handsome face, though his colour had improved at least. He looked to be in his late twenties with a strong, square jaw, his beard showing thick and dark after days without shaving. His hair was jet black with a tendency to curl. Charity pushed it back, out of the way.

"There, there," she soothed, remembering nights caring for John and Jane during childhood illnesses, and more recently Kit as he thrashed and sweated, burning up with fever.

Kit would scold her if he knew she was here. He'd instructed that the fellow's care be seen to by Mr and Mrs Baxter but waking up to Mr Baxter would give anyone a migraine and poor Batty had enough on her plate. It wasn't because he was a handsome man and Charity was beyond curious about him. Not at all. It was her Christian duty to play the good Samaritan. Her name reminded her of that daily though, if she was being honest, she often cherished less than charitable thoughts about her fellow man.

It had been three days since they'd found him, and he'd woken at odd intervals, murmuring incoherently. Kit had been with him on those occasions and said nothing sensible had passed the fellow's lips, least of all his name. So, a stranger he remained.

It was another warm day, the summer in full bloom as June gave way to July. Charity reached over to the basin of cool water on the bedside table and wrung the cloth out once more. As she turned back to press it to his head once more she gave a gasp of surprise.

A pair of startling blue eyes stared at her, bright and lucid and at such odds with his colouring. They were a pale blue, a rather unnerving shade, piercing as they watched her.

"My, you gave me a turn," Charity said, covering her heart with her free hand and blushing a little. She might live in the middle of nowhere, but the impropriety of being in a man's bedroom alone was not lost on her. "How are you feeling?"

He blinked, and she could not help but envy his thick, dark eyelashes as they swept down and briefly hid those disturbing eyes.

"Thirsty," he replied, his voice guarded.

Charity supposed he was bound to feel rather out of sorts and peculiar after such a tumble. She put the cloth down, reached for the water, and poured him a fresh glass. As she had before, she raised his head with her arm before placing the glass to his lips. He drank the glass dry but refused a second and closed his eyes as she settled him back against the pillows.

"How does your head feel?" she asked, her heart beating a little faster as getting answers to her questions became a possibility. Then she remembered how he'd landed here, and anxiety spiked in her chest. What if he remembered too, and blamed poor little John?

"Like a horse kicked it. Repeatedly," he added, somewhat terse. "What happened?"

"Y-You fell," Charity said, praying God forgive her for not being entirely truthful. "I expect a rabbit or something startled your horse and you lost control. You hit your head on a rock when you fell."

A contemptuous look swept over his face and his gaze grew cold. "Nonsense. I'm an excellent rider."

Charity opened and closed her mouth in surprise, a little taken aback. "Well, nonetheless, you *did* fall and hit your head."

As if to confirm her words he raised his hand, fingers touching the dressing that wrapped around his head. He grimaced.

"How long?" he demanded, frowning.

"Three days ago," Charity said.

His frown deepened but he said nothing, staring around the room with increasing confusion.

"Where the devil am I?" His breathing grew rough and he moved to sit up, trying to use his bruised arm to lever himself and exclaiming with pain as he discovered the injury.

"It's all right," Charity said, keeping her voice calm. "You're safe. You're at Brasted Farm, though what on earth you were doing out here we have no idea. We're miles from anyone."

"Brasted Farm," he repeated, his breathing still heavy as he shook his head. "I don't remember. I don't know...."

"Well, don't fret over it." She smiled, hoping to chase the fear from his expression. "Let's start with an easy one. I'm Charity Kendall, and whom do I have the pleasure of addressing?"

To her dismay, the terror and confusion on his face only grew. His eyes widened as he took a deep breath before replying.

"I don't know."

***

Baxter shook his head and took the clay pipe from his mouth. He blew a cloud of smoke into the room and narrowed his, wagging the pipe stem to punctuate each word.

"Fellow's up to no good. Too smoky by half, he is. Don't believe a word. Hah, can't remember who he is? Don't want to, more like."

Charity ignored the voice of doom in the corner and turned to Kit. He was staring into space, a rapt expression on his face.

"How strange," he said, looking rather intrigued by the prospect. "Imagine, waking up one day and not having the faintest idea who you were. All your worries, responsibilities... all gone."

With a snort, Charity folded her arms and glowered a little. "Well, you needn't sound so envious," she said, her manner tart and rather irritated. "I'm sure we all know you'd rather be elsewhere than here, but what shall we do about him?"

Kit returned a reproachful look but gave a shrug. "What in blue blazes can we do? Uncle Edward said head wounds can do peculiar things to a fellow. Well, here's your proof."

Mr Baxter snorted, muttering under his breath, relishing the misfortune they were about to bring down on their heads by not heeding his advice and throwing the unfortunate fellow out onto the moors.

Charity sent him an impatient glare and turned back to Kit. "But there might be people worrying about him. For all we know there's a search party out looking now."

"And?" Kit demanded, reaching for the book he'd been reading before she'd interrupted him. "What of it? If there is they'll get here, eventually." He flicked through the pages to find his place and then sighed as Charity kept her gaze on him. "Oh, very well. We'll make enquiries. It will mean going into town though."

"As if you mind," Charity said with a snort. Getting out of the house and among any kind of civilisation was Kit's idea of heaven. The only reasons he stayed in this out of the way place were sincere attachment to his family and the conviction that a poet ought to lead a solitary and difficult life to feed his muse... or some such nonsense. Charity wasn't sure to which reason he gave the most credence.

Kit grinned, nodding. "True enough. I'm starved of intelligent conversation. Not that I'll find much in such a backwater as

Tillforth but still." He dropped his book to the floor to save himself from the cushion she lanced in his direction.

"Intelligent conversation my eye," Charity retorted, nettled, even though Kit was laughing now, and she knew he'd said it on purpose to rile her. "Drinking too much and acting the fool with that other young buck you call friend, I'll wager." With a dignified sniff of displeasure, she turned her back on him and returned to her sewing while he chuckled and picked up his book, unrepentant. Ah… brothers.

***

"I've brought you some lunch. Oh!" Charity looked around in surprise as she discovered the bed empty and their mystery guest standing at the window.

She'd known he was a big man, but somehow seeing him standing in their little guest bedroom brought it home with some force. He was tall, with broad shoulders and long legs. All lean muscle and an air of restless energy that clung to him. She felt he was a man who hated to be idle, and bored easily. Kit had lent him a clean shirt as his had been bloodstained but the stranger was broader, and the material stretched tight across his back.

He'd been quiet the last few days and she imagined the unpleasant sensation of not knowing who he was had cast him adrift, leaving him unsettled and anxious. She suspected he was not a man who was neither meek nor docile; those cold blue eyes told her as much. Inevitably, his true nature must show itself sooner or later and—from the rigid set of his shoulders and the look on his face–perhaps today was that day.

"If it's more bread and cheese, please don't trouble yourself," he said, with a dark timbre.

"It is," Charity said, placing the tray on the bed. "With some good pickle and a slice of apple pie."

He made a sound of disgust and Charity's temper flared. "This is not a wealthy household, Mr *whoever you are,*" she snapped.

"We live simply here, and you are eating into our supplies. One might think you'd be grateful to be fed at all."

"Might one?" he retorted with contempt. "And where is here?" Charity folded her arms, wondering if he was used to people crumbling and running away from him when he glared at them so fiercely. "I've told you that. Kit even showed you on the map. It's not our fault you don't remember anything about where you were or what you were doing here."

She watched as he let out a breath, staring out of the window at a landscape that seemed to stir no memories for him.

"Do you remember nothing at all?" she asked, wishing to help him if only to get him out from under her roof. He was an unsettling presence and Mr Baxter's dark prophecies about him seemed to fall a little too close to home. "What did your home look like? Do you have brothers or sisters... a wife?"

This last question hung in the air and Charity wished she could take it back lest he believed she was interested in the answer.

He turned back to her, a mocking glint to his gaze that suggested that was exactly how he'd interpreted it.

"I'm not married," he said, amusement lacing a voice that was decidedly upper class. "That much I'm sure of." He paused, his face growing darker. "I... I don't think I have any family."

Charity felt her sympathies rise despite her irritation. To be alone in the world would be hard indeed. She took a step closer to him. "How can you be sure?"

"I can't, damn you!" he shouted, making Charity flinch at the fury of his words. He sucked in a breath and clenched his fists. "I can't even remember my name," he said through clenched teeth. "So how can I be sure of anything? I only know what I *feel* to be true."

Charity glared at him. She was always ready to help someone in distress, to do what she could to make another's lot easier to bear, but never had she found someone so ungrateful for her efforts.

"Well, sir. Your lunch is there. Eat it or don't, but remember you take the food from our mouths. I'll bid you good day." She turned and stalked from the room, only just resisting the urge to slam the door on her way out.

In future she'd let Mr Baxter deal with the blasted fellow, as Kit had wanted. Charity turned and stomped back down the stairs, resolving to put the thankless man from her mind.

***

Dev watched the young woman as her eyes flashed with temper. She bade him good day with much the same tone as she might send him to the devil, and he admitted to a surge of satisfaction. Riling her was the only interesting part of his day.

Giving the tray she'd placed on his bed a look of disgust, he laid down beside it. He felt as weak as a kitten, and standing made his head throb in time with the deep bruising on his shoulder and arm. Added to his physical condition, the fear he might never come to his senses lingered and nauseated him. He glared around the small room with disgust. Whoever he was, he knew this kind of living was not what he was used to. The coarse bread and plain fare they had served him was dull and unfamiliar. A look at the clothes he'd been wearing when they'd found him was enough to consolidate this theory. So, he was rich and powerful. The certainty that he was accustomed to being obeyed without question was a truth he wasn't about to deny.

He cursed out loud, the obscenity lingering in the quiet of the room. If he had to spend much more time here he'd lose what was left of his mind. Bored beyond belief, he found himself irritated, restless, and yet without enough energy to even stand for over ten minutes. He rather wished Miss Kendall would come back and pick a fight with him. At least it relieved the endless hours.

Charity and the Devil

Dev glowered at the tray on the bed as his stomach made a sound of protest. Reasoning that some food would settle his stomach, he reached for a slice of the coarse brown bread and the generous slab of cheese. He dipped the cheese into the pickle and took a bite, chewing and scowling at the same time. Beggars could not be choosers and, for now at least, he was a beggar. The idea did not make him feel better.

He turned his thoughts back to Miss Kendall and considered her, as there was little else to occupy him. She was attractive, in a simple and rather rustic manner. Tanned from working outside, her cheeks glowed with ruddy good health. He knew there were calluses on her hands as he'd felt them upon his skin when she'd raised his head to drink. She would find ridicule if set amongst the females of the ton. Those ladies with fine, porcelain complexions that never saw the sun and hands as soft as downy feathers, would look at her in disgust. He grinned as he imagined Miss Kendall's words if he suggested as much. He'd see those dark eyes flash with fury again, that was for sure. She'd been desperate to tear him off a strip earlier, to tell him exactly what she was thinking. Strange to say it, but he'd been rather disappointed she hadn't. He would have to try harder next time.

He was not to get the opportunity. She did not reappear to remove his tray, nor to bring his dinner. Instead, her brother came. He'd learned that they were twins, which was not at all obvious. Though they shared the same thick, dark hair and darker brown eyes, Kit had none of the robust good looks of his sister. He was as tall as Dev but finer in build; slender in fact. He was handsome for sure, with the kind of pale skin, flushed cheeks and bright eyes Dev had seen before. Consumption, then. He cut a rather rakish, romantic figure: a man that women would pine for, if given half a chance. Dev wondered why in the name of God he'd buried himself here in the middle of nowhere. Even without a penny to his name, the fellow could live a pleasant life in town under the patronage of some wealthy widow.

Then, to his revulsion, he'd discovered the fellow was a poet. A poet! Good Lord, he'd have women swooning at his feet if they discovered that on top of his romantic looks.

Dev had never been one for books. He had found his talents at school lay in physical activity, and he regarded intellectuals of any flavour with deep suspicion. From the guarded and distrustful narrowing in young Mr Kendall's eyes when he called, the feeling was mutual.

So, Dev spent the next few days alone, sleeping, and eating such rustic fare as they bestowed upon him. He hoped to restore his strength and escape with all haste… until one afternoon, when a small boy poked his head around the door.

"Hello," the boy said, a nervous expression on his tanned, freckled face.

"Hello to you," Dev replied, scowling, wondering if they would force him to play nursemaid now. "What do you want?"

The boy edged into the room, a thin wooden box clasped in his hands. "Nothing, only I remember how bored I was last year when I was sick and… well, no one else seems to like you, so I thought you might like a game of dominoes?"

Dev's eyebrows shot up and he gave a bark of laughter. The boy's honesty amused him, not that he'd imagined anything else to be true. The household believed him a damned nuisance and he thought them beneath him. It was hardly a secret. Still, the boy had a point. He was bored out of his mind.

"Why not," Dev replied, gesturing to the small table pushed against one wall with a single chair beside.

The boy shot him a grin and between them they moved the table closer to the bed.

"I'm John," the boy informed him as he drew up the chair and Dev sat opposite on the edge of the bed. "Pleased to meet you…?" He held out his hand, leaving a gap for Dev to supply his name.

Dev sent him a dark look and the boy flushed.

"Oh, yes. I forgot. Is it very odd, to not know your name?"

"What do you think?" Dev demanded, rolling up his shirt sleeves. "And if you intend on asking fool questions all afternoon, you can take your dominoes and find the door."

"Goodness, you *are* rude," John said, wide eyed and rather impressed if his expression was anything to go on. "Charity would clip my ear if I dared speak like that."

Dev's chuckle rumbled around the room. "Do you think she'll clip mine too?"

"I should say so," John replied, his young face earnest. "She hates rudeness above all things."

The idea of the young woman trying such a thing made Dev grin. Oh, he'd like to see her make the attempt. "Well, we shall never know, as your sister is clearly too frightened to face me again."

This time it was John's startled laughter that rang out as he lifted his gaze to Dev's in astonishment. "Charity? Frightened?" He stopped laying out the dominoes, his eyes alight with mirth. "Sir," he said, his voice grave though his lips twitched still. "You surely do not know my sister."

Chapter 4

"Wherein the devil makes work for idle hands."

John came again the next afternoon. Bored with dominoes, Dev decided it was time the young fellow learned a real game and taught him to play whist instead even though it was normally a four person game. He also persuaded the boy to bring him a bottle of claret. John confided to him that Kit would tan his hide when he discovered it missing as it had been a present from their uncle. Dev assured him it was worth the sacrifice. It wasn't the best quality of course, certainly not what Dev was used to, but at this point anything of an alcoholic nature was welcome.

At Dev's insistence John also hunted down a button box and Dev assigned the larger coat buttons as guineas, the mother-of-pearl buttons as crowns, and the smaller, ebony buttons as a shilling a piece.

By the end of the afternoon John owed him almost fifty guineas.

"Bother," John said, casting his cards on the table in disgust.

Dev rolled his eyes. "Come, come," he said, disapprovingly. "You're up to your neck in the river tick, your pockets to let, surely you can do better than that?"

John frowned, perplexed, as Dev gathered the cards up again. "Sir?" he queried.

"A young man ought to cuss with confidence," he said, shaking his head in dismay at the boy's lacking education. "Enough to make the devil blush," he added, enjoying the way John's eyes widened in awe. "At the very least a loss like that deserved a *hell and damnation*."

John's mouth dropped open and he gaped at Dev. "Charity would have my hide if I even dared—"

Dev snorted, narrowing his gaze at the young man. "What are you, a man or a mouse? Are you going to let a woman tell you what you can and can't say?"

To Dev's surprise, John did not give an indignant reply as he might have expected, but pondered the question.

"If it were any other woman, I'd say you have a point, sir," he said, watching as Dev dealt a fresh hand. "But Charity...."

He sounded doubtful and Dev could not help but laugh.

"By God, the woman rules the roost with a rod of iron, does she not?"

"Oh no, sir," John said, quick to defend his sister. "Charity isn't at all like that, only she says manners and respect for others are the defining quality of any gentleman."

Dev picked up his hand but gave the boy a curious look. "Does she now?"

John nodded, reaching for his own cards. "Yes, sir."

"What happened to your parents?" Dev asked, curious how Miss Kendall and her older brother found themselves acting as parents to two younger siblings.

"Dead, sir," John replied, matter-of-factly with his eyes on his cards.

"I gathered that much," Dev replied impatiently. "Dead how?"

"Oh." John looked up, clearly unused to such direct questions about a subject Dev suspected most people tiptoed around. Tiptoeing was not in his nature. "Consumption," he said, returning his attention to his cards.

"Like Kit?" Dev asked.

A flash of emotion crossed the boy's face before it shuttered up. He gave a taut nod.

"When did they die?" Dev asked, wondering how long Miss Kendall had overseen the household. For despite her brother's presence, in matters pertaining to the family and the house and its day to day running, Charity Kendall was Lord and Master, skirts notwithstanding.

"Just after Jane was born," John said, frowning over his cards. "Charity says it was a harsh winter. The birth weakened our mother and she never recovered. Her death hit our father hard from what Kit told me. The illness took hold and he died not long after her."

For a moment the troubling picture of a young Charity nursing her dying parents and caring for a newborn and a three-year-old boy flickered behind Dev's eyes. He suspected she was in her mid-twenties now, so seven years ago she'd have been eighteen, if that. Dev watched the boy, intent on his cards now, and wondered if he ought at least express his sympathies. He suspected the child had heard it all before though, and it would change nothing.

"Come along, then," he said instead, impatiently as John looked up at him. "I haven't got all day. Are you playing this game or not, you young varmint? I intend to wipe the floor with you."

John grinned at him, his freckled face full of amusement. "Damned if you will, sir," he said, the curse word leaving his mouth with gusto.

Dev snorted and gave an approving nod. "That's more like it."

***

The next morning, Dev's head felt a little less like it might roll from his shoulders and hit the floor at the slightest provocation. That being the case, and having spent another idle morning and most of the afternoon going out of his mind with boredom, he ventured down the stairs.

Charity and the Devil

John had been busy with chores and so hadn't had time to win back the rest of the money he'd lost. It amounted to a rather startling seventy-five guineas now but Dev could tell that the boy was coming about. He'd won two of the last five hands and Dev had taught him a few of the tricks the unscrupulous could use to prey on greenhorns who knew no better. If the boy wanted to play such games, it would be as well to know the pitfalls that lay in wait for the inexperienced.

Raised voices reached his ears from what he suspected was the door to the kitchen. Miss Kendall's familiar and somewhat strident tones were easy enough to identify.

"Well, whoever this dreadful Blackehart fellow is, I hope he finds him. With luck he'll challenge the damned rakehell to a duel and bloody well shoot him through his shrivelled-up heart."

Dev's eyebrows raised at the vehemence with which she had spoken the words. For a woman who disapproved of swearing she had a rather impressive vocabulary.

"Charity Kendall!" The sound of an older woman's censorious voice quieted the clamorous din of whatever was being discussed.

"I'm sorry, Batty," Miss Kendall replied, sounding anything but. "But the man is a scoundrel and it would serve him right to reap what he's sown."

Dev could hear pans clattering as someone moved about the room.

"If this Blackehart owns the man as people are saying, everything makes perfect sense."

"How does it?" Mrs Baxter asked.

Dev frowned, glad the older woman had raised the question he couldn't ask. The name *Blackehart* had started his heart thudding in his chest, but he was damned if he knew why.

"Because that's why the viscount is selling the farm." Kit's voice this time, grim and angry.

The conversation carried on behind the door as Dev's chest grew tighter and their words circled his brain. There was something familiar about whatever it was they were talking about, something that made his skin prickle with alarm and recognition.

The kitchen door swung open, making him give a guilty start as Miss Kendall stepped through, almost walking into him.

"You!" she exclaimed, anger in her voice.

Dev's mind was still reeling, but he could not help but note the fact her dress was old and faded, the sleeves rolled up, showing sun-browned arms. Her hair tumbled about her face, dishevelled and wild, and her cheeks glowed, flushed from the heat of the kitchen. There was a floury smudge on her chin.

Caught off balance by the heat of her anger, Dev took an involuntary step back as Miss Kendall advanced on him.

"You," she repeated, stabbing him in the chest with her finger. "I want a word with you."

"I am at your service, madam," Dev replied, sneering and retreating into his iciest manner, trying to find himself on surer ground.

"He's ten years old, for heaven's sake! Is it normal, for a man of your age and experience to corrupt a little boy when you are a guest in someone else's house?" she demanded, her dark eyes filled with rage.

"What the devil are you on about?" Dev replied as Miss Kendall snorted and folded her arms, glaring at him with such contempt a lesser man might well have blanched.

"Gambling, swearing, and drinking too!" she threw back at him with the righteous indignation of a priest casting the devil into hell.

Dev stared at her for a moment before throwing back his head and laughing.

Charity and the Devil

"You think it's a laughing matter?" she exclaimed, looking very much like she wanted to put her hands about his throat and squeeze.

"No," Dev said, shaking his head. "Not in the least. The boy ought to have learnt such things on his own account by now but being stuck in the middle of nowhere with a harridan and a *poet* has deprived him of a proper upbringing."

To his immense satisfaction the virago before him stared with a shocked countenance, open-mouthed and speechless. Seeing Miss Kendall stunned into silence was quite a treat. Naturally, it didn't last.

"A proper upbringing?" she repeated, the words faint, though the glint in her eyes promised retribution. "I suppose that's the upbringing you were given, *Mr Nobody?* If so, that explains a great deal about the kind of shallow, arrogant, pompous… morally lacking…."

To his amusement she floundered, her fury running ahead of her tongue as she searched for a sufficiently dire description of his lamentable character.

"Rakehell?" he supplied, raising one eyebrow in query.

"If the cap fits," she snarled, unfolding her arms and clenching her fists.

For a moment Dev wondered if she might strike him. The desire to do so shone in her eyes.

"One day," he said, ensuring his voice remained the bored drawl of a man who believed the conversation beneath him, "if you do your job well and don't tie the lad to your apron strings forever, he will venture out into the world. He'll be eager for a taste of life, as all young men are. Do you think it better for him to go into that world prepared for the tricks that might be played on him and with conversation that will welcome him into the company of like-minded young men?" He tilted his head to better observe something that might have been a glimmer of doubt in Miss

Kendall's eyes. "Or would you send him into the world unprepared, an innocent lamb to the slaughter?"

"He's *ten*," she repeated, her voice implacable. "I'm not expecting him to catch the next mail coach to the big city just yet."

"No, indeed," Dev replied, affable now. "Yet I am only here for a short time, God willing." Miss Kendall snorted, looking as unimpressed as a woman who dressed as a serving maid could look when addressing a man far above her station. She did a remarkably fine job of it. "And you did all this out of the goodness of your heart, I suppose?"

It was Dev's turn to snort now as he returned a scathing look. "Don't be ridiculous. I was bored out of my mind. I had to do something."

Miss Kendall opened her mouth and shut it again, rendered speechless for the second time that afternoon.

"Stay away from John," she said, her tone quiet but furious. "No more gambling, swearing, and certainly *no drinking*!"

She turned on her heel and headed back into the kitchen, banging the door behind her.

"Oh, for the love of God!" Dev shook his head. Wondering why the devil he was bothered, he slammed his palm against the door and followed her in. "He had barely a third of a glass, *with water*!"

Miss Kendall turned around in shock. He suspected no one had ever dared pursue an argument in the face of her temper before, and that drove him to push even harder.

"He wanted to feel like a man instead of a little boy for once in his sorry life!"

To his astonishment, Miss Kendall just stared at him, her eyes filling with tears. Before he could say anything further she fled the kitchen. Dev stood there, wishing there wasn't a creeping sense of guilt working its way under his skin. Damn, but the woman put his

Charity and the Devil

hackles up. It was her fault not his, he reasoned, wondering why that didn't make him feel better as a tsking sound came from the far side of the room.

"Well, then. You're the mystery man who's setting the house on its ears, no doubt."

Dev turned to find a short, stout woman regarding him with curiosity

"Sit yourself down," she commanded, gesturing to the table.

Dev did as she told him, wrong footed once more and at a loss for any other options. The woman bustled about and placed a frothing tankard of ale before him, along with a slice of what might have been game pie. Dev's eyes lit up as his mouth watered in anticipation, and he took a large bite.

"Mmmm, meat," he mumbled through the crumbliest, lightest pastry he'd ever tasted. "One more mouthful of cheese and I feared I would squeak," he admitted, reaching for the tankard of ale.

The woman snorted, pushed her curly grey hair back from her flushed face, and chuckled. "Aye, and whose fault is that, then? That's what you get for complaining in this house."

Dev frowned at her and she shook her head.

"The doc said to keep you on simple fare for the first few days. After you complained about it, Charity decided it would do you good to keep to the same diet rather longer."

"Ah." Dev snorted. *Touché, Miss Kendall.* "I see."

He ate the rest of the slice in three large bites and pushed his empty plate away as the woman pulled up the chair beside him. She placed a full basket before her and two empty bowls. She slid one bowl in front of Dev, who stared at it and then at her.

"If you're well enough to go battling Miss Kendall and eating my pie, you're well enough to lend a hand. Get to it," she added, gesturing to the basket full of short, fat, green pods.

"I beg your pardon?" Dev replied, stunned.

"Surely you stole peas from the garden as a lad?" She picked up a pod and squeezed it. The bright green casing gave a soft pop and split open, revealing a row of juicy peas, nestled vivid and jewel-like in their silky container. She reached for another and handed it to him.

Dev stared at her, and then took the pod, curious despite himself. She grinned at him as he popped the casing.

"Satisfying, isn't it?" Dev ran his finger along the pod, scattering the peas into the china bowl as the woman had showed him. Strangely enough, she was right. He reached for another pod, and popped it open, this time stealing two peas. They were fresh and sweet, full of sunshine.

"Here, none of that," she scolded, though there was laughter in her eyes. "You want to eat my pie, you work for it, scape grace."

For just a moment her words transported Dev to his childhood and the last nanny he'd had before they had sent him away to school. An image of his father swam behind his eyes and the wash of hurt and loneliness that followed it stunned him. What the devil? How could he remember that and not his own name? He let out a breath, surprised and unsettled by the memory.

"Come along. then," she urged, watching him with something that might have been concern in her warm eyes.

Dev cleared his throat and scattered the rest of the peas into the bowl.

"You're Mrs Baxter?" he asked by way of conversation as he reached for another pod.

"I am," she said, her stubby fingers working far faster than Dev's. Her bowl already had a gleaming pile of peas in the bottom. "Batty they call me," she said, rolling her eyes, though it was clear the affection nickname gave her pleasure. "My husband, Ralph Baxter, works here too. We've been here since we were first married. Worked for their grandpa to begin with, after his wife died, then for their parents, and now for them. 'Bout forty years, I suppose."

She sent him a curious glance, frowning a little. "You reckon you were born in these parts? Can't tell by your accent.

Dev laughed and gave a shrug. "I don't know for certain, but yes, I think so. The landscape feels like…." The word *home* came to mind, only to be dismissed. It didn't feel like home, but it felt familiar. "Like I know it well."

"Young John likes you," Mrs Baxter said, her voice mild though there was a shrewd look in her eyes as Dev turned to look at her.

"Miss Kendall, on the other hand, does not," he replied, his tone dry.

"Well," Mrs Baxter said, getting up to pour herself a tankard of ale, "you can hardly blame her for that. You're not exactly a gent, are you?" She turned and gave him a narrow-eyed look. "And there's little point in telling me I'm no lady. I know it better than you, so you can hold your tongue."

Dev did just that, torn between amusement and indignation.

"You weren't far out, mind," Mrs Baxter said, her inflection softer now as Dev frowned. "She does coddle the boy rather. He knows the land well enough to go hunting alone but she won't let him, and there's no harm in him learning to cuss and play cards if you ask me. She's afraid of messing up though, trying to be mother and father to the lad and after everything it's not surprising. She lost so much, so young, and what with Kit…."

He watched, alarmed as the woman's voice grew thick, but she took a deep drink of her ale and cleared her throat.

"Well, anyway. She's the motherly sort and she's so afraid of failing them, of doing the wrong thing. It plays on her mind." Mrs Baxter sighed and set down her ale, returning her attention to the peas. "Poor thing never had the chance to consider her own future, between her parents and Kit, and running this place." Mrs Baxter looked up at him. "She's no idea what it is to let her hair down, to have fun or not be the one in charge. Never got a glimpse at romance either or even dreamed of falling in love, I reckon. Kit went away to school, you see, and Charity stayed here, bringing up the little ones and keeping the place going."

Dev stared at the pea pod in his hand, lost in thought until Mrs Baxter elbowed him.

"If you want dinner at any point this evening...." With a huff, Dev returned to his work.

Chapter 5

"Wherein if you can't say anything nice… hold your damn tongue."

By the time dinner was ready, Charity had rediscovered her equilibrium. The day to day running of the farm usually soothed her temper, and if perhaps she'd spent a little too long explaining her irritation to the pigs so be it. They were good listeners and it had made her feel better. There was little doubt in her mind that their *guest*, for lack of a better term, was a rake and a scoundrel. What such a man had been doing in these parts alone, and at such an hour of the morning, she could not imagine. The suspicion he knew Lord Devlin, and had perhaps even been on his way to visit him, was something that inspired no further warmth for him. He was just the kind of rude, hateful person she could imagine carousing with the viscount. Living in the middle of nowhere as they did, little gossip about the outside world reached their ears, but tales of Devlin's excesses were legend.

The nagging suspicion that his words about John might have had a grain of truth to them did not ease her rage. If she was honest, that fact only made her even angrier. How dare he come in here with his snooty voice and hands that had never seen a day's work in his life, and criticise her efforts to raise her family as she saw fit?

She took a deep breath, aware that her equilibrium was rather more lost than she'd realised.

Hurrying out of her workaday clothes she washed in cool water, grateful for the shock of the damp cloth against her hot skin. Charity slipped on her only 'best' dress, a simple white cotton gown, tidied her hair as best she could, and hurried downstairs.

The fragrant scent of roast chicken stuffed with herbs drifted from the kitchen as pushed open the door.

"It's all done, dearie," Mrs Baxter said, waving her away. "Go and sit, Baxter's just taken the potatoes in."

"You're a wonder, Batty. Thank you." Charity smiled, guilt at having abandoned the poor woman in her temper making her feel crosser than ever with the wretched man occupying the guest bedroom. Still, at least she didn't have to look at him... over dinner.

Charity halted in the doorway, gritting her teeth at the sight before her. John looked up and grinned at her from beside her nemesis.

"Look, Charity, our guest is well enough to join us now. Isn't it splendid?"

Charity's jaw tightened further as the despicable man quirked a dark eyebrow at her. She refrained from answering. As her mother had always said, if you can't say anything nice....

They all sat and endured as Mr Baxter cleared his throat and read a passage from the bible. Charity always wondered how he reconciled his beliefs in supernatural creatures and omens with his love of the good book, but he wasn't one for philosophical discussions.

"I think Pipkin is a lovely name," Jane commented once the sermon was over and grace had been said. The little girl reached out to take a slice of bread from the basket beside her. "I had a rabbit called Pipkin."

"It's hardly a man's name, you goosecap," John replied, giving his younger sister an impatient look. "I think Arthur is a good name." He turned to their guest, whose pale blue eyes rested on him with amusement.

"Like the king?" he said, lifting his gaze to meet Charity's eye over the table.

Charity and the Devil

She glared at him and turned her attention to Kit instead. Her twin's lips quirked as he carved the chicken He'd left the kitchen before her encounter with Satan himself, but no doubt he'd heard of her little outburst by now.

Charity held her tongue as the devil helped himself to their food and the rest of the family joined in the game of naming their nameless guest. Irritation simmered beneath her skin, especially when Mrs Baxter bustled in with a bottle of wine, filling the intruder's glass for him.

"Why, thank you, Mrs Baxter," the fiend replied, all charm and insincerity. "This is, without a doubt, the finest roast chicken I've ever tasted."

He flashed the woman a dazzling smile and Charity watched in awe as Batty actually blushed. *Blushed!*

"How would you know?" she asked tersely as she cut into the admittedly tender flesh of her own dinner. "If you can't even remember your own name?"

Those pale eyes swivelled to rest upon her and Charity stared across the table at him, refusing to lower her gaze. She wasn't about to be put off by that stare. Even if it was... unnerving.

"I have discovered over the past days that certain things—" He lifted his wine glass to his lips and closed his eyes, savouring the aroma before taking a sip. "—a taste, a smell, a familiar phrase... a touch... these things can trigger a memory."

"And Batty's chicken made you remember what, exactly?" Charity challenged.

"That I was grateful beyond words it wasn't cheese," he replied without hesitation.

John snorted, covering his mouth with his hand and even Kit grinned.

The traitor!

"So, shall we call you, Arthur?" John asked, looking up at the wretched man as if he was deserving of his innocent hero worship.

"No," Charity replied, butting in. "Let's think of something that suits his character," she added, giving as sweet a smile as she could muster.

"Charity," Kit warned, his voice so low that only she could hear.

Charity ignored him, tapping a finger to her lips, apparently lost in thought.

"Let me see. Arthur is too... regal," she murmured, satisfied by the flash of something dark and angry in those pale eyes. "Archibald... no, Alan...." She shook her head and then grinned, giving a triumphant look. "I have it." Pausing for dramatic effect she held the dreadful creature's gaze. "Attila."

John gaped at her, no doubt wondering about all the lessons in politeness she'd drummed into him over the years. Kit groaned as Jane tugged at her sleeve.

"Who's Attila?" the little girl asked

Charity watched as the recipient of her insult sat back in his chair and reached for his wine, twisting the stem between long, elegant fingers. He looked amused, outwardly at least, but vengeance shone in his eyes. Charity's heartbeat picked up.

"Attila was the greatest barbarian ruler to ever live," Dev said, his tone nonchalant as little Jane gasped, turning big eyes on Charity.

"A barbarian?" she queried as Charity squirmed, wondering if she'd been a little hasty. "That doesn't sound very nice, Charity."

Charity cursed as the olive-skinned male across the table raised one eyebrow, the movement so slight as to have been imperceptible if she'd not been staring straight at him.

"I'm sure your sister only meant to imply that I seem like a capable man," the wretch drawled, never dropping his gaze from her face as her cheeks burned. "Worthy of being followed by millions and ruling an empire."

"Oh," Jane said, her sweet face clearing. "Is that what you meant, Charity?"

Charity gritted her teeth before forcing her face into the parody of a smile. "Of course, Jane," she replied, simmering. "Whatever else could I have meant?"

Jane let out a breath and returned to her dinner. "Oh, good. I thought for a moment you meant to be rude. Attila *is* a good name though. Shall we use it?"

A choking sound came from the end of the table and Kit held out a hand. "Apologies, went down the wrong way," he spluttered, covering his mouth as his shoulders shook with mirth.

Charity glowered at her twin and tried desperately to change the subject. "Did you discover anything else of interest, Kit, on your trip into town?" She turned back to Attila, as she was determined to think of him from now on. "My brother has been making enquiries on your behalf, sir. In case there was news of any missing persons."

He looked at Kit with interest. "I did," Kit replied, helping himself to peas. "But I'm afraid to no avail. There was no news of anyone lost or missing."

"*No one* misses him?" Charity said, her voice mournful and sympathetic as she placed a hand against her heart. "Oh, how strange."

Those pale eyes narrowed once more, that cruel mouth twitching, and she imagined it was killing him to play the role of polite guest that he had adopted for the evening. More fool him for trying to hide his true nature.

"Well, it doesn't matter. You can stay as long as you like, can't he Charity?" John asked, with all the naïve innocence of a boy who didn't realise he was condemning his big sister to hell on earth. "You always say how much you enjoy visitors."

"Thank you, Master John," Attila replied, baring his teeth. It may have been a smile, but it made Charity shiver. "You are a kind and gracious host."

"I found something though," Kit hurried on before Charity could reply, apparently only too desperate to move to safer ground. He got to his feet and went to the sideboard where a small parcel lay, wrapped in brown paper. Kit removed the paper and set it on the table, held up by the wine bottle.

"Oh," Charity exclaimed in surprise as she stared at the small painting. "It's exquisite."

Kit beamed at her and nodded. "Knew you'd like it," he said, approving. "Old Jacob thought I was mad for buying it, but I knew you'd see it."

"Old Jacob has a point," Attila replied, staring at Kit's wonderful discovery with consternation in his eyes.

Charity snorted. Well it was hardly surprising. The man was a barbarian, a Philistine. The painting was not anything that would be deemed fashionable it was true. It was neither pretty nor romantic. Instead it sought reality. The old woman had led a hard life, every line of it engraved on her haggard face. The painter had captured her with such skill Charity could see her curiosity at being painted as she stared out of the picture with an almost suspicious frown.

"Why would anyone want a picture of that gnarly old woman on their wall?" the barbarian demanded, not getting the point at all. "It's enough to put one off one's dinner."

"I doubt it," Charity muttered, having noted the vast sums the fellow could eat. To be fair, he was a big man, but still....

"It's art," Kit replied, staring at Attila as if he'd crawled out of a cheese wheel.

Ah, at last, her brother saw the barbarous brute for what he was. All it had taken was a discussion about art. She should have known.

"It's hideous," Attila replied, frankly as John snorted with amusement.

"It's honest," Charity replied, matching his timbre. "It doesn't hide what it is, nor does it present the sitter in a flattering light purely for their own adulation. It's not done for the sitter's self-consequence, nor that of the artist. It reflects truth, real life as it is. Not some prettied up, nauseating representation of the worthy poor and their humble but beautiful simplicity."

Kit beamed at her and Charity felt a glow of pride at her brother's pleasure in her words. It seemed she had been listening when he ranted about art, poetry, and literature. Charity turned to regard Attila, who was giving her a curious look she could not read. He drained his glass and gave a shrug, unimpressed by her impassioned speech.

"I bow to your superior knowledge of art," he replied, though she felt the implication in his mocking undertone that a woman who'd never been very far from the farm she'd been born in couldn't know anything about anything, let alone art. "However, I still say it's ugly."

He smirked, and Charity clasped the knife in her hand a little tighter.

"I dare say, sir," she replied, conversationally as she made a show of returning to her dinner. She paused then, looking him in the eye. "Beauty is in the eye of the beholder, after all. I'm sure there are numerous things in the world that many people would consider handsome, and which I would think grotesque."

She held her smile as Kit's foot pressed down on her toes, hard. A kick would be delivered next time, if she didn't hold her tongue. Charity well knew her twin's tactics.

Attila was quiet, and for a moment she thought perhaps she'd gotten the better of him.

No such luck.

"I don't believe you, Miss Kendall." Those pale blue eyes were glittering intently now. "I believe you would pretend indifference for the sake of being thought an independent woman with an original mind. But you'd know the truth... in your heart. You admire and desire as much as anyone else." He lowered his voice, leaning towards her a little. "Such thoughts might even keep you awake at night."

Charity felt the blush as it crawled up her neck. Of all the outrageous, shocking, dreadful things to imply....

Kit cleared his throat and stood up, wielding the carving knife and glaring at Attila in rage as John and Jane looked back and forth between them all, aware of the strange undercurrent but confounded by what was going on. Giving their guest one last look of fury her twin pasted a smile to his face. "More chicken, anyone?"

***

Dev left the dining room aware of the most peculiar sense of contentment. The meal had been tremendous, he'd meant that. Mrs Baxter and Ms Kendall were wonderful cooks and everything from the succulent chicken, to the summer pudding she'd served with thick cream, had been a delight. He couldn't ever remember eating so much. Well, he couldn't remember much of anything it was true but still, he felt... replete.

Then there had been the company. What little he sensed was true about his own life, he felt certain he had endured it alone. There had been no warm, annoying, loud and laughing family around him like the Kendalls had here. Something that might have been envy wormed its way into his chest and he squashed it. Such thoughts were pointless.

Miss Kendall, however, had proved herself a worthy adversary. Sparring with her had been rather enjoyable, in a somewhat twisted way, perhaps. Good Lord, but she had a tongue on her that one. Attila, indeed! He gave a grunt of amusement despite himself. He'd gotten his own back, though. The blush that had bloomed over her when he'd implied she admired him, made him wonder. He hadn't even meant it. The woman had made her animosity clear from the outset. Dev hadn't believed for a moment she had any feelings of a romantic nature for him.

He wasn't a fool, however, and neither was he blind. He knew he was a handsome man. Perhaps his name and history escaped him at present, but he didn't doubt he was a man who knew his way around a woman. That being the case, he still found himself surprised by her interest. Perhaps she despised him so, not only because he was rude and obnoxious—he would not deny it—but because it angered her to find herself drawn to him. The idea was intriguing.

It was something he would need to consider... and investigate.

Dev opened the door to the garden, needing some air before he returned to his room. He breathed in the warm, perfumed air with pleasure. Night scented stock wrapped its fragrance around him and he let out a sigh of content. A muffled curse beside him was the first indication he wasn't alone.

"Forgive me, Miss Kendall," he said, as he turned to see the moonlight casting its silver light over her upturned and irritated face. Despite her obvious annoyance he had to admit she looked rather lovely in the moonlight, her skin silvered and ethereal, large eyes glittering. "I did not intend to disturb your evening."

She snorted, a rather prosaic sound that hardly suited the romance of the situation.

"Really? I thought it was exactly what you had intended."

The words were tart, and she folded her arms over her chest as she stared daggers at him.

Dev grinned, chuckling at her obvious aggravation. "At the risk of sounding like a five-year-old, *you started it.*"

"I did not!"

Dev stared at her and she huffed, folding her arms a little tighter.

"Well, all right, I did." Her lips compressed with the admission. "But you were sitting there looking so damn smug and self-satisfied that a saint would have been hard-pressed to resist, and I'm no saint."

"I'm glad to hear it." Dev infused the words with his most seductive tone, curious to see what effect this had on Miss Kendall. To his increasing enjoyment, her eyes widened, and she moved away from him.

"I'll bid you a good evening then, sir."

She turned and hurried back inside, but Dev wasn't ready to let her leave just yet. He followed her in.

"Don't you mean Attila?" he taunted, though the words softened with his amusement rather than sounding annoyed. They were back in the dining room, now cleared and empty.

Kit had retired as the ugly painting had inspired him to write; something equally grim, no doubt. Charity had ushered the children to bed earlier, and Mr and Mrs Baxter were busy in the kitchens.

They were all alone.

"Or should that be Mr Hun?" he mused, watching her in the moonlit room as she turned to face him. "I haven't given you leave to use my name, have I? We should need to be better acquainted for that."

Her eyes narrowed and she gave him a curious look. Had anyone ever flirted with her before? He wondered, stuck here in the back end of beyond as she was.

"I have no desire to become better acquainted, thank you," she retorted, primly. "I have had a surfeit of your acquaintance, in fact, and can only hope to reduce it as soon as may be."

Dev chuckled, a low, dark sound that rumbled around the gloomy space. He took a step closer and he heard her intake of breath.

"I don't believe you," he said, enjoying the look in her eyes. They were wide now, and a little startled, like a young doe caught unawares. "I saw the blush that stained your skin when I suggested you thought of me at night." He took another step as she mirrored him by backing away. "Did I hit a nerve, Miss Kendall?"

"Certainly not," she retorted, though there was a breathless quality to her voice he found less than convincing.

Dev grinned. Oh no, this little hellcat was not immune by any means. Rather more pleased than was good for him, Dev took another step towards her.

The missile came from nowhere, smashing a bare inch to the left of his temple against the wall beside him. Cold, sharp shards of porcelain exploded, prickling against his skin like tiny needles. His heart raced, sweat breaking out over his skin as the smashing china transported him to another time, another place.

Dev caught his breath, backing up as the memories rushed in, tumbling over each other as his identity returned to him alongside a lifetime of bitterness and hurt. He found the wall at his back and leaned into it for support, standing among the debris as the door opened and Kit appeared, holding a candle aloft. He looked between them, seeing his sister's worried face and Dev huddled against the wall. A mixture of suspicion and concern filled his dark eyes as he stepped into the room and glared at them both.

"What the devil is going on?"

"I lost my temper," Charity said, staring at Dev with a mixture of frustration and curiosity.

With irritation he noticed something that might have been concern in her expression. He didn't want her pity, that was for certain. Not the woman he was about to throw from her home by selling it from under her.

His heart thudded: a strange, heavy sensation that echoed in his throat. Blackehart. Miss Kendall's words rolled back to him.

"Whoever this Blackehart fellow is, I hope he finds him. With luck he'll challenge the damned rakehell to a duel and bloody well shoot him through his shrivelled-up heart."

My God.

He'd missed his meeting with Blackehart. He'd missed his opportunity to explain his plans and buy some time, and now the man was looking for him, and none too pleased about it if Dev knew anything.

Damnation.

Wrath blazed beneath his skin as he realised the woman before him was entirely to blame. The insulting, not to mention libellous letter she'd written had brought him here, and this was the result. Well, there was no help for it. He needed to lie low until the sale completed. When the money was in hand, then he'd face Blackehart and hope having the money was enough to avoid finding himself dead in a dark alley. A lifetime of looking over his shoulder did not appeal.

Dev looked up as Kit handed him a glass of brandy. "Are you all right?" he asked, something between suspicion and interest in his inflection. "You look like you've seen a ghost."

"Something of the sort," Dev replied, knocking back the drink in one large swallow as he attempted to marshal his thoughts. He needed a plan, and fast. "To be honest…." Dev cringed a little; honesty was the furthest thing from his intentions. They would throw him out on his ear if they knew the truth. "I'm not feeling all that well. If you would excuse me. Goodnight, Mr Kendall, Miss Kendall."

He suppressed the urge to glower at the woman as he stalked from the room, feeling aggrieved all over again. Blast her to hell. He was in the devil of a tangle, and it was all her fault.

Chapter 6

"Wherein the kitchen is the heart of any home."

Charity looked at the frosty faced butler and refused to be intimidated.

"Well, when do you expect him back?" she demanded, holding onto her temper by a thread.

"I'm sure I couldn't say, *madam,*" he replied, looking her over with contempt, the dried up, miserable old muck worm.

Charity drew in a breath, about to give him a piece of her mind, when Mr Ogden appeared.

"Miss Kendall," he said, his eyes full of warmth for her.

"Good day to you, Mr Ogden," she replied, matching his warmth and politeness for no other reason than to nettle the butler. "I was hoping to catch the viscount at home."

"Alas, you are unlucky once again, Miss Kendall," Mr Ogden replied, his words filled with sympathy. He at least understood her situation. "I'm afraid the viscount has returned to London. He intends to remain there until…."

He hesitated, and Charity gave a derisive snort.

"Until they have dealt with this unpleasant situation for him," she finished, gritting her teeth.

Mr Ogden held out his hands, his expression pained. There was no use being angry with him, she knew that. He was as much at the viscount's mercy as she was. He dismissed the butler and offered her his arm.

"Will you take a turn about the garden, Miss Kendall?"

Charity and the Devil

Charity didn't much want to do anything of the sort. Her thoughts were not pleasant and making polite conversation rather too much of an effort. However, she did not wish to be rude, so she pasted a smile to her face and took his arm as Mr Baxter glowered at her from the cart. Well, he'd just have to wait.

The gardens at least were a joy, something of a balm to her jagged thoughts. As the days passed and their impending eviction grew ever nearer, she felt increasingly out of control. It was a sensation she despised. If there was something she could do, action she could take, then she could at least be useful. There was nothing worse than being forced to sit and watch while those you loved….

She forced the old memories away. There was no point dwelling, and she'd always been a 'live for the day' kind of woman. She knew first-hand how short and fragile that day could be in a cruel world. It had been her vow to ensure that the rest of her family lived long and happy lives, untainted by such worries and fears as seemed to prowl her heart in the early hours of the morning. Yet Kit's health was already fragile and now this.

Stop it, she commanded herself, blinking back tears.

"If there was anything I could do."

Charity looked up, startled from her maudlin thoughts by the sincerity of the man beside her. She blinked and forced that fake smile once more.

"I know that, Mr Ogden, please don't reproach yourself. You've been nothing but kind."

"Kind and useless," he said, with a heavy sigh as he guided her down a neat gravelled path. "But my employer is a fickle, vain and selfish man, and no amount of pleading your case would move him. I must confide he became dreadfully angry with me. I feared he might strike me at one point, ranting and raging as he did. I thought perhaps he would dismiss me entirely."

Charity gasped, appalled not only that the man had taken such risks on her behalf but also shocked that he would betray his employer in such a manner. "But Mr Ogden, I... I had no idea. Oh, my dear sir! I beg you will not put your employment in such jeopardy. My goodness, if you had lost your job on our account...."

Guilt rolled over her as Mr Ogden returned a serene smile and patted her hand.

"If I could have swayed his decision, it would have been worth it."

Charity swallowed, noting the look in the man's eyes with dismay and turning away from him. Oh, dear. His admiration was growing marked and she didn't know how to deflect his attentions without causing him hurt or embarrassment. Though she knew she ought to be flattered and pleased by his consideration of her, there was something about the man that made her uncomfortable. Try as she might she couldn't put her finger on what it was. He was educated, kind and had good prospects and yet ... he made her skin crawl. Why was that? He certainly wasn't unpleasant to look at.

She'd had no dealings with men before, being sheltered at the farm and too taken up with keeping everyone fed and raising the children so she couldn't be sure. Not understanding what else to do, she simply ignored the tender look in Mr Ogden's eyes and pretended she hadn't seen it. Was she being foolish though? Selfish even?

If she married well, at least she could keep John and Jane safe and at her side and afford the best care for Kit when he fell ill again. It was what Kit had wanted her to do though he had at least hoped she would find a love match. Marrying Mr Ogden did not give her such heady ideas. Love would not be found with a man like him, though perhaps she could find security and maybe even contentment if she tried hard enough.

The thought made her heart flutter in a not altogether pleasant manner.

Charity and the Devil

She stole a glance at the man at her side. He was at least fifteen years her senior, but she could not deny he was a good-looking man. Not precisely handsome, not like their aggravating house guest, but well made with strong, even features. He was taller than her and broad though, to her irritation, she compared him once more to the ill-mannered lout occupying the spare bedroom. Naturally the fiend was taller and broader. Thinking of the man made her temper flare to life again. Had the devil been planning on seducing her last night? The thought made her heart thud; no mere fluttering for that wretch, but rather a full-on military tattoo that erupted in her chest.

"I'm afraid all this upset has made you unwell, Miss Kendall. You look quite flushed." The worried tone of Mr Ogden only made her flush harder as she dragged her thoughts from their disturbing path.

"I think you must be right, Mr Ogden," she muttered, lying through her teeth and grasping the opportunity to quit his company. "If you'll excuse me, I must get out of the sun and go home. I… I find I'm feeling rather faint."

Being a gentleman, Mr Ogden was adamant about escorting her back to Mr Baxter and the cart and would have insisted on conveying her back to the farm himself in the viscount's own carriage if Charity hadn't put her foot down. There was something about his solicitous nature that got under skin and made her want to shout at him. She couldn't fathom why as he'd been nothing but kind, but he made her feel like a delicate flower who might wilt in a sudden gust of wind, and it drove her mad.

Delicate she wasn't.

Short tempered, pig-headed, stubborn, and rash were all words that could be rightfully flung in her face. Delicate? She was about as delicate as a hammer. Charity snorted while Mr Ogden grew smaller in the distance, and the cart rumbled its way back home.

***

"He needs to go," Kit said, his voice insistent now.

"That's all well and good," Charity replied, ladling boiling hot jam into jars and trying not to scald her fingers. "But how can you throw a man out who doesn't even know who he is, or where he lives? It's not exactly an act of charity, is it?"

Kit pulled a face at her and stuck his finger into the blob of jam she'd dripped onto a cool plate to see if it would set. "Charity be damned," he said, smirking at her as he licked his finger clean.

Charity dropped the ladle into the pan and mimed clutching at her sides with hilarity. "Ha-ha," she said, deadpan, retrieving her ladle before it sank into the sticky red mixture and disappeared. She sighed, wondering where they would be when they ate this year's batch of strawberry jam. Somewhere, scrabbling for survival? Uncle Edward had pledged to help them, but he had five daughters of his own and was far from a wealthy man.

Kit sighed. He sat back in his chair and studied the kitchen table as though it held all the answers.

"Why are you so keen to get rid of him anyway?" Charity asked, frowning at her brother. "I mean, apart from the fact he's rude, obnoxious, and the most unlikable man it's ever been my misfortune to come across?"

She watched as Kit glanced up at her, something in his expression she couldn't decipher which was troubling. Usually she could read her twin like a book. He shrugged and looked away from her.

"Well, for a start I don't like the way he looks at you so make sure you're never alone with him."

Charity raised her eyebrows at him, wondering if he'd run mad. The man couldn't stand her. Yet then she remembered his seductive tone of voice the other night. The one that has so unnerved her, before she'd thrown something at his head at least.

Charity and the Devil

"There's something about him I don't like," Kit continued. "Something...." He let out a breath, running his hand through his hair. "I don't know, perhaps Mr Baxter is right for once and he'll bring us trouble?"

Charity snorted and returned a scathing expression. "Even a stopped clock is right twice a day," she muttered, making him laugh.

"True enough." He sat forward and reached for the loaf of bread he'd brought to the table earlier, before the jam had even finished cooking. He cut a thick slice, buttered it, and then gave Charity an expectant look, all puppy dog eyes. She sighed at him.

"You're worse than John!" She dripped a little more onto the china plate and Kit lost no time in transferring it to his bread. Charity shook her head, laughing. "It's still hot, it will melt the butter and you'll burn your mouth."

Kit shrugged and bit into the bread anyway, sucking in a breath and fanning his hand in front of his mouth as she'd predicted. She snorted, amused. Kit always had been the impatient one, wanting everything now, vibrating with the desire to see, to experience, to know. Full of vinegar, her father would have said. A smile curved her mouth, though it was a sad one, full of regrets.

"Don't look like that, Charity," Kit said, his voice low. "It breaks my heart."

Charity rearranged her face and glanced at Kit. "I was just trying to remember if I'd fed the pigs this morning," she retorted, lying again.

Kit sighed, and she turned away, knowing he didn't believe a word. That was the trouble with being twins; he knew her mind as well as she knew his.

"Something smells divine."

They looked around as their nameless guest appeared. Charity bristled, all her senses on alert as his large frame filled the doorway.

"Oh," she said, her voice scathing. "You're up are you?"

"So it appears," he replied, smiling at her.

At least, he bared, white, even teeth looking like he might rip her throat out, but she assumed he'd meant it to be a smile.

"Have some bread and jam," Kit invited, pulling out a chair and ignoring the look of fury Charity sent his way.

Typical of Kit. He didn't trust the man or want him here, but he'd not lose the opportunity to talk to someone new.

Charity watched out of the corner of her eye as the man sat himself down and then waited, expecting to be served. She frowned, biting back her annoyance. He was someone used to being waited on. His accent spoke of culture and money as clearly as the clothes they'd found him in. Once again, she wondered what he'd been doing out here in the middle of nowhere. Surely, he'd been on his way to see the black-hearted viscount?

With a huff, she cut him two slices of bread, as he was obviously incapable, and threw them on a clean plate, sliding it towards him. "Help yourself."

"Thank you so much."

That unsettling baring of teeth was given again and she shivered, remembering an illustration of a tiger in an encyclopaedia she'd studied as a child.

"Are you feeling better?" Kit asked him as he managed to butter his own bread without the help of a valet or a butler or something.

She hoped he spilled jam down his shirt, then she remembered it was Kit's shirt and she'd have to wash the blasted thing.

Charity and the Devil

He scraped what was left of the jam off the plate and nodded, though he looked a little ill at ease now.

"I... I am," he said, glancing up at Kit and nodding his thanks. "In fact, I remembered a little about myself."

Hallelujah.

Kit brightened considerably at this information, sitting up and giving the man his full attention.

"Not much," the fellow added, apologetic as all their hopes crashed to the ground. "But I remembered that my name is... David."

"David?" Charity repeated, narrowing her eyes. "You don't look like a David."

There was a flash of ire as he returned a quelling look which likely terrified chamber maids and footmen alike. "Nevertheless."

"Well, that's... a start," Kit said, glancing at Charity who knew he was inwardly cursing just as loud as she was. "Nothing else?"

Nothing helpful, he didn't say, though she could hear the words hanging in the air.

"A last name, perhaps? Or where it was you were going to, or coming from?"

David shook his head and held out his hands in a defeated manner. "I'm terribly sorry, but no," he replied, not looking nearly sorry enough to Charity's mind. "Nothing else."

"Do you know Viscount Devlin?" Charity demanded, folding her arms and glaring at him.

There was a flash of something in his eyes, but she couldn't say what. Recognition, maybe?

He was quiet for a moment and she assumed he was considering the question.

"I know of him, yes," he replied, the words a little cautious. "But no, I don't believe I know him personally." He paused, taking an inordinate amount of time to spread a perfect layer of jam into every corner of his bread. Once satisfied, he cut the slice in half and raised it to his mouth. "I hear he's a devilish fine fellow," he mused, studying the slice with a nonchalant air. "Quite a one for the ladies."

"Devilish," Charity sneered. "Now that I can believe."

Despite herself she watched as he bit into the bread, closing his eyes with pleasure as he chewed. Her gaze slid to his jaw where his beard was coming through heavily now. Kit had lent him his shaving gear but perhaps the useless man couldn't do it by himself. She imagined sliding a razor down the strong line of his throat and felt her mouth grow dry. As she forced her gaze from him she caught Kit staring at her in consternation. A blush prickled up her own throat and she turned away, annoyed with herself.

Charity scraped the last of the jam from the pan and decided she'd do well to keep as far from David as possible.

***

Dev, or David as he'd now styled himself, hung about the kitchen and generally made a nuisance of himself for the rest of the morning. If he was to avoid Blackehart there was no other option but to stay until the farm sold. It wasn't for much longer at least. If a sliver of guilt wormed its way into his heart at the fact the Kendalls were sheltering the instrument of their doom, he did his best to suppress it. Everyone had their troubles. They'd make a new life somewhere else.

Why, though, had no one come looking for him? Why wasn't the countryside full of stories of the missing viscount. It was more than a little odd. He wasn't popular, especially with his staff. Dev was not such a fool as not to know it, but surely *someone* would have missed him? Unless perhaps the news had been kept quiet? But why?

Kit had left them to go off and write poetry or something dreary and Dev found himself left with the women. Despite feeling he ought to be appalled by slumming it in such a fashion, he found it all rather fascinating.

Miss Kendall was clearly infuriated by his presence but Mrs Baxter, who had bustled in with a basket of eggs and had made him welcome, fussing over him and giving him samples of the tarts she was making and asking him for his opinion. This only aggravated Miss Kendall all the more, which amused him no end.

It was the first time he'd really had the opportunity to watch her. She always seemed to be out about the farm, occupied with something or other. The young woman was always in motion, though, and he found his eye drawn to her as she moved around the kitchen. It was no wonder her hands were so rough. Looking after their family was not something she would leave for Mrs Baxter's sole care. It seemed there was work enough for more than two as they spoke of an endless list of jobs that needed attention. As soon as the strawberry jam was done, and the jars left to cool, Miss Kendall washed and prepared a huge basin of gooseberries. Dev had always been rather partial to gooseberries and wondered if they were all destined for jam.

He'd never in his life spent time in the kitchens before, never even considered the work involved in preparing a single meal, let alone thinking ahead about preserving stores for the winter. His food simply appeared on the table and he ate it with little thought for the time and effort it might have taken. He knew, of course, that his own home had substantial kitchen gardens and hot houses for the more exotic fruits, like pineapples. Nothing so unusual would ever have been seen here, that was for sure.

Mr Baxter appeared at one point and was roundly scolded by his wife for tracking dirt into the kitchen. Mrs Baxter handed him a cup of tea and then ushered him out again as fast as possible, as he muttered about the likelihood of the sow birthing her litter in the next few days. Dev smirked as Mrs Baxter shut the door on her husband with a huff of annoyance, and then wished he hadn't as she caught his expression. Narrowing her eyes at him, she fetched a sharp knife and a large basin of potatoes.

"If you're going to clutter up the kitchen, you'd best make yourself useful instead of sitting there looking ornamental," she said, a challenging glint in her eyes.

Dev opened his mouth to protest but caught the look of disgust in Miss Kendall's eyes. She'd already made several scathing comments about his unshaven state, which he had to admit was annoying the hell out of him too. Not that he couldn't do it, only that he couldn't do it well. He was damned if he'd come down the stairs cut to ribbons. That she thought him useless and unable to fend for himself was as irritating as it was ridiculous. He was a gentleman for heaven's sake! He had a valet for such menial tasks and he'd never lifted his hand to work a day in his life.

Gentlemen *didn't*.

There were rules about such things. Yet, the idea rankled, and so he picked up the knife and a potato with a grimace.

"Not that much!" Mrs Baxter exclaimed, shaking her head and tutting at him. "There's more potato for the pigs than for us if you cut that much off!"

Chastened, Dev glowered a little, ignoring Miss Kendall's snort of amusement, and set about improving his skills.

Chapter 7

"Wherein even a devil can't drown a fluffy little kitten."

The next day, Dev found the kitchens deserted. A note on the table instructed him that there was bread, cheese, and ham in the pantry, and that he should help himself. From the terse tone of the note he gathered that Miss Kendall had written it. Mrs Baxter, Miss Kendall, and John had gone to market and would not be back until that evening.

Dev rubbed at his beard in irritation. There was little enough to amuse him here but at least getting under Miss Kendall's skin afforded him some entertainment. Without her prickly presence, or Mrs Baxter fattening him up like a Christmas turkey, he felt rather at a loose end.

By half past ten he was going out of his mind with boredom and things got so bad he decided he'd try to read a book. Dev hated to sit still for more than half an hour at a time in normal circumstances, too much nervous energy fizzing beneath his skin to allow such peaceful repose. As a gentleman he might have eschewed work in all its forms, but that was not to say he was idle. He rode and fenced, boxed and socialised, drank too much, slept too little, and spent too much time in the company of scandalous women.

If he was being honest, he'd have to admit that he had never felt better than he had the past few days. Now that his bruises were healing and his head had stopped thudding, he felt rested. His liver was certainly thanking him as it seemed there was little in the way of strong liquor in the house. The dark circles had gone from under his eyes, and the jaded, rather dissipated look he'd noticed growing marked in his face over the past few years was fading with good food and a proper night's sleep.

In fact, he felt disgustingly healthy and in need of something physical to do. He was damned if would risk running into Mr Baxter, though. The man looked at him as if he were a malevolent spirit and made peculiar signs with his hands when he thought Dev wasn't looking. Dev was certain they were meant to ward off evil. Not that he cared what the mad old fellow thought of him, but he was damned if he'd endure another lecture from the Bible. It reminded him too much of his father's words for comfort.

So, a book it was. With a resigned sigh he pushed open the study door, as the few books the house seemed to possess lived here, and was roundly cursed as he set foot in the room.

"Damnation! Didn't I say I was not to be disturbed when I was working?" Kit looked up from a desk littered with screwed up pieces of paper, a tattered quill in his ink-stained hands. "Oh," he said, as he saw Dev standing in the doorway. "It's you."

That didn't seem to be a positive statement, but Dev was never one to be put off by rudeness. In fact, he viewed it as a challenge. That being the case, he closed the door behind him and hovered, craning his neck to look over Kit's work.

"Can I help you with something?" Kit demanded, gathering his papers up and stuffing the crumpled pieces in the bin.

"Not a thing," Dev replied, smiling.

Kit sighed and narrowed his eyes at him. "Look, I don't like you, you don't like me. So, do us both a favour and bugger off. I've got work to do."

Dev chuckled and wondered just how much trouble the twins had gotten into as children with their outspoken natures.

"So, you're a poet?" he asked, leaning back against the wall and folding his arms.

"I am," Kit said tersely. "What are you?"

There was a suspicious glint in his eye, but Dev grinned at him and shrugged.

"A gentleman," he replied, his tone affable.

Kit snorted, a disparaging sound that Dev would normally have taken exception to, but he *was* riling the fellow on purpose, and he didn't want to get thrown out for breaking his host's nose.

"Your notion of a gentleman and mine are not necessarily the same," Kit said, smiling through his teeth in a manner that made a parody of his polite tone.

"I have no doubt of that," Dev replied, accentuating his cut glass accent.

"Just stay away from my sister," Kit growled, the sudden fury in his voice taking Dev a little by surprise. Surely, he didn't think...?

"*Miss Kendall?*" Dev repeated, all at once a little on his guard.

"Of course, Miss Kendall!" Kit exploded, throwing down his quill so that ink splattered several clean sheets of paper. "I've seen the way you look at her, like you'd eat her in one bite."

Dev gaped at the man, wondering if he was touched in his upper works. Perhaps there had been a little flirtation but ... "Are you mad? Or just deluded? I mean I've heard of poets having vivid imaginations but really!"

"Oh, don't come the innocent with me." Kit got to his feet in one smooth movement, shoving back his chair and moving from behind the desk. "I know your type, with your looks and your money. You think any woman is yours for the taking and you don't care what becomes of them when you grow tired and move on." The young man got up, stalking closer, his expression furious now. "Well, not *my sister.*"

Dev had to admit he was rather impressed. He'd thought the young man a spineless sort—intellectuals often were, in his experience—and to see him defend his sister, albeit for no good reason, raised him in Dev's estimation.

Nonetheless.

Dev drew himself up to his full height and squared his shoulders. They were not far off in height, but Kit's uncertain health had deprived him of the breadth that Dev carried with ease.

"Your sister cannot stand the sight of me," Dev said, biting out the words in a precise manner, as if he was explaining to someone with a mental impairment. "And I assure you the feeling is mutual. The idea that there is anything of… of a… *romantic* nature is quite frankly ludicrous."

Kit took a step closer, his voice low and angry now. "Damn you, David, or whatever your name is. I see the way you watch each other. The air is so thick when the two of you are in a room you could cut it like cheese."

Dev opened his mouth, but Kit didn't let him speak.

"She's had a tough time, sacrificed everything for the rest of the family, and she has no more notion of men than a kitten of a lion. She's innocent, and I intend to keep it that way, so keep away."

Dev gaped as Kit snatched his work from the desk and stalked from the room, slamming the door as he went.

Well, that had been unexpected.

Miss Kendall had been watching him? A frisson of excitement ran down Dev's spine, which he rather suspected had not been the outcome her twin had been hoping for.

If he was honest with himself—a rarity, it was true—her virtue was something of a lure. That surprised him more than anything else. Virgins had held no interest for him. Far better an experienced woman who knew what she was about than having to teach someone what was what. Far too much hassle.

Yet being the first to ever kiss those lush lips... would she taste as tart as her sharp tongue suggested, or sweet?

The frisson grew stronger, prickling over his skin, desire heating his blood as the idea took hold.

Damn it. No.

Dev clenched his fists and let out a breath. He was a bastard all right, and turning this family out on their ear to save his own sorry hide was something he was quite prepared to do, though he admitted that the tiny sliver of guilt was just a little heavier than it had been. Yet if it was between himself lying dead in a ditch and the Kendall family being upended and moved, then they could damn well start packing.

Seducing Miss Kendall before they were evicted, however? No. There were limits to his villainy, though it surprised him to discover it. That was a line he would not cross.

***

Dev wandered the farm after his confrontation with young M Kendall, eager to rid himself of the restless sensation burning beneath his skin. He needed something to do and he needed it fast. Ogden had been correct. He'd never taken the slightest bit of interest in the running of his estate or any tenants living upon it. He could see the farm was in good order. Many of the pigs they reared were out to pannage, foraging the moors and woodland but the farrowing sows were kept in the piggery and were fat and healthy. There were also a good number of chickens, geese, turkeys and ducks, as well as a cow and at least a dozen goats. The house itself was sturdy and in excellent repair, with signs of recent work to the slate roof visible. Apart from one paddock which needed attention, all the fences were strong and, even to his inexperienced eye, the cultivated fields were well tended. He didn't have the faintest idea if they were growing wheat or barley but to his uneducated gaze it looked good. It was a rare thing, in this part of the world, to have land fit for anything but grazing. He suspected many years of hard graft had brought them to this point.

Pleased that he'd inspected the place whilst evading the dour companionship of Mr Baxter, Dev walked on further. The sun was high now, burning the back of his neck. He strode away from the farm and up the hill that lay behind, enjoying stretching his muscles. The terrain became rockier and he climbed, pausing for a moment to admire the view as the countryside stretched on into the infinite, or so it appeared from this vantage point. It was a harsh and rugged beauty, not the soft greens and rolling hills he'd found further south when he'd travelled the country.

Dev drew in a breath, wondering why the landscape spoke to him today when it had felt so unwelcoming before. Could he find a home of sorts in this isolated landscape rather than constantly escaping to London? Another question reared its head. Did he care about the fate of the Devlin name after all?

He'd been so certain he wanted to grind his prestigious name to the dust, to cast their history to the four winds and laugh as he did it. His father had been so damn proud that it had seemed a fitting tribute. Yet now, at the eleventh hour, his resolution wavered.

Was he such a child that he would continue to destroy his own life, his ancient heritage, just to spite a man who was no longer around to see him do it?

He'd always thought so, but now….

Dev hesitated, thinking it over for once instead of just carrying on with the promise he'd made himself so many years ago. He wondered what Miss Kendall would think of such a destructive vow and snorted as he conjured her disgusted expression. Good Lord, she'd give him a dressing down for wasting such an opportunity. She'd not do anything so careless and criminal as to throw away a moment of her life.

No, she'd fight for it, tooth and nail.

Unbidden, the image of her dark eyes softening came to him; her mouth forming a smile just for him, shy and sweet instead of a thin line of displeasure. He allowed the image to grow as he imagined taking her in his arms, taking her lips….

God damn it!

Irritated, he carried on climbing up the hill.

***

By the time Dev had returned to the farm, he was hot, sweaty, and not in the best of humours. Although he'd walked far enough to take the edge off his desire for physical exertion, the image of Miss Kendall, pliant and willing in his arms, was difficult to shake.

So, it was with a less than enthusiastic reception he greeted little Jane as she threw herself against him, wrapping her arms around his legs and wailing like a small but determined banshee.

"Whatever is that racket for?" he demanded, looking down in horror as the little girl stared up at him, fat tears streaming from her big brown eyes.

"Please, Mr David, please, *please* don't let him do it."

"Let who do what?" Dev said, perplexed as the child reached for his hand and tugged him forward.

She was strong for a tiny slip of a thing and kept a tenacious grip on his fingers as she pulled him in her wake.

"There!" she said, with a theatrical flourish the great actor Kean himself would have approved of as she pointed the finger like an infuriated soothsayer.

He almost expected a crack of thunder to sound overhead, such was the desperate energy vibrating from her slender frame. Instead he saw Mr Baxter dangling a tiny grey kitten over the open mouth of an old grain sack.

"He's going to murder them, Mr David!" she wailed, clutching at his arm now and sobbing as though her heart would break.

Oh, for the love of everything holy....

A pitiful mewling sound reached Dev's ears and he knew he was sunk. Though he'd deny it if asked and ignored anything small and fluffy on principle, buried down deep he had to acknowledge that he had a soft spot for animals. His parents had never allowed him a dog as a child. His mother's nerves would not endure barking, and she disliked cats. The only animals that his father kept were useful hunting dogs that would likely bite your finger off given half a chance, and horses, naturally.

Pets were an indulgence that the late viscount had not approved of, concerned that they would scratch the polished wood floors and ruin the furniture. No amount of pleading on Dev's part as a boy had changed his mind.

He had once kept a kitten for a short while, unbeknownst to his father. A wild thing it had been, taken from the stables and hidden with care. The feral creatures could roam the stables at will as they kept the mice down and out of the feed. His father had discovered the poor creature and drowned it.

"Now then, Miss Jane," Mr Baxter said, dropping the kitten into the sack and closing his fist around the opening. "We've been through this. They got no mama, no one to feed them. They can't survive on their own and it's crueller by far to let the poor mites starve."

"I got no mama either!" Little Jane shot back at him, and Dev found himself rather impressed by the strength of her argument. She was clearly of Miss Kendall's blood. "Shall you put me in the sack and drown me too?"

Mr Baxter rubbed a weary hand over his face. "Don't you twist my words now," the fellow said, looking increasingly put upon. "You had Miss Kendall and Mr Kit, not to mention me and Mrs Baxter. Plenty of folk to look after you!"

"I can look after the kittens! *I can!*" she shouted, stamping her foot in fury. "Tell him, Mr David."

Imploring, she turned glittering, guileless eyes upon him and Dev cursed under his breath.

"Well, couldn't she?" he asked Mr Baxter, rubbing the back of his neck and wishing the lot of them at Hades, kittens and all.

Mr Baxter returned a scathing expression. "That young'un could sleep through a thunderstorm that would rattle the brain in your head. There's no way on earth she'll wake to feed kittens, and I ain't doing it, that's for good and certain." The man placed a gnarled hand on his hip, the squirming sack still writhing in the other.

Jane wrapped her arms around Dev's thigh and began to cry. Not the theatrical, wailing sobs she'd started with, rather the quiet, pitiful weeping of a child who knew she had no power in a world run by adults.

Hell and damnation.

"Give me the sack," Dev said, wondering if he'd gone completely off his head. If anyone ever heard about this....

Mr Baxter stared at him, dumbfounded. "If you think you can bully me into—"

"Just give me the damn sack," Dev roared, fed-up to the back teeth of the whole affair by now. "I'll feed the blasted creatures."

Mr Baxter held the sack out to him, his expression so puzzled it was almost comical, as Dev snatched it from his grasp and stalked into the house.

Jane followed at his heels like a lamb, as Dev muttered obscenities under his breath and ignored the expression of stunned adoration shining in her large, brown eyes.

***

"I don't believe you."

Charity stared at Mr Baxter, who seemed torn between quiet bewilderment and consternation.

"Go and look then!" he retorted, throwing up his hands in exasperation. "I tell you now, the two of them are in the barn, feeding the wretched things our cream!"

Pausing for long enough to cast the man a doubtful expression, Charity hurried off. This she needed to see.

They'd done their business in record time at the market and had made good time getting back too, so were home rather earlier than expected. She suspected it was for this reason alone that she caught them.

David had placed the kittens in the in the tack room so they could close the door and keep any of the barn toms out. He made a sort of nest by fluffing up straw and corralling the kittens in by piling more sheaves around them. David sat in the straw, heedless of the damage to his fine boots, and held a tiny grey bundle of fluff in his large hands, while Jane encouraged the kitten to suckle from a twisted bit of muslin dipped in cream.

"That's it," David said, his voice quiet and encouraging, though whether he was speaking to the kitten or Jane she wasn't sure.

"It's drinking at last," Jane said, excitement in her eyes as she cast him a look of admiration. "This one is much weaker than the others, isn't it?"

"Yes," David replied, smiling at the kitten. "It will work like this until it's stronger, then you can feed it from a teaspoon."

Charity felt something lurch in her chest at that smile. Drat the man. Why did he have to go and be kind to defenceless animals? It was so much easier to hate someone who treated his horse with contempt or kicked puppies. Not that she was sorry he'd rescued the kittens. She'd tried her best to harden her heart over the years—farming was not for the tender hearted, that was for certain—but she could no more have drowned the kittens than Jane could… which was likely why Mr Baxter had waited until she'd gone out to deal with them.

Charity and the Devil

She shifted from behind the barn wall, craning her neck to get a better view.

"Oh, Mr David, you are clever," Jane gushed, clinging to his strong arm with her small hands. "How did you know what to do?"

Charity watched as the man hesitated before he answered. "I had a kitten once, when I was around your age," he said.

"Oh," Jane sighed and snuggled up to him, and Charity could now see that the four other kittens were asleep in his lap. She bit her lip against the exclamation that burned on her tongue. "That explains it. What was it called?"

"Dinah," he replied, stroking the tiny kitten's head with one large finger before placing it with its brothers and sisters. "She was black, with one white paw."

"Awww," Jane said, giggling, her dark curls falling over the sleeve of his shirt. "Mr David?"

"Yes?"

She rested her head against his heavy arm, staring up at him in such a way that Charity felt a lump rise to her throat. "Thank you so much for rescuing them for me."

David frowned, then sighed. He rubbed the back of his neck and looking as uncomfortable as any man could. "You're welcome," he said gruffly.

Jane beamed at him and then looked up as John's voice echoed around the yard.

"Oh, John's home! I must tell him what you did."

Before he could protest, Jane ran from the barn, hurrying past Charity without noticing she was there.

Chapter 8

"Wherein our hero is held at knife point."

Charity watched, still astonished, as David picked up the kittens and arranged them in the nest he'd created.

"I never would have believed it unless I'd seen it with my own eyes."

Charity bit back a laugh as David jumped at the sound of her voice. He grunted and turned his back on her until all kittens were snuggled into a fluffy pile.

"That was very kind of you," she said, meaning it, the gratitude in her voice too audible.

Little Jane didn't have much in the way of toys and though she adored and idolised her big brother John, his rough and tumble games of war and hunting were not always to her taste. The kittens would be something for her to love and play with, if they survived, when the big boy games became too much. She prayed David would not grow tired of caring for them as Jane would be devastated now if they died. With chagrin Charity acknowledge that she'd end up looking after them herself before she saw Jane upset.

David still said nothing, and she sensed rather than saw his unease. He got to his feet brushing straw from his clothes and sighing over the state of his boots.

"I… I was wondering if you'd like me to shave you?" The words were out before Charity had time to think them through and she wished to take them back.

Charity and the Devil

His cool blue eyes lit with astonishment and something else she could not interpret, though it made her heart thud a little harder. He rubbed his hand over his beard and grimaced, and she knew she was correct in believing he didn't like being unshaven.

"You don't have to do that," he said, sounding rather terse as he looked away from her, a frown drawing his dark brows together.

My, he looked forbidding when he scowled. She remembered him moments ago, petting the kittens, and bit back a grin. She thought perhaps his black-hearted image had been tarnished for good now, though he could scowl all he wanted.

"I know I don't *have* to," Charity said, rolling her eyes and tutting. "I was being kind. It's what people do for each other… normal people at least, ones with manners," she added, folding her arms as she saw the irritation flash in his eyes. "You were kind to Jane and the kittens, you didn't have to do that either, so now I'm being kind to you."

He glanced over at her, and she smothered a grin, amused by the rather perplexed cast to his expression. She watched as he frowned, fighting some internal battle, but he rubbed at his beard again and gave a taut nod.

"You know how?" he asked, his tone sceptical. "Or are you just hoping for an opportunity to cut my throat?"

Charity laughed.

"You'll just have to put your life in my hands, won't you?" she said, enjoying the chance to taunt him a little. "But yes, I know how. My father hated to be unshaven and when he and mother fell ill…." She shrugged, pushing away memories of her father's emaciated frame in the last days of his life. "Kit too, when… when he's not well enough," she added, wishing and praying that those terrifying days would never revisit this house. She wasn't sure she would survive the loss of her twin. No one else must leave her. Never.

David cleared his throat, bringing her back to the present. "Yes, then. Thank you," he replied, sounding a little as if the words were unfamiliar to him. "I would appreciate it."

Charity nodded. "You're welcome. I'll come up in a moment, if that's all right?"

He nodded his agreement and turned away from her.

"Did you really have a kitten called Dinah?" she asked, wondering if he'd made it up or if it was something he'd remembered about his life. "You remember her?"

"Yes," he said, avoiding her gaze. "Small things are coming back. Seeing the kittens brought the memory to mind, I suppose."

That made sense at least and she was glad his memory was still returning. She could not imagine how lost it must make one feel, not knowing who or where you belonged. Perhaps that was what made him so bad tempered?

"You must have been fond of her, to have remembered that," she said, wondering why she was keeping him talking, unwilling to let him go. He seemed somewhat unbalanced by his act of kindness, though, and she wanted to press him before he retreated behind sarcasm and bad manners. That he inevitably would seemed obvious enough.

"I suppose," he said, gruff now, impatient to leave.

"Did you keep her with you a long time?"

He let out a breath, and she could see he'd had enough.

"No," he replied, the word terse and a little annoyed now as he turned on his heel. "My father drowned her."

Charity watched as he walked away, the breath leaving her in a sigh. "Oh."

For the first time, she wondered if perhaps the man's life hadn't been of the gilded and polished quality she'd supposed. She'd heard the cut glass of his accent, seen the impeccable tailoring of his clothes, and assumed his life was one of pleasure and ease. Was she so far from the truth?

What if he'd been treated badly? What if he'd been lonely, unhappy? She imagined him as a little boy, the same age as Jane, without someone to save a beloved kitten for him, like he'd done for her little sister. Was that why he'd done it?

Charity frowned, wishing she wasn't so eager to know. Mr Baxter was right. The man was trouble, trouble of a sort she could ill afford to get involved with. Offering to shave him had been an idiotic idea. Even now the thought of her hands on his bare skin made her own heat, although she still lingered in the cool shadow of the barn.

Still, she'd done it now and she must keep her word. Hoping she could do it without cutting his throat as she'd promised, she thrust her trembling hands under her arms and stalked into the house.

***

Dev opened the bedroom door to find Miss Kendall carrying a tray with a jug of hot water and a steaming damp towel. He'd laid the spare shaving kit her brother had lent him out and put a chair by the window so she'd have good light.

She came in, avoiding his eye and he frowned, tamping down a rather peculiar prickly sensation in his gut as she brushed past him. He felt as nervous as a virgin in a whorehouse and he couldn't fathom why for the life of him. Miss Kendall was the virgin here. It ought to be her blushing and trembling, for heaven's sake. He was a man of the world, to put it mildly.

So why did thoughts of her hands on his skin make his nerves leap?

Because you've sworn to keep your damn hands off her, a terse voice retorted in his head. Ah. Yes. That would be it. Nothing worse than having an itch you couldn't scratch and now the wretched creature was about to make things a damn sight worse.

Dev watched as she set about preparing to shave him, noting the high spots of colour upon her cheeks. He hid a smile, pleased that she was suffering nerves too. Was she eager to put her hands on him, he wondered? Or was that just maidenly anxiety at the impropriety of being in a man's room alone?

He wondered if Kit had any idea she was here and dismissed the notion. If his earlier outburst was anything to go by, the fellow would suffer an apoplexy. She'd get the scolding of her life when he discovered what she'd done. He glanced up at her again, wondering if she knew. She must know her brother would disapprove.

Yet here she was.

The thought puffed him up a little until, and with rare humility, he wondered if perhaps he was over-inflating his own appeal? The woman did seem to do as she pleased no matter what her brother said. Perhaps Kit's opinion simply didn't matter?

"Sit down then, please," she said, with that brisk, no nonsense tone in her voice that he well recognised, though there was a faint tremble to the words.

Moving with deliberation, he kept his gaze on her as he stepped closer, noting the way her colour rose further. Oh yes, she was unsettled. The idea pleased him, and he bit back a grin.

Dev seated himself in the chair, tilting his head back as she placed the steaming towel over his face. He sighed. It felt good, though having his head at this angle wasn't comfortable.

She removed the towel and lathered up the brush, applying the soap to his face. She was careful not to touch him more than necessary and continued to avoid his eye.

"You really do have a valet, don't you?" she said, as she reached for the razor, opening it with care.

Dev nodded. No point in denying it. "Yes."

"Do you remember his name?"

Jacobs.

Dev frowned, wondering if he should make a name up or pretend he couldn't remember such details. He did not rely on his valet as much as Miss Kendall might suppose, but the fellow always shaved him far better than he could manage himself. His beard was thick and unruly and, on the occasions when he had tried to do it himself, he'd ended up covered with tiny nicks. It was not a good look.

"I don't remember," he said at length.

The fewer lies he told, the less likely he'd get in a tangle by forgetting something.

"Lean back," she instructed him, which he did for a moment before straightening again.

"I can't stay like that the whole time you shave me," he protested. "It hurts my neck."

She tutted at him impatiently. "Well, how does your valet do it?" she asked. "I've only ever shaved my father and Kit in bed so it's easier."

She turned an intriguing shade of scarlet as she realised what she'd said, and Dev swallowed his laughter. That was a cheap shot, though, and he'd not take it. Too obvious.

"I lean back against him," he said with a slight shrug, though the thought of resting his head against her breast was rather too inviting for his peace of mind.

"Very well." She bit the words out, unwilling but resigned and Dev leaned back.

He closed his eyes, knowing that watching her was a recipe for a cut throat, no matter her assurances. After an initial hesitation and a sharp intake of breath as he rested his head against her, she began. He was unsurprised to find her touch sure as she shaved him with almost as much skill and dexterity as his own man.

"It's very coarse," she commented as she reached over to clean the blade before beginning on his neck.

"Yes."

"Do you have foreign blood by any chance? Your skin is so dark."

Dev nodded as she moved back to carry on. "Yes. Italian."

Damnation.

He bit his tongue. He shouldn't have told her that. Few people knew or remembered that his grandmother had been Italian but, although it wasn't a secret, he must have a care.

"But you still don't remember your family name?" she asked.

He dared to glance up at her, cursing the puzzled look in her eyes and his own foolishness. "No."

"My uncle said amnesia does funny things to the mind," she said, quietly, almost as if she was reassuring herself as much as him. "I suppose he's right."

"So it seems," he murmured, hoping he'd escaped any further questions.

"There," she said, wiping the last of the soap from his face with a smile. She stood back to admire her handiwork, and Dev saw that flush rise on her cheeks again. He returned her smile, holding her gaze and running one hand over his smooth jaw.

"That feels wonderful," he said, the words low and intimate, though he hadn't intended it to be.

There was something in her eyes; an appreciative glint that made his thoughts stray into dangerous territory.

Miss Kendall looked away from him, busying herself in gathering the shaving things together and cleaning the blade of the razor. "I'm glad," she said, a tart note to her voice. "But you needn't think I'll be doing this every day. You must learn to do it yourself, you know."

"Yes," Dev replied, his tone solemn. He smiled at her as she turned her back on him, knowing she did it so he couldn't see how he'd flustered her, and he *did* fluster her. "I will, you have my word."

"Good." She turned back then, holding the tray before her like a shield. "Well, then I'll... I'll see you at dinner."

She paused, not moving, as though she'd forgotten what she'd meant to do.

"You will," Dev agreed, amused now as he saw her swallow. She wanted to leave, but she didn't. The realisation made him smile, warmth unfurling in his chest.

"It's not much tonight, as we've been out," she continued, her tone almost apologetic. No, no, that would never do. "Nothing cooked, at least. Just cold meat and such like."

"You mean to say I won't have a cooked meal?" he demanded a deliberate thread of irritation to his words.

Her temper flashed in her eyes. "Not unless you cook it yourself, no!"

The words were curt and snappy, and Dev grinned at her. There she was, his little hellion.

"Oh!" she huffed, realising he was teasing her. She stalked to the door, leaving without another word while Dev held it open. He watched her walk back down the hallway, admiring the sway of her lovely behind as she went.

***

Dev yawned and stretched. He had officially lost his mind. There was no other explanation. It was three in the morning and here he was, feeding kittens. If any of his cronies from town discovered that the hard living, hard drinking viscount they knew had been reduced to such indignity, he'd never live it down.

Once he'd encouraged the little grey runt of the litter to drink his, or her, fill—Dev wasn't sure which—he laid his head back against the straw. It seemed pointless to go back to bed when he'd need to come back in a few hours anyway. The straw wasn't so uncomfortable. With a sigh, he closed his eyes.

***

Charity stared and stared, but could not decide what to do. She'd assumed, after hearing him tiptoe down the creaky stairs around midnight, that David would have had enough of his angel of mercy routine and decide the kittens could wait until a decent hour of the morning. When she had heard him tread the stairs once more at three am, she'd admitted astonishment. Feeling sorry that the poor man was getting no sleep at all, she'd decided to go for him, assuming he'd go again around six am. She was always up and doing by then anyway—a farm was no place for lay-a-beds—and so she had thought to allow him a lie in and had risen at five thirty, expecting to send him back to bed. Except she couldn't... because he was asleep in the straw, with the kittens in his lap.

She bit her lip, wondering how long she dared just stand and stare at him. It was a view worth studying, in her opinion.

Charity had experienced little of the male of the species. Oh, there was her brother and she'd brought John up from a baby, so she knew what the basic anatomy looked like but... well, she'd never seen a man like this before. She knew Kit was a beautiful man, but he was slender and built on finer lines than this fellow, and he was *her brother*. Ugh.

David, though. She swallowed, her throat feeling tight and rather dry. His head lolled back against the straw and she admired his rather obstinate, square jaw, and the strong line of his throat. His hair stuck up in odd places, dishevelled, with bits of straw caught in the thick black here and there and, as her gaze travelled over him, she saw black hair on his chest too where his shirt gaped open. He'd pulled on breeches and boots, but his shirt was open, falling a little from one heavy shoulder to expose a dark nipple. He was exquisite. Masculine beauty at its finest, not that she had anything to compare it to, but suddenly it was hard to breathe.

Wondering how she dared, Charity tiptoed closer, kneeling in the straw beside him. She'd come to feed the kittens, so he could sleep, and he was sleeping so... she'd feed the kittens and not disturb him. There was no law about admiring the scenery while she did it.

She reached, intending to pluck one kitten from his lap when a large, dark hand darted out, wrapping around her wrist.

Charity squealed, staring at Dev whose eyes were now wide awake and staring at her.

"Oh, it's you," he said, looking a little bewildered, and smothering a yawn, perhaps not as awake as he'd first appeared. "You startled me."

"Sorry," she said, swallowing as he still held a tight grasp on her arm. "I came to feed the kittens, so you could get some sleep but... you were still here."

"Oh," he said again, as Charity realised how close he was.

Her gaze fell to his chest, to the smooth expanse of warm skin and the dark, wiry hair she felt the sudden desire to run her fingers through. She dragged her eyes back to his, only to find them amused and dark with some emotion that sent her skin prickling with awareness.

"I must have fallen asleep," he murmured.

She watched as his eyes dropped to her mouth, and he licked his lips.

"Could I have my hand back please?" She'd intended her words to sound annoyed but, somehow, they were more squeaky than imperious.

"Depends what you want to do with it," he said, running his thumb over the pulse that was thudding beneath the skin at her wrist.

The low, masculine timbre of his voice made her breath shorten. That mocking tone that implied he knew well she was an innocent who had strayed into dangerous territory fired temptation and indignation within her at the same time.

"I came to feed the kittens," she repeated, the words breathless despite her best efforts.

The look in his eyes reminded her of barn cats when they had a mouse cornered in a dark place, but then the intense expression fell from his eyes and he looked away, releasing her hand.

"So you did." He seemed tense suddenly the teasing quality gone and a harder set to his jaw. He picked the kittens up, one by one, and put them back in the straw where they mewled and crawled over each other. "They're all yours," he said, terse now as he got to his feet, brushed off the straw, and left her alone in the barn without a backwards glance.

Charity let out a breath, not knowing what to think. Disappointment at his abrupt departure was not something she ought to feel, his company not something she ought to look forward to. He would leave soon enough, and she did not need or want a broken heart. It was better this way. She ought to thank her lucky stars he didn't wish to toy with her affections or seduce her. Whether she would was another matter.

Chapter 9

"Wherein there's sweetness enough to tempt a saint, never mind a devil."

Dev sat beside his bedroom window, too tense to sleep. Below him, the farm was a hive of activity, the cockerel shouting his head off while the chickens showed off, cackling over who laid the first eggs. The cow was lowing, rubbing her head against the fence post, impatient for milking, while the rhythmic sound of Mr Baxter sweeping the yard was a constant shushing in the background.

The sun rose behind it all, fecund and golden, tinting the sky a hazy pastel tone as tiny puffs of white cloud drifted upon a lazy breeze.

He inhaled, willing the simmering in his blood to dissipate and leave him be. That flickering sense of anticipation to see her again disturbed his peace of mind and threatened to make him a villain in every sense of the word.

Waking to find Miss Kendall so close to him, her eyes on him with such open appreciation… it had fired his blood. Dev had felt the tumult of her pulse beneath her skin, seen the eager flush to her face. He could have kissed her then. She would have allowed it. He could have tumbled her into the straw and….

Dev gritting his teeth. *No.* There were limits. He was hiding away here when all the time he had set the wheels in motion to remove them from the property, from the only life they'd ever known. The shadows in the young woman's eyes were easy to see, as was the tension in her shoulders when discussions moved to the future and what they were to do. Dev always made himself scarce during such conversations, as though he was giving them privacy, when he was in fact escaping the burden of guilt that was growing heavier the longer he stayed.

Mr Baxter was a miserable old buzzard, but he seemed genuinely fond of them all, in his own way, and no one could deny he earned his bread. All the jobs that the women could not manage fell to him and Dev could tell it was wearing him down, though he said nothing. It was clear he was not as young as he had once been. He ought to be filling the wood store, which was dwindling, but chopping wood was hard graft. The old fellow had also mentioned the fencing around the horses' paddock needed repair. Yet now they lived in a quandary, not being able to spend time or money on a place they were leaving. So, Mr Baxter had agreed to cobble something together to last the weeks they had left. Dev had noticed the quality of the workmanship around the place and knew it would rankle with a man who took pride in his skills.

Mrs Baxter worked from dusk till dawn and everything she did Miss Kendall matched her and then some. The two women cleaned and cooked, made and mended clothes, and dealt with the laundry. Mrs Baxter milked the cow and Charity the goats. They tended the large kitchen garden and made preserves and pickles and jams, curing meat and making butter and cheese. Some produce they sold whilst they stored the rest for the harsh winters ahead. Winters here were cruel and could keep a body indoors while the snow lay thick at the door for weeks on end.

Kit hadn't the stamina for physical work, which might have made Dev sneer if he couldn't see how much it gnawed at him, and how honestly Kit wished he could have been of more use. He helped where he could but tired easily, his pale skin becoming flushed, that rather strange feverish glint in his eyes. He did however, bring the most income into the place, such as it was. The young man had been full of himself last night as he brought news that his work was to be published in a rather radical paper called *The Examiner*. The pride in his sister's eyes at his success had shifted something in Dev's chest, which still ached as though someone had pried back one of his ribs.

What would become of them when they left the farm? Would they move to a city? Their uncle lived in Bristol. Thoughts of Miss Kendall confined to the narrow streets of Bristol and far from the rugged wilderness of the hills she loved made him uncomfortable. She had too much energy and life to survive any lodgings Kit's earnings could pay for. They'd not be able to afford one of the better areas. How far from the slums would she live? Unease stirred in his chest and he tried to push it away. Perhaps the sea air would do Kit good?

As the guilt lay a little heavier, he wondered what she would do if she discovered his identity, discovered that he was the cause of their distress? He pushed the idea away, uncomfortable with the sensation that pulsed through his him.

With a frown. he returned his gaze out of the window, and watched as Miss Kendall strode towards the kitchen garden with a fork and an empty basket. He saw her smother a yawn as she went, pushing a dark lock of hair from her face and tucking it behind her ear. She'd left her bed early so he could sleep. The thought stuck in his throat.

Decision made, he hauled on his clothes and hurried down the stairs.

***

Charity looked at the rows of potatoes and sighed. It was a job she rather enjoyed, seeing the smooth rounded shapes rising out of the dirt. At this time of the year when the skins were fragile they tasted as sweet as early summer. Buttered and cooked with mint there was nothing better. Today however, lethargy pulled at her bones.

She loved it here. She loved every hard-won inch of this land.

They'd tucked memories into every corner, every nook and cranny, and now and then Charity would unearth one, long forgotten.

There was the apple tree she'd got stuck in when she was five years old, and her father had climbed the gnarled roots to fetch her down again. Over there, down by the stream, was where Kit had pushed her into the icy water when she'd teased him for having a crush on a girl in the market. She'd been wearing her best Sunday dress and he'd been sent to bed with no supper. She'd snuck some up to him later, filled with remorse.

They'd all been born in the large, master bedroom here, which, even now, lay empty. Though Mr and Mrs Baxter had encouraged Kit to take it, now he was master, he couldn't bear to do it. It had the best views and the most space, but he said it didn't feel right. When he in turn had given it to Charity, she'd also refused. Some ghosts still lingered even if their presence was a warm one. She wondered if they were clinging to the past, hanging on to something which was long gone and could never return. Perhaps Kit was right. Perhaps, at last, it would force her to face the real world, and to live in it. The thought was frightening, unsettling, and her spirits tumbled a little further.

Everything would change. It had already begun. Even her own thoughts differed from before. She'd been perfectly content hating their nameless houseguest, but then he'd not only found a name, he'd rescued helpless kittens and made her little sister happy. It was so unfair. How could she fight that? He'd taught John to swear and cuss and gamble, which she was still unsure about but… he had to become a man one day. He needed a father figure and Kit always had his head in the clouds.

Yet her growing fascination with the dangerous, blue-eyed devil had already led her feelings onto unmarked paths, into forbidden places where snares and brambles awaited. Her instincts told her to keep clear of him, that he would only cast her further down a road she ought not to follow. Except she had never even been kissed before, never known what it was to feel a strong pair of arms around her. She had thought she had enough in her life, that she was content, but then the wicked viscount had moved to evict them, and David had arrived and stirred up her heart with as much ease as Mrs Baxter stirring a pot of soup.

Here she was, almost an old maid at twenty-five years old, with a ready-made family and without the faintest idea of what it was to be in love.

With a sigh she squared her shoulders and lifted the fork. Daydreaming and maudlin thoughts would not get her anywhere. The potatoes would not dig themselves.

"May I help with that?"

Charity gasped, too lost in her own head to have noticed anyone walking through the garden.

"My, you startled me," she said, wishing that alone accounted for the way her heart was pounding as David walked towards her. "I thought you were having a lie in?"

He shook his head and held out his hand to take the fork from her. "How could I lie abed when you are working your fingers to the bone?"

"You managed it well enough up till now," she said, flushing as she heard the tart note to her voice. For once she hadn't meant to be so confrontational.

She saw a flicker of guilt in his eyes but to her relief he came about, squaring his shoulders. "I was regaining my strength," he said, his tone dignified.

Charity snorted, deliberately provoking. Thank God he hadn't apologised. The kitten incident was bad enough. She looked him over. "You look strong enough to me," she said, and then cursed as the blasted man smirked at her.

"I'm so glad you noticed," he murmured.

She glowered at him, folding her arms. "Well, on you get, then," she snapped, huffing. "But do mind your delicate hands. I wouldn't want you to get blisters."

David opened his mouth to retort and then apparently thought better of it, narrowing his eyes as he lifted the fork. "You're digging these up?" he asked, pointing at the thick green leaves of the potato plants.

"You don't know what they are, do you?" Charity said, grinning at his ignorance.

David thrust the fork into the soft soil after sending her a look of disgust. "I pay people to do this sort of thing," he said, his tone scathing. "And if you don't want my help you only need say."

"No, no," Charity said, giving him a condescending smile. "I should be pleased to educate you. These are potatoes. Repeat after me now. Po–ta–to."

"Funny," he said, shaking his head as he shook the earth from the tines of the fork. "Hilarious, you are."

Charity nodded, smug. "I know." She was enjoying herself enormously.

"Oh, look," he exclaimed, grinning and sounding surprised as the purple skinned potatoes showed themselves like jewels in the soft earth. "Is that what they look like? I've never seen them uncooked."

"Really?" she said, shaking her head in wonder. "They're called Fortyfold. They're tasty. We'll have some for dinner."

"Excellent." He bent down and picked them from the dirt.

Charity stamped on some strange, soft sensation that rolled through her chest. He looked ridiculously pleased with himself as he bent to collect the tubers, placing them in the basket for her. Good Lord, but what disparate worlds they inhabited. He'd never dirtied his hands before, never seen the source of where his dinner came from, and yet the pleasure he took in the discovery warmed something inside her. There was an honest sense of delight shining in his eyes as he reached for the fork and started on the next plant.

"How many do you want?" he asked as he began to dig again. He paused, his expression quizzical. "Miss Kendall?"

"Oh." She started, realising she'd been staring at him and not answering the question. "Well, fill the basket for now and we'll take those to the kitchen. There are peas and beans to pick after," she added, brisk as she dragged her gaze from the too small shirt that grew taut over his broad chest as he dug.

Swallowing and turning her back on him so she couldn't see his self-satisfied expression, Charity hurried off to fetch another basket, and left him to his work.

***

It was strangely therapeutic, snapping the beans off and throwing them down into the basket. The vines rose into the sky, scaling the supports given them, scarlet flowers bobbing bright against the blue sky as a warm breeze teased them into motion. Miss Kendall couldn't reach the highest ones, so they worked together. Unable to resist the temptation, he often stood behind her, reaching up while she worked lower, so close they almost touched. Now and then he allowed his arm to brush against hers, wondering if she felt the simmering heat between them as he did.

The scent of her lifted as the breeze toyed with her hair, loose curls falling down her neck. It was far from the exotic, sophisticated perfumes he was used to. She was far from the experienced, jaded creatures he'd desired before now. Yet desire surged beneath his skin all the same, no matter how he tried to keep it at bay. She smelled wholesome, if such a thing were even possible. Her innocent perfume filled his senses: the bread she had baked that morning, clean linen, and soap, and the faintest trace of roses. How could such simple things combine to create something so intoxicating?

There was a peace that came with this work, too, and he understood the pleasure he saw in her eyes when she looked around at the garden bursting with produce. Yet now and then there was sorrow in her expression, when he thought perhaps she remembered she must soon leave it all behind.

That strange, unwelcome ache behind his ribs was still there, insidious and crafty, getting under his skin. Once or twice he caught himself rubbing his chest with the heel of his hand, as though he could ease the guilt away.

He watched as she bent down to move the basket along, and the movement pushed her breasts forward. They strained at the neckline of her gown, plump and mouth-watering. Dev swallowed hard as the desire to reach around her and cup them in his hands slammed into him. Heat prickled over his skin, making him sweat harder than the summer sun that beat down on the back of his neck. He tore his gaze away, only to notice how her skirts clung to her behind, showing the curve of her bottom.

Oh, God.

Dev closed his eyes, willing the image to leave his mind, but then he heard her curse and opened his eyes in time to see her stumble. She fell, her back to his chest, and he caught her, sucking in a breath at those lovely curves he'd just admired touching the growing discomfort beneath the placket of his trousers. Without conscious thought his arms went around her, one hand splaying across her stomach, the other at her hip.

"Easy there," he said, his voice sounding low and unsteady

She stilled, and he had the distinct impression she was holding her breath.

He looked down over her shoulder and discovered his mistake as he noted the rapid rise and fall of her breasts. Her bottom pressed against him, so close that he wondered if she could feel his growing desire. Would she understand what she did to him? His fingers tightened a little upon her hip as he fought the urge to pull her closer still and illustrate it further. He waited for her to curse, to turn and slap him and give him some stinging set down. But she didn't, and he didn't know if he was glad or not. He wanted to kiss her, to hold her, but instinctively felt there was danger here, for his own heart as much as hers.

God he was a bastard. A fact he'd always relished. Until now. Damn his awakening conscience. He should let her go and apologise, yet she wasn't moving away from him, hadn't protested his touch. The hand at her stomach moved, tentative at first, and he watched it as though it had a mind of its own. It moved to her waist and then slid higher, so slowly. He felt her breathing hitch as his thumb grazed the underside of her breast.

The scream that rent the air was high and bloodcurdling and they both jolted as the moment shattered.

"Jane!" Charity cried, moving before Dev had even registered the fact it was the little girl who had screamed.

She hitched up her skirts, running through the gardens as Dev shook himself out of his daze and followed her.

They thundered into the yard and the sheer relief in his heart as he saw the child was whole and unharmed was alarming to him. Her brother, however, was another matter. His clothes were torn and filthy clothes, he'd skinned both knees, his nose was dripping blood down his shirt, and he had the beginnings of a remarkable black eye.

He held two fat rabbits in one tight fist, the knuckles bruised and raw.

"John! Oh, John!" Charity fell to her knees in the dirt, running her hands over the boy, checking for broken bones. "Where does it hurt, love? Who did this to you?"

John turned scarlet at his sister's fussing, his lips trembling as her concern battered down his obvious desire for bravery, to be a man.

"Stop mollycoddling the boy," Dev snapped, exasperated as John sent him a pleading look. "He's fine. Nothing more than a few cuts and bruises."

Charity turned on him, astonished and angry. "This is none of your concern," she said, her tone furious as she reached for John's hand. "Come along, love," she said, her voice soft now. "Come into the kitchen and I'll clean you up, good as new. Batty baked shortbread this morning and you can have as much as you can eat." She smiled at him, ruffling his hair, and Dev saw the shock in her eyes as the boy snatched his hand away.

"I'm fine," he said, his voice trembling a little but his chin jutting with determination. "I can clean myself up."

With something that might have been remorse in his chest Dev watched the incomprehension in her eyes.

"But what happened?" she asked, annoyance flickering in her expression now as she saw the rabbits in his hand. "I thought I told you not to walk the moors on your own. It's far too dangerous. We discussed this!"

"No," John replied, growing obstinate now. "You told me I couldn't. There was no discussion, and I was only checking my snares." His voice grew strident, his cheeks flushing deeper as his emotions rose, a dangerous glitter to his eyes. "I caught two, look," he said, holding them up to show Dev and bursting with pride.

"And did they put up a fight?" Charity demanded, her hands on her hips as her own temper rose.

John returned a look of disgust and the similarity between the two siblings in that instant was startling. Good Lord, they were all stubborn as mules. "No. But three gypsy boys did. They tried to steal them from me, but I stopped them." He stood taller, squaring his shoulders. "I fought them and made them run away."

"What?" Charity exclaimed, horrified.

Dev's heart sank as he realised what she'd say.

"You should have let them have the blasted rabbits, John. You could have been hurt! You *have* been hurt. We don't need the silly rabbits anyway!"

Dev winced, knowing just how deep that would have cut the boy's fragile pride.

"Don't be ridiculous," he said, his voice hard as he wondered what the devil he was playing at. Antagonising Charity was not in his best interests, but he couldn't bear the mortification in the boy's eyes. It was all too familiar. Memories stirring in the dark recesses of his mind. "They're fine, fat rabbits, and they were his. No man can let another take what belongs to him. You did right, John. Well done."

For a moment something in Dev's heart squeezed as he saw the gratitude in the boy's eyes.

"Oh, you bloody men!"

Charity turned on him and Dev took a step back. He'd known she'd be irritated with him. but the fury in her eyes was rather more than he'd bargained for.

"There were three of them! He could have been badly hurt and left for dead. They might have killed him! They might have had knives. People can do terrible things in the heat of the moment. Do none of you ever *think*?" she shouted, moving closer giving him a hard shove, both hands flat on his chest. "You just react, don't you? You never think of the consequences, you never give a thought to those who care for you, those who get left to cope with the mess you leave behind." Her voice quavered, and she snapped her mouth shut, her jaw growing rigid. "Fine," she said, throwing up her hands. "You obviously have more experience at raising children, so go ahead. You deal with it. You deal with all of it. *I quit!*"

Dev and John exchanged glances, neither one of them knowing what to say as the enraged figure stalked from the yard. She went through the gate, slamming it shut behind her, and kept walking.

"Sorry," John said, his voice quiet. "I didn't mean for you to get into trouble, sir."

Dev snorted, giving the boy a rueful look. "It's kind of my *raison d'être*," he replied, deadpan, smiling as the boy frowned at him. "It's French. Means my 'reason to be'."

"Oh." John grinned at him. "They are fine though aren't they, sir?" he said, holding his rabbits like a trophy. "I couldn't let the other boys take them."

"Indeed not," Dev agreed, laying his hand on John's shoulder. "Quite right too. It's the principle of the thing, a matter of honour."

"Exactly!" John said, standing a little taller now. "I had to stand up for myself."

Dev sighed, wondering if he was about to make matters a whole lot worse. "You know, I do a little boxing myself. I... I could give you some tips." The words sounded rather grudging, and Dev didn't know why he was offering at all. It was none of his affair. "If you'd like?" he added, half hoping John would refuse.

The boy's eyes grew wide and round, his mouth falling a little open.

"If I'd like?" he repeated, his voice faint and more than a little incredulous.

The worshipful look in his eyes made Dev feel more unsettled than ever.

"Oh, sir! I'd like that above all things."

"Hmph," Dev said, frowning, uncomfortable with such undeserved adulation. He moved forwards, gesturing for the boy to head towards the house. "Well, come along, then. We must get you cleaned up, so your sister can see it's not so bad and calms herself down."

"It's not her fault, sir," John said, all at once growing serious. "She worries, you see. After mother and father, and what with Kit...."

He trailed off, and Dev could see the fear in his eyes.

Charity and the Devil

"I know," Dev said, nodding. "I quite understand. You are a lucky young man to have a woman like her to care for you. She'd fight your battles for you if she could, but you must not let her."

John nodded gravely. "No sir. I know it."

Chapter 10

"Wherein pleasure is often a sin, and sin...."

Dev helped John clean up his cuts and bruises, though there would be a deal of mending for the women to do to repair the split seams and tears in the clothes he removed.

Once John had settled in the kitchen with a glass of milk and a plate of shortbread—well, he *was* only ten—Dev looked around for Charity.

On his second visit to the kitchen Mrs Baxter looked up from skinning the rabbits, a shrewd glint in her eyes. "You'll not find her. If she's gotten herself in a pelter, she'll go down to the river until her temper settles."

"Oh," Dev said, a little unnerved at being seen to be looking for her. "She won't be back for lunch?"

"Doubt it." Mrs Baxter left the rabbit and washed her hands. "Why don't you take her something to eat? Apologise for whatever it was you said to set her off."

"Apologise?" Dev baulked at the idea. He'd never apologised for anything in his life before. "She was wrong!"

Mrs Baxter tutted at him and shook her head. "Maybe so," she replied, giving him a stern look. "But she does the best she can, for everyone."

Dev watched as she filled a wicker basket with bread and cheese, slices of pie, and a jug of ale.

"She's not usually quite so unsettled as of late, but she wants everybody happy and healthy, and she loves this place to her last breath. Leaving it is tearing her apart."

Charity and the Devil

Dev frowned at the jagged feeling in his heart as Mrs Baxter held the basket out to him and for a moment he considered refusing. This was not his affair. Miss Kendall had said as much. Why should he care?

Mrs Baxter raised an eyebrow at him and, feeling much put upon, Dev reached out, took the basket, and stalked out of the kitchen. He found her down by the river as Mrs Baxter had predicted. By the time he reached her his boots were sodden. It never ceased to amaze him that, no matter how dry the summer, Dartmoor was always wet and boggy somewhere. The moors were treacherous, even to those who knew them well. It was all too easy to get lost and wander into a moss-covered bog. Sometimes you got nothing more than wet feet, other times the moss might conceal a granite crevice so deep a man could disappear without even a splash and never be seen again. Yet it was beautiful. Beautiful and dangerous, like the gleam on a sword, and it bred stubborn, hardy, wilful creatures, like the hot-tempered hellion sitting on the rock down there.

Dev sighed, noting her hunched posture, her knees brought up to her chest and her arms wrapped about them. Her head was resting on her knees, her face turned away from him. He wondered if she would continue to rant at him as he drew closer, and found himself shocked when she just looked up, her eyes full of despair, and turned away again.

"I brought you some lunch," he said, hovering and feeling ill at ease. He had no right being here. How the devil was he supposed to make her feel better? Yet the desire to do so crawled beneath his skin. She should be mad as hell and spitting fire. Instead she looked like a rag doll that had lost all its stuffing.

He sat down beside her and opened the basket, at a loss for anything else to do.

"I'm not hungry," she mumbled.

"Oh, come on," he said, forcing a light-hearted note into the words he was far from feeling. "You're always hungry."

She snorted but didn't comment, didn't grow angry at the teasing insult or retaliate. Dev sighed.

"I'm sorry," he said, finding he meant it.

He was still certain he'd been in the right, but he could have been tactful about it, and he couldn't bear to see the misery in her eyes. It made the ache in his chest grow heavier, the guilt at what he was doing to this family harder and harder to ignore.

"What for?" she asked, her voice dull. "Being right?"

He felt his eyebrows rise at the admission and she cast him a rueful look, her eyes overly bright.

"I don't know what to do for him." she said, her voice catching.

The sound was like a metal lure, tearing through the tender flesh of his heart and pulling taut, dragging him out of the dark depths and towards the surface, towards something he didn't know how to escape.

"He needs a father, he needs better than I can give him." A fat tear rolled down her cheek and she wiped it away, the gesture angry and impatient though another just followed the same path. "They all do."

"Don't be foolish," Dev replied, wishing he hadn't come looking for her. He was out of his depth. He didn't do comforting teary females, certainly not *innocent* teary females. "You've done everything you possibly could. More than anyone could expect of you."

"But it isn't enough." She looked up at him then, her soft brown eyes so full of sorrow he wanted to take it all away—all the hurt, all the uncertainty—but he couldn't. "I'm so frightened."

Charity and the Devil

The admission shocked him, knocking the breath from his lungs. He had thought Miss Kendall the indomitable, thick skinned type, a woman who wore sensible shoes and had chapped hands and knew how to run a farm. Except here she was, soft and so very beguiling.

Before he knew what he was doing—before the thought had even become a thought he could dismiss because it was beyond foolish—he had taken her in his arms. He gathered her up, swinging her legs around so she sat upon his lap, and laid her head on his shoulder. He stroked her hair, rubbed circles on her back and made the soft reassuring noises he used to soothe his horse as he let her cry. He had no idea if it was helping as he wasn't used to being kind to weeping women, but it was the best he could do. There was nothing he could say. He could not pretend that it would be all right. He could not give her hope that the sale of the farm would not go through, for he knew better than anyone that it would. Guilt and desire warred in his chest and he had never hated himself more.

Hell and damnation.

He wished he'd never come here. He wished he was still in blissful ignorance of the heartache and trouble he was causing a family who had already seen their fair share of both. Yet, here he was, with the redoubtable Miss Charity Kendall clinging to *him* for support and comfort, when all along he was the devil at the heart of it all, the maggot writhing in the apple, spoiling everything.

"I-I'm sorry, I've made your shirt all wet," she said, hiccoughing and trying to regain her composure.

"Not to worry, I have other shirts."

"No, you don't," she said, contradicting him as ever. "That one's Kit's."

Despite everything, he laughed. "Dreadful, argumentative creature," he said, though there was warmth and affection behind the words.

She grinned and let out a little laugh herself, uncertain and somewhat shy as she looked up at him. Her gaze fell to his mouth and his body was at once on alert. He wondered if she had the slightest idea what she did to him, what she invited by looking at him so. Somehow, he doubted it.

Dev swallowed, promising himself he'd look away, that he'd break the tension that was simmering between them.

"I've never been kissed before, you know."

Oh, hell.

The words were little more than a whisper, yet he felt them resonate in his bones, felt the spark they created and the flare of the tinder that was his dry, dusty, shrivelled up heart bursting into flames.

"You ought not say that," he said, striving for control. He was the bastard who had caused her whole family's trouble. He would not compound his villainy, he would not fall that far into the darkness.

"Why not? It's true." She stared at him, her eyes guileless, strangely trusting for all the animosity she had cast his way.

"Because it's as good as an invitation," he said, the words terse as frustration seethed beneath his skin. The sun warmed his back and, for once, the surrounding ground appeared soft, dry, and thick with moss. A comfortable bed for a tumble, and a willing partner… God, he wanted that.

"I know it is. I'm not as innocent as all that." She smiled at him and the sight of it was like a blow to his guts, winding him.

"You shouldn't…." he began, trying to find the strength to remove his arms from around her, to ignore the invitation in her eyes before he crossed an unforgiveable line. "You mustn't…."

But she reached up, coiling her arms about his neck.

"Make me feel something," she said, pleading in her voice. "I'm so tired of being frightened and angry and lonely. Make me feel something else, something new.... *Please.*"

It was the *please* that undid him, that unravelled any grasp on right or wrong. The lines had blurred now, and he no longer knew which way was up. He knew neither who he was nor wanted to be... except he knew that he wanted to be the one who kissed her first. He wanted to be the one she dreamed of and sighed over, the one who made her feel everything a kiss could be. He could give her that at least, as she'd asked for it. Just a kiss, nothing more. He'd make it sweet and tender and everything a first kiss ought to be, and then he'd let her go.

Dev reached out his hand, cupping her face and wishing his heart wouldn't leap so as she turned into his caress, closing her eyes. Such trust, such a gift she would give him. He lowered his head, reminding himself of his intentions and holding his own desires in an iron grip. Sweetness, innocence, and tenderness, he reminded himself, but as his lips brushed hers the fire burning in his heart licked at his skin, blazing higher.

His breath caught, but still he held back, pressing his lips against hers again and again: a dozen kisses, light as a butterfly's wing, every bit as tender as he'd promised. With careful touches, he encouraged her lips to part, his tongue inviting, teasing. Yet Charity was not the kind to shrink from life, from experience, or from a challenge. He ought to have known that by now.

She opened her mouth to him, pulling his head down towards her. The fire blazed brighter and hotter. It swept through his blood as he pulled her closer, wanting and needing, devouring everything in its path and burning for more, and the more he took the more she offered.

His grip on control slipped and his position on the rock was simply not good enough. He needed to touch her everywhere, every part of him with every part of her, nothing between them. The desire for it, for her, the burning need drove every coherent thought from his mind as he tumbled her onto her back on the moss. She drew a breath as she saw him move over her, braced on his arms, and he searched her gaze for any sign of doubt, waited for her to tell him no, but found nothing except longing.

"Kiss me," she said, tugging at his neck.

Dev ducked his head, pressing his mouth to the tender skin beneath her ear and she moaned, arching beneath him. He trailed damp kisses down her neck, across her collar bone as one hand moved to cup her breast. Oh, sweet mercy, she was so soft, so pliant and willing, and he was as hard as the rocks that the river swept over. Desire was raging faster than the water rushing past them, tumbling through his thoughts and sweeping aside all his good intentions. All he could think of, the only thought in his head, was of sinking into her softness and wiping the sorrow from her eyes, watching her come apart for him, writhing beneath him as he loved her.

"Yes," she murmured, her hands tangling in his hair. "Yes, David, make me forget it all."

David?

The name that didn't belong to him jarred and he stilled. He had wanted to be the one she sighed for, his name on her lips as she found her pleasure with him... except he was a fraud, an imposter, and quite possibly the most despicable bastard in the whole of the country.

He pushed away from her, getting to his feet and putting as much distance between them as he could.

"What is it?" she asked, bracing herself on her elbows as she stared at him, perplexed by his sudden retreat.

The movement pushed her breasts forward, straining the neckline of the simple gown she wore, and Dev cursed, rubbing a hand over his face as he tried to get a grip on his sanity. He dared to glance back at her. Desire flushed her cheeks, her mouth swollen from his kisses, her hair in disarray... she had never looked lovelier.

He cursed and strode down to the water, scooping up icy handfuls and throwing it over his face and the back of his neck. He wiped his face on his sleeve, aware that no amount of frigid water would put out the fire she had lit.

"David?"

"Don't!" he snapped, not wanting to hear the evidence of his lies and duplicity upon the lips that had kissed him so tenderly. He snapped his mouth shut, hating himself for the confusion in her eyes. "Forgive me," he said, the words rough. "You don't understand what you are doing, what I want from you."

"Of course I do," she said, smiling at him. She held out her hand, inviting him back down to lie beside her. "Come back to me, David."

"No!" He turned his back, that name twisting something dark and ugly in his gut, and he cursed whatever perverse pleasure fate had taken in landing him in this situation. Somewhere someone was having a good laugh at his expense, he was sure of it. "You're sweet, Charity," he said, closing his eyes against that sweetness as it threatened to unravel his sanity. "Sweet and innocent, and I'll not ruin you when you haven't the slightest idea of what you're doing."

She gave a huff of laughter, sitting up and favouring him with a look of indignation.

"Don't be an idiot," she snapped. "I'm nothing of the sort and you know it. I may not have any experience with men, but I take the cow to be serviced by our neighbour's bull. I do run a farm, if you hadn't noticed. Procreation is rather an important part of it and I'm perfectly aware that the male of the species has one thing on its mind, no matter *which* species." Her tone was tart and frustrated now, perhaps embarrassed now as her cheeks were scarlet. "I knew what I wanted, and so did you. I see no reason for you to get all chivalrous about it."

She stalked off, brushing moss from her skirts as she went, and Dev stared after her, torn between rage and the desire to wrestle her to the ground and show her just what it was she'd been asking for. He gritted his teeth, reached for the untouched picnic basket and stalked after her.

"Well, forgive me for trying to be a gentleman," he yelled after her. "I should have known not to have bothered on your behalf, Miss Hellion!"

She turned on him, hands on hips, dark eyes flashing. "Oh, for heaven's sake! Stop acting like you're the injured party. You were just terrified I would cry all over you and beg you to marry me the minute we were done. Well, not on your life," she threw at him, the sneer he was all too familiar with making a spectacular reappearance. "I'd not marry a worthless rake like you if you begged me. All I wanted was to forget my troubles, just for a few minutes, but no, that was beyond your capabilities."

She folded her arms, glaring at him, and Dev wondered if he'd ever been more furious in his entire life. If he had, he couldn't recall it.

He stalked up to her, so close they almost touched, and slid his hand behind her neck, lifting her head and making her gasp, her eyes widening.

"If I'd have taken you as you'd asked, it would have taken a damn sight more than a few minutes," he said, the words hard, angry, and full of repressed desire. "I was trying to have a care for you, to not take advantage of the situation when you were upset and vulnerable, but if you are so desperate for a good tupping, by all means lie down and spread your legs. I'm only too happy to oblige."

The slap was hard and ferocious and made his skin burn, but at least it knocked some sense into him. With regret he watched as

Charity and the Devil

she ran back up the hill towards the farm and wondered where the hell he'd gone wrong.

Chapter 11

"Wherein proposals are made and our hero suffers a shock."

Dev avoided her for the next few days, working around the farm. Seeing as he had a willing pair of hands and a strong back, Mr Baxter pounced on him and set him to cleaning out the barn, the cow-shed, the goats and, the final indignity, the pigsties.

Strangely however, Dev found he didn't mind. Admittedly, the stench was breathtaking, but the work was satisfying. He rather enjoyed shaking out the new straw over the cleaned floor, the scent of last summer's sun floating around him like the dust motes that caught the light. Heated thoughts of Charity in that same straw with her skirts around her waist plagued him at regular intervals, and nothing he could do would make them leave him be, so he worked harder. If they wondered what had got into him, no one asked, happy enough to accept his help, and so he worked like a man possessed.

He was, he realised, exactly that: possessed by the need for Charity Kendall, by the image of her behind his eyes, spread out beneath him, all willing warmth and invitation. At the mercy of his libido, he worked until he sweated, until his body was too exhausted to act on its desires. By the end of the day he ached from his labours. He'd given up the journey from bed to barn and, lying in the straw with the kittens to make feeding them easier, he slept like the dead.

It didn't help.

Thoughts of her invaded his dreams and, when the kittens woke him, mewling to be fed, he found himself hard, and aching in a way that had nothing to do with mucking out barns. Cursing and irritable, he rose with the dawn and washed in cold water; anything to rid himself of the ever present and desperate desire that crawled beneath his skin, wearing him down and pushing at his good intentions.

Dev wiped his face on his shirt sleeve, sneering at his own arrogance. Good intentions indeed. His good intentions were not to ruin a young woman whose life had already been brought to disaster at his hand. Just because he'd not allowed himself to steal her innocence along with her home, didn't make him any less of a fiend and he knew it.

The days passed, marked by the simmering tension between them. They didn't speak any more, avoiding each other whenever possible. Yet there were still heated looks exchanged across the yard, across the dining table at night, eyes filled with anger and frustration and... *need*. That she still wanted him despite her anger was obvious. He felt her gaze on him when he worked, the knowledge burning him from the inside, temptation licking at his skin, his willpower devoured in the flames until it was nothing but ash. Yet as his desire burned hotter his guilt increased, and as the inevitable sale grew closer, he only despised himself more.

He trudged back to the house to get breakfast. He'd been turning over a neglected part of the garden since daybreak, readying the soil to sow cabbages, though he didn't know why. They all knew they would not be here to harvest them in the spring, but some stubborn sense of hope still clung to Charity. She didn't want the garden to be devoid of produce if by some miracle the miserable viscount died of dissipation before the sale could complete. That she was talking about him made a peculiar despondency settle in his bones. He was tired, he realised. Tired of lies, of pretending to be a good man, and tired of the truth of who he really was.

He glanced down at his hands, finding the palms blistered, calluses beginning on his fingers after their recent introduction to what real work felt like. They gave him a sense of satisfaction, which seemed odd as they were sore as hell, yet for once he felt he'd done something worthwhile. For the first time in his life he'd done something to build rather than destroy, no matter that planting cabbage wasn't exactly something to stand the test of time. At least he wasn't pissing his fortune up the wall. That was something.

As he got closer to the house, his nose detected bacon frying, making his stomach twist and clamour. By the time he turned the corner he was salivating. He wasn't sure what made him stop—some sixth sense, perhaps—but he darted out of sight just in time.

His steward, Phillip Ogden. was on the doorstep, talking to Charity.

Dev peered around the corner, pressing himself against the wall and straining to hear what they were talking about.

"So there really is nothing to be done?" Charity said, and Dev could hear the last of her hopes as they died in the dull tone of her voice.

"Come, Miss Kendall," Ogden said, taking her arm and guiding her to a bench in front of the house. "Come and sit down, you've had a shock."

Dev ducked back out of sight as they drew nearer to him. He heard Charity's skirts rustling as she sat.

"I can't tell you how very sorry I am," Ogden continued, his voice low and confiding. "I tried once more to remonstrate with the viscount in my last correspondence, to make him reconsider the callous nature of his actions, but I'm afraid he is a violent man, and a powerful one. I confess I fear his reprisals. In any case, his reply was formed in the coarsest, most vulgar terms, with which I won't sully your ears."

The lying bastard!

Dev gritted his teeth. God damn the man. He'd always known Mr Ogden was a slippery character in terms of his attempts to work around him, but Dev had believed the man was working in his best interests out of loyalty to the title. Apparently not.

"Oh, Mr Ogden, no. I begged you not to intervene on our behalf," Charity replied, her voice trembling now with the effort not to cry. "Truly, you have been more than kind and I should have been horrified if you'd been in any way harmed or lost your job on our account."

"I must be honest, Miss Kendall," the lying toad said, sincerity dripping from his voice. "I did it for selfish reasons."

"Whatever do you mean?" Charity replied, innocent that she was.

Dev's heart thudded in his chest. No. No, surely not.

He could almost see the supercilious smile on the man's face as he said the words that Dev knew would follow.

"I had hoped that... if I could save your family's home, perhaps you might look kindly upon me."

Dev experience a surge of fury that chased the breath from his lungs. The desire to reveal his presence and shake Ogden until his teeth rattled was so fierce he had to clench his fists and pressed his head back against the granite wall so hard it would leave bruises. The pain steadied him. He couldn't interfere, could not let Ogden see him. If he did, Charity would know everything and Dev would never get the chance to explain, to apologise... though what the bloody hell he'd say he couldn't fathom. There was no explanation past the fact he was an unutterable bastard, no apology he could make she would care to listen to. Yet he had to try.

Their conversation had moved on and Dev closed his eyes, knowing only too well what would come next.

A rustling sound and Charity's sharp intake of breath suggested that Ogden had gotten to his knees.

"Miss Kendall, you must be aware of my deep regard for you, for the years in which I have held your lovely countenance in my heart. I admit, I never dared to hope, not until now, what with the disparity in our ages, but... might you do me the honour of becoming my wife?"

Dev's heart stuttered, the permanent ache that sat beneath his ribs now less of an ache and more akin to a knife wound. The shock of it startled him, the depths of the wound more profound than he could have known.

Say no. Say no. For the love of God, say no.

He couldn't breathe. His lungs had locked down tight, and there was an ache in his throat that wouldn't let him swallow.

Charity, please, love, say no.

"Mr Ogden." Charity's voice was faint, her shock audible. "I-I don't know what to say."

Yes, you do, Dev begged her, his silent prayer repeated over and over as he realised just how much it would hurt to see her marry his steward. He'd never believed himself capable of caring for someone else, had always thought he was too twisted, too cruel to give a damn about anyone but himself. Yet the Kendalls had shown him what it meant to be family, and the longing to remain a part of it hit him square in the chest.

"I have told no one this," Ogden carried on, with what sounded like a smug tone to Dev's ear, "but I have secured new employment. I cannot continue to work for such a wicked, dissipated rakehell as the viscount. He is a vile bully, a libertine who seeks nothing but oblivion in vice, squandering his fortune and sullying his father's good name. His treatment of you was the last straw, and so I have been making discreet inquiries."

"Oh?" There was trepidation in Charity's voice now and Dev swallowed hard, wishing he could dispute the words of his steward on this too, accuse him of being a liar once more.

To his shame, however, he recognised the description only too well. He had wealth and status, yet he had nothing that Charity would value.

"Lord Brady has offered me a position with him in Yorkshire. It is not such a prestigious name to be sure, but the position comes with a handsome house, quite large enough to accommodate your siblings, and I would offer Mr and Mrs Baxter a position there much as they have here, if that would meet with your approval?"

Dev heard a muffled sob and Ogden's exclamation of sympathy.

"I fear I have overwhelmed you," he said, sounding too damn pleased for his own good.

Dev gritted his teeth. Charity wasn't overwhelmed. She was never overwhelmed. She took every damn thing in her stride. Her tears were because she didn't want to marry a man she didn't care for, but Dev knew—just as Ogden did—that she had no choice.

He felt sick, in physical pain, as if his guts had been caught in a giant hand and twisted.

Charity and Phillip Ogden.

Married.

Regret was a weight that dragged at his heart, regret for everything Charity would have to give up, for all the family would lose. All of it his doing. He wanted to make it right. If he was honest, he wanted far more than that though. He wanted Charity to be his, to love him and turn to him when the world grew harsh. He wanted to protect her from anything that might hurt her. Especially Phillip bloody Ogden. Thoughts of the bastard laying his hands upon her spun in his mind, visions of that lying prig taking her innocence, the prize she had offered to *him*, and he'd rejected. A prickly sweat broke out over his skin. He didn't know what to do. Numb and cold, he *could* do nothing more than stand and listen, waiting with his heart in his mouth for her inevitable acceptance.

"I am truly honoured by your proposal, Mr Ogden," Charity replied, and the words were careful, her voice trembling now. Dev inhaled, preparing himself for the pain he knew would come. "And... and I am most grateful but... I cannot give you an answer today. I-I need a little time to think things over."

"But surely...." Ogden began, a thread of laughter in his voice, as if he could not believe she hadn't snapped at his offer. "Surely, in the circumstances...."

The man was stunned. Dev couldn't believe it either. Ogden's offer would save them, and all Charity would need to do was sacrifice her own happiness. It wasn't as if she hadn't done that already. Dev knew she'd do it again in a heartbeat. So why did she hesitate?

Surely not because of him?

His heart gave an uneven thud in his chest, the ache beneath his ribs pulsing, expanding, pushing at the confines of his chest. The sensation was terrifying. Dev had never cared for another human being in his life before. Why the hell should he? No one had ever cared for him. His mother had been an opium addict and spent more time speaking to hallucinations than she did to her own son, and as for his father....

Dev swallowed, forcing the painful memories away as he'd learned to do over the years. He shoved them way down into a deep, dark pit where they could not hurt him anymore. Yet, as terrifying as they were, he could not do that with his feelings for Charity. Those feelings were too bright, shining with honesty and truth, and they refused to be consigned to the dark where he kept everything else that might make him think about his life, that might make him actually feel something.

"The sale won't complete for at least another three weeks," Charity said now, and the firm tone of her voice was one Dev recognised, she would not be swayed.

Good girl, he thought, closing his eyes. Don't let him bully you. Perhaps there was time … "I will give you your answer in ten days."

Ten days! So little time to… to do *what?*

"Ten days?" Ogden objected. "Why so long?"

Because she doesn't want you, you stupid bastard! Dev wanted to scream the words in the man's face, and keeping out of sight was killing him. The first opportunity he had, he would dismiss Mr Ogden and break the fellow's nose. Not necessarily in that order.

Mr Ogden had no choice but to agree to her terms, as Charity would not budge and, to Dev's unending gratitude, no amount of wheedling on Ogden's part would change her mind. He listened as they walked away, as Charity bid Ogden a good day and his horse trotted back down the lane, away from the house.

Dev let out a breath, though his chest still felt locked in a vice.

Ten days.

What the bloody hell could he do?

***

Dev watched her over dinner. She'd told no one of her proposal, he was certain. That she was thinking of it was obvious, though. She was quiet and distracted, barely opening her mouth to speak which was so out of character that even Jane remarked on it and asked what the matter was. Charity just smiled and pleaded a headache. She said she was worrying about the trip she must take to her Uncle's to discuss where they would live. That she was leaving the next morning and would be away four nights was another blow that Dev could have done without. There was so little time left. He didn't want to miss a moment with her. Though it appeared his vivacious spitfire was gone already, buried under the weight of her fears.

The only time she became animated was when the subject turned to Lord Devlin.

"I heard he'd reduced his father's fortune by half within two years of his old man's death," Kit was saying, shaking his head as he tucked into the succulent chicken and ham pie Mrs Baxter had served them tonight. "I mean… how is that even possible? It must take serious work to spend that much money. The fellow is single minded, I'll give him that."

"He's wicked, that's what he is," Charity said, setting down her knife and fork with a clatter. The hairs on the back of Dev's neck prickled and he forced himself to keep his eyes on his plate, though the food had turned to ash in his mouth. "He's wicked and cruel and, what's more, he's a damned coward!"

"Language, Miss Kendall," Mrs Baxter scolded as she bustled in with a carafe of wine and set it between him and Kit. "And keep your voice down. Mr Baxter had too much sun today, the old fool. I told him he ought to keep his hat on. He's in bed and sick as a dog."

"I'm sorry, Batty, forgive me, but it's still true," she said, her words threaded with such anger that Dev couldn't swallow for the guilt that had lodged in his throat. "If Devlin wants to act with such callousness he could at least have the courage to look us in the eyes and tell us his intentions in person. If a man is ruthless and cruel, he should at least admit it to himself, to do what he does with intent and damn the world. At least I could respect a man who faced me, even if I despised him. But the viscount hides behind letters and his steward and—"

Her voice broke and the silence rang out over the table. Mrs Baxter moved towards her, hugging her as Charity struggled not to cry.

"You're wrong, love," Kit said, sighing as he reached out and took her hand. "He's not a coward, he just doesn't care. We are nothing to him. He cares no more for us than for the trees or the rocks upon his land. We are here, and if it no longer suits him to have us here because we are in his way, then he'll cut us down or dig us up. I doubt he would even remember our name if someone asked him."

Dev felt sick. He stared at his plate and knew he could not eat another mouthful if his life depended on it. Kit had the right of it. He'd not cared. Not until Charity had insulted him so deeply that he'd wanted to retaliate. He hadn't cared that he'd driven her to it. He hadn't thought about them at all.

Everyone returned to their meals, giving Charity a chance to compose herself. Dev pushed the food about on his plate, eating nothing as Kit tried his best to turn the conversation to something a little more light-hearted.

He looked around as Jane tugged at his sleeve, her eyes big and round.

"Will we be homeless, Mr David?" she whispered to him, and Dev wondered how much more guilt his heart could contain before it split open under the strain. "It's just that... Mr Baxter said we won't be able to take the kittens to the city but... but they're so little."

Dev grasped her hand under the table and squeezed. "You won't be homeless, Jane, and I will look after the kittens if you can't. Don't worry."

The relief in the little girl's eyes was instant, her trust in him absolute. She was just like her sister, more worried for the fate of her kittens than for herself. Jane smiled at him and sighed, returning her attention to her dinner.

Dev got to his feet, pushing back his chair as everyone turned to look at him.

"Forgive me," he said, his voice sounding odd and scratchy. "I... I think perhaps I had too much sun today as well. I'm feeling rather unwell. If you'll excuse me."

"Oh, you men! I told you both, you must wear a hat, no matter how sweaty it makes you!" Mrs Baxter's scolding voice followed him out of the door as he hurried away, away from the concern he didn't deserve, away from the guilt and the lies and the horror of what he was doing to them.

Chapter 12

"Wherein storms are forecast."

Dev lay in the dark of the barn, breathing in the perfume of a previous year's dry summer's heat upon the surrounding straw, listening to the night creatures hunting, their prey scurrying for their lives. Somewhere an owl hooted, its companion calling back to it on the other side of the farm. Beside him the soft huffing of the kittens was just audible as they slept, contented now they'd filled their tiny stomachs with cream.

The barn doors were open to the night, to let in some air after a stifling afternoon. The storm that had been threatening all day was almost upon them, and Dev watched the dramatic flicker and flash of the lightening as it lit the skies. It was not a night to be out on the moors. The wind picked up, stirring the dust and straw just inside the barn and, a bare moment later, the heavens opened.

The noise of the rain was staggering after the quiet of the night. It fell like fury, as if it could wash away every trace of humanity from the face of the earth and leave it clean and refreshed. Thunder cracked overhead, the noise rumbling through the earth, echoing through Dev's chest. It felt like judgement, like condemnation from above.

Dev didn't believe in God. He'd prayed too often as a boy and never been heard, yet he felt as though the righteous anger of a vengeful deity was being thrown down from the heavens, for him and him alone.

Something had to be done. He had to save the farm. Yet, if the sale didn't complete, Blackehart would come for him. Dev didn't know how much of the rumour about the man was true but, having met him, he was willing to believe every word. Built like a mountain, he exuded power. They said the scar that lined his face was given to him in the workhouse as a boy, and Blackehart had killed the man for it. He'd been twelve. The self-proclaimed king of crime, he was one of the most dangerous men in the country, and no one incurred his wrath and lived to tell the tale.

Another crack of thunder shook the ground beneath him and Dev got to his feet. The temperature was plummeting, and the kittens would get cold if he didn't shut the doors and keep the wind at bay. Soaked the instant he set foot outside, Dev secured the doors against the wind that fought to tear them from his hands. A horse screaming caught his ears and he turned his head towards the sound.

"What the devil…?"

Dev ran towards the paddock as a slim figure in a white nightgown became visible, playing tug of war with a horse strong enough to trample her in its terror.

As he grew nearer, he saw the lightening had hit a tree and a heavy branch had tumbled down, breaking the already fragile fence lining the paddock. The Kendalls' horses had got free, spooked by the storm. Fortunately, Dev's high strung mount was securely tethered in the barn. Charity had caught the roan by slinging a rope about its neck. The thunder made the creature wild, and it reared, showing the whites of its eyes and kicking out with its front legs.

"Get back!" Dev yelled, snatching the rope from her hands, terror in his heart the thrashing hooves might strike out at her. "Go back inside," he instructed, yelling over his shoulder as he fought to calm the petrified horse.

"Goliath is out too," she shouted over the din of the storm. "I have to look for him."

"No! I'll go," Dev shouted back at her. "Get indoors before you catch pneumonia."

He glimpsed an impatient eye roll before the horse he was fighting took his attention once more. Damn the woman!

It took some time to calm the creature enough to get it inside and out of the weather. Charity returned as Dev headed back outside, soaked but triumphant as the more docile bay trotted meekly by her side.

"I thought I told you to get indoors," Dev snapped. "I would have seen to it."

Charity snorted as she led the horse into the stall. "We survived before you got here you know," she said, her tone dry as she reached for a handful of straw and wiped the sodden animal down. "Besides, she'd have been halfway to Plymouth by the time you'd got the other one sorted."

"God, you're stubborn," Dev said, sighing and rubbing a hand through his wet hair, not sure if he was criticising her or full of admiration.

She laughed, and the sound filled his chest. He wanted her to laugh always, to look at him and smile because he was the one she turned to when things became difficult, because she trusted him. It was a simple enough desire, but one so far out of his reach he didn't know where to begin. He moved about the barn, closing the weather outside and lighting a lamp. His trousers were sticking to him and he felt chilled to the bone. Charity must be frozen too, though he knew if he insisted she get dry and let him see to the horse he'd get torn off a strip, so he held his tongue.

She finished rubbing down the big bay and left the stall, and Dev's brain stuttered to a standstill as he looked upon her in the lamplight. The nightgown she wore was sodden and almost transparent as it clung to every part of her. The outline of her breasts and the darker circles of her nipples were clearly visible, as was the darker triangle at the apex of her thighs.

"Thank you for your help," she said, closing the stall and then looking at him with a quizzical expression. "What?"

Dev couldn't have formed a reply if his life depended on it, but the look in his eyes must have been answer enough. He saw the breath snag in her throat, the flush of colour that suffused her skin. His blood heated further as she looked him over in turn and he remembered he wore only his trousers, as he'd stripped his shirt off to sleep. The desire in her eyes was blatant and honest, and he wished with all his heart that she knew the truth of him, instead of wanting a man who didn't exist.

Dev stood balanced on a precipice, with the devil on one side and all his hopes and dreams on the other. He could have her now, he could make her his in every way, or he could hold back and try to put things right, hoping when she finally discovered the truth ... she could find it in herself to forgive him. Dev knew it was a forlorn hope and, if he gambled and lost, he would never know what it was to love her. He might never have another chance to touch her and show her everything he was feeling. All the emotions he had no hope of voicing, as he barely understood them himself, would be revealed with such ease if he could only touch her.

Dev cleared his throat and tore his gaze from her, knowing the sight had been engraved behind his eyes for all eternity. "You... you should go and get warm," he said, his voice sounding strange and too loud now that the storm had died down. "The worst of it has passed us by. Goodnight, Miss Kendall."

The storm was dying down now, and he could hear nothing but the steady patter of the rain outside, the thunder gone. He walked away from her and checked on the kittens before rearranging the blanket he slept on. Once it was straight, he sat down and pulled off his boots, listening for the sound of the barn doors opening and closing. It never came.

He started as the cold cotton of her nightgown touched his back, followed by the damp warmth of her body as her breasts pressed against him. Her hands rested on his shoulders, her head against his.

"Am I so unappealing?"

Charity and the Devil

There was uncertainty in her voice and Dev hardly dared breathe, let alone move. He closed his eyes, appealing for help. *God in heaven, I'm trying my best here. If you do exist, for the love of everything holy, give me strength.*

"You are as far from unappealing as it is possible to get, you foolish creature," Dev all but snapped as the edges of his sanity unravelled.

"Then why do you keep turning away from me?"

Dev laughed, but it was a desperate sound with nothing remotely amusing about it. He moved away from her, unable to think with her body so close to his.

"Because you don't know who I am," he shouted, frustrated beyond anything he'd ever endured. "How can you put such trust in me to… to give yourself to me, when you don't know the first thing about me?"

She gave him a pitying look, such warmth in her eyes Dev wanted to howl at the unfairness of life. Except it wasn't unfair. He'd been due a reckoning. If this was the fates giving him his just deserts, then they couldn't have devised a more perfect torture. It was a torment of the most exquisite variety.

"But I do know you," she said, her voice soft as she inched closer. She reached out a hand, placing it upon his arm and Dev felt the heat of her touch upon his skin as though she scalded him. "I know you are the man who rescues kittens to please a little girl, a man who hadn't the faintest idea what a potato looked like, but who was so delighted by the discovery he wanted to know every other plant in the garden. A man who wouldn't take advantage of a woman in a moment of distress." She pressed her cold cheek against his and whispered as though she was sharing a secret with him. "I know you are not so black-hearted as I first believed, as perhaps you believed yourself…."

"Stop it!" Dev shook her hand off and rubbed his own over his face as the guilt threatened to choke him.

What would she say if he revealed who he was? Would she still believe he could change? He swallowed as the truth settled in his stomach, cold and heavy and all too real. No. She would not.

Her hatred for the viscount had gone beyond mere anger and dislike. The name Devlin had become the embodiment of everything that was cruel and unjust in the world, and she would never forgive him if he told her now. He had to make amends first. If he proved the truth of his words, then, *perhaps*... if he begged hard enough, then she might forgive him.

"I am a bad man, Charity," he said, with more honesty than any words he'd ever spoken before in his life. "I've done things you would despise me for, and it is not until now, knowing how you would despise me for them, that I realise how bad I have been."

"But... but you don't remember," she said, puzzlement in her eyes.

"I remember." He sucked in a breath, wondering how much he could tell her without having her guess the rest. He looked away from her, away from the shock in her eyes, wishing he could walk away from his past and start over, but it wasn't possible. Was it? "I remember," he said again, his voice low as anxiety twisted his guts in a knot. "And I am ashamed of everything have done."

"Oh, David."

She moved towards him, to comfort him even after his confession, and Dev held up a hand to force her to stay back. If she touched him again, he would lose his mind.

"But why? Why didn't you tell us?"

Dev wondered what her reaction would be if he told her the truth. *Because I wanted to hide here until it was safe, until the money from selling your home from under you was in my hands, and then... because I never wanted to leave.*

Instead, he prevaricated.

"I'm no fit man for you, Charity, though it kills me to admit as much."

She stared at him and Dev knew she had no reason to trust in him. He gathered his courage all the same, trying to forget the words she'd thrown at him when he'd refused to make love to her. *I'd not marry a worthless rake like you if you begged me.* Was that still how she felt? Had this simply been another chance to bed him, to forget her troubles for a night, before she did what was sensible and married Mr Ogden?

"I am everything you supposed me to be," he said, hearing the loathing and bitterness behind the words. "A worthless rake who'd never done a day's work in his life, but I want to change. I want to be more than that."

Dev met her troubled gaze, trying and failing to judge the look in her eyes. He hoped she could hear the sincerity behind the words, hoped she'd seen the willingness in him to be a different man over the past weeks, enough to put her trust in him when good sense must tell her to run and not look back.

"There are things I must do but, if you can wait for me, I will return for you. I promise."

"You're leaving?"

Dev nodded, knowing it was the only way. "I must."

Her expression was one of bewilderment, frustration and confusion as she shook her head. "But I can't give you time. I don't have any, you know I don't. The farm will be sold in just a few weeks and… and Mr Ogden has proposed to me." She dropped her gaze, which relieved him, at least he didn't have to feign surprise.

"I've told him I need to think about it but… Oh, David, it solves everything. He will have a large house, room enough for all of us. He's even offered Mr and Mrs Baxter a position and you know they'd never find another, not at their age. I confess that alone has cost me many sleepless nights. How can I refuse him?"

she demanded, and it was a real question, a desire for him to give her an escape. "How can I say no, knowing everyone would be safe and cared for—"

"Because you don't care for him," Dev said, his voice rough. "You don't love him or even desire him, and you'd be miserable, you know you would."

Her eyes glittered, and she swallowed hard, yet that independent spirit still shone through.

"Who says I love you?" she demanded, a little indignant. "We hardly know each other."

Dev smiled. Good Lord but he was caught, his heart snagged on a hook, and he wasn't even struggling to get away any more. The stubborn tilt to her jaw, her desire to have the last word, her warmth and kindness; he loved everything about this woman. He loved her. The truth of it stole his breath.

"I know that," he said, when he could speak again. The revelation filled his chest, warm and heavy and solid. It was the most frightening thing he'd ever experienced. "And I'm not saying you do." He gave a bitter laugh, shaking his head. "I'd be astonished if you did after all the dreadful things I've said to you, but… I'm not giving up hope that *you could*. If I tried hard enough."

He reached out his hand, touching her cheek with his fingertips for a moment before letting them fall away. It was all he dared. "I can be very persuasive, you know."

Her expression softened for a moment and she let out a reluctant huff of amusement. "I don't doubt it," she said, the words a little tart but warm all the same. She looked up at him from under her lashes. "I like arguing with you. More than I like talking to most other people."

The admission made the warmth in his chest expand further, He watched a rueful smile curved the corners of her mouth and gave a startled laugh.

Charity and the Devil

"As do I."

"Oh, David, what shall we do?" she said, clutching her arms about herself. "Is that even your name?" she asked and then cursed as she saw the truth on his face. "You lied to me," she said, her voice full of sorrow.

Dev held his breath as he saw the disappointment in her eyes. Had he played this wrong? Should he have kept silent until he could reveal the whole truth? He was only giving her more reasons to run from him.

"How can I ever trust you?"

There was such anguish behind the words Dev felt his throat ache, it was hard to swallow, harder to form the words he needed but he forced them out.

"I don't know." He rubbed his hand over his face, suddenly exhausted, worn down, yet he must fight for this, for her. There was no other way. "I don't know why you should trust me. I can't give you one single reason which would make any sense other than I pray you will." He moved towards her and clasped her hands. "This... these feelings in my heart, they're foreign to me, Charity. I've never known the like before. The desire to please someone other than myself.... It's new and strange, and bloody terrifying if you want the truth."

He gave her a twisted smile. "I can tell you this much. I am a wealthy man, I can take care of you, and your family, and Mr and Mrs Baxter too, only... there are things I must do first. I will tell you everything else you want to know when I return, I'll reveal every corner of my black soul if you'll only give me a chance."

Charity withdrew her hands and got to her feet. "And how do I know you'll return?" she demanded, her voice brittle with anxiety. "What if I wait and you get cold feet? What if Mr Ogden doesn't want to wait any longer and you don't return at all? I'll have lost everything. Not just me, but everyone. We'll be right back where we started."

"I won't, love," he said, begging her to believe in him when everything she now knew must force her to question every word he said. "You can trust me, I swear it."

"I don't know," she said, her voice faint now as she shook her head. "I don't know what to do, who to trust. You've just said everything I want to hear, but how can I believe you after all the deceit? I *want* to believe you though. I want to more than anything."

Dev watched as she clutched her arms about herself. She shivered, her slender figure so full of sorrow it broke his heart. He got to his feet and pulled her into his arms, holding her tight, rubbing circles over her back and she sank into his embrace with a sigh.

"I know it, and I can't defend who I was, only who I want to be. This is where you belong though, with me. You know it as well as I do."

Charity looked up at him then, fear and desire and confusion shining in her eyes. "Is it?" she replied, as though she really wanted an answer. "It is what I want," she admitted, reaching up to touch his cheek. "But is it what I need?"

She moved back, out of his embrace and he let her go, albeit with reluctance.

"I need to think. Perhaps it is as well we are apart for a few days. It will give us both some perspective. Will you stay until I return at least?" He saw her hopeful expression even as his plans for the coming days fell apart. "Mr Baxter is quite unwell, it seems. I think he'll be abed a few days. Kit will make himself ill trying to do his work as well and...."

She stopped as her voice quavered, and Dev longed to pull her back into his arms just as he cursed his luck. He needed to get his affairs in order but, if Charity was to trust him, he could not abandon her the first time she asked for his help. He could write to Ogden at least, tell him to stop the sale of the farm. It would give him a little breathing space. Blackehart would never know he was here, though it would mean risking a visit to the post office in Tillforth where he could well be recognised, but there was little choice.

"All right, love," he said, nodding his agreement. He moved closer and she allowed him to kiss her cheek. "Go to bed now. I'll see to the farm while you're gone. Don't you worry."

She nodded her thanks and Dev watched her leave the barn, her slender frame weighed down with worry and doubt. One day soon he'd see those cares lifted from her shoulders. He'd make sure she had nothing to worry about ever again. He would care for her family and make everyone safe, just as she longed for. Kit would see the best doctors, and he would spend his days making sure his beautiful hellion wished to throw things and row with him alone, because the making up afterwards would be spectacular. He'd make sure of it.

Chapter 13

"Wherein hopes and dreams and fears hang in the balance."

The next morning, Dev escorted Mrs Baxter and Charity into Tillforth. He drove the cart with Mrs Baxter and Charity huddled next to him. Sadly, Mrs Baxter was in the middle but perhaps that was for the best.

Mr Baxter had been meant to accompany her to visit her uncle, but he was still too unwell and the dampness after the storm had set Kit coughing and hacking this morning. Though her twin had insisted he was perfectly able to go, it was clear Charity would worry herself sick about him if he did, so Mrs Baxter had offered to go in his stead. Kit had insisted on coming as far as the village, though; he was expecting a letter to be awaiting him at the post and seemed jittery with excitement. He was riding Goliath, trotting beside the cart as they followed the track into town. Dev noted the flush in his cheeks with misgiving, but he was a grown man and as stubborn as his sister.

Mrs Baxter fussed the entire journey, explaining what there was to eat and how Dev should prepare it. She seemed to think they'd starve, though he'd seen the pantry and knew it was stacked floor to ceiling. There was enough there to survive an apocalypse never mind four days without her. He let her words wash over him, his own worries too profound to linger overlong on hers. They'd live on cheese if it came to it. He'd done it before.

As the small market town of Tillforth got closer, Dev's fears only grew. He was known here, though it was unlikely anyone would recognise him now. Dressed like any common labourer, despite Mrs Baxter's protests that he should smarten himself up a little to go to town, he looked nothing like a viscount. His best chance of remaining incognito was to look as different as possible and he'd done just that. He'd not even shaved, though he was rather expert with a razor now, and had tied a kerchief around his neck in a rough knot, pulling a battered old hat Mr Baxter had lent him down low over his eyes.

"Now he wears a hat," Mrs Baxter grumbled, as she looked at the misshapen thing with horror. "When I think what a fine gentleman you looked when we found you," she added with a heavy sigh.

"I've changed," Dev replied, meaning it. He glanced over at Charity, but she avoided his eye as she'd done all morning. Not that he could blame her. Heaven alone knew what she was thinking. He only hoped this journey they were making was a waste of time.

Charity's uncle had written to say he'd found a small house near his own. He would help them with the rent as far as he was able, but the onus would now be on Kit to earn enough to keep them. Dev hoped to God his own plans came to fruition, for the reality of the family living off a poet's income was enough to make his breath catch in his throat.

Once they'd seen the two women safely to the mail coach, Dev and Kit hurried off to the post office. He pulled his hat low and kept his head down, hoping to avoid scrutiny.

Dev let Kit go to the counter first. He had correspondence to post and Dev waited as he walked back to him clutching a letter and looking anxious.

"Here goes," he said.

Though Dev gathered it had something to do with his poetry, he didn't know what the young man was so agitated about. Kit's bark of triumphant laughter made the elderly lady who had taken Dev's place in the queue jump out of her skin and she sent him a reproachful look before continuing with her business.

"I'm going to be published!" Kit exclaimed, his face glowing with triumph and a rather feverish look that Dev knew would worry Charity.

"You've been published before?" Dev replied, wondering why this was different.

Kit shook his head. "Only in journals," he said, waving the letter in Dev's face. "This is different. They're publishing a book of my poems. A whole book, and I get a healthy advance!"

He flashed Dev a glittering grin and went to leave the post office.

"Wait," Dev said, grabbing at his arm and wishing Kit had allowed him to bring the post home with him as Charity had wanted. "Where are you going?"

"To celebrate, of course," Kit said, giving an incredulous laugh. "I've friends here and I want to share my good news. You get off back to the farm when you're done, I'll see you back there for supper."

Dev frowned, knowing Charity would not like this in the least. "Don't you think you ought to come home with me now?" he said, feeling on shaky ground. Kit was a grown man and Dev would be the first to tell him to mind his own business if the situations were reversed, but Charity had left him in charge and… he didn't want to let her down. "Perhaps wait a day or two to celebrate. You're looking a bit feverish."

An expression that Dev well recognised entered the young man's eyes. Strange how they never looked like twins until their tempers were lit, then the similarity was downright eerie.

"I'll do as I please, Mr David," he said, his tone even. "Even if you've persuaded my sister you're not a worthless scoundrel, I'm still her guardian. Remember that."

"What the devil do you mean by that?" Dev demanded aware they were in a public place but not liking the implication one bit.

Kit stared back at him, the brightness of his eyes giving Dev even more to worry about. "I don't know," he said, a troubled note lingering behind the words. "But you've more secrets than any man has a right to if I know anything. I don't trust you."

Dev snorted, holding the man's gaze. "No more should you," he agreed. "But your sister means the world to me. I have only her best interests at heart. You have my word on it, for what it's worth to you."

Kit stared at him a little longer and it was rather unnerving. The man had a piercing gaze, so intense Dev wondered if he was somehow unravelling his secrets.

"Very well," he said at length, and nodded. "I'll take you at your word. For now."

He turned, and Dev put his hand on his arm again, stopping him.

"I really do have your sister's best interests at heart, Kit," he said, wondering why he was so worried. Surely the young man knew his limits? "And she'd never forgive me if I didn't talk sense into you. There's rain in the air and another storm brewing if I know anything. Come home with me now. When that feverish look has gone and the weather fine again you can come and celebrate until you're insensible. I'll even fetch the cart to carry you home."

"A tempting offer," Kit said, flashing his charming smile again. "But *carpe diem* and all that." He gave Dev a friendly smack on the shoulder. "Stop looking at me like I'm about to fall off my twig, for heaven's sake. You're not my mother, nor my sister come to that, and I'll be back by supper. My word on it."

There was nothing else for Dev to do. He'd tried his best. Short of giving the fellow a whack on the back of his head, he couldn't stop him. With a sigh, Dev rejoined the queue. The letter he had penned to Mr Ogden was in his hands, and he hoped the woman behind the counter would not wonder why a man who looked like a farm labourer was sending letters to Lord Devlin's steward.

To his relief, though the woman gave him a curious look, she was more interested in the elderly lady who stood behind Dev. That they were desperate to gossip was obvious, and Dev paid his money and left them to it as fast as possible and with a sigh of relief.

At least now the farm would be safe. Ogden would stop the sale on Dev's instructions. The man had proved himself a backstabber but a written instruction would be hard to ignore. Dev himself was far from safe though. He had an idea of how he could make things right with Blackehart: a deal he could surely not refuse. Yet he knew the man's reputation all too well. Dev had reneged on an agreement and that meant losing face. In Blackehart's world, it was as good as a death sentence.

Dev shuddered and prayed he'd come out of this alive. For the first time in his life, he *wanted* to live. He had a future he wanted to grasp with both hands and hold on to for all he was worth. Killing himself slowly with drink and sordid living was the furthest thing from his mind. At long last he realised the greatest revenge he could have on his father was not to ruin everything the man had achieved, but to make a success of his own life. Perhaps he would be a father one day and—The thought stopped him in his tracks in the middle of the main street, and he had to apologise as an elderly gentleman ploughed into the back of him.

A father.

He might have a family if Charity was foolish enough to marry him.

Dev stopped breathing. The thought was a new one, fresh and startling, and a foolish grin curved over his mouth as he imagined her carrying his child. The ache below his ribs intensified and he rubbed at it with the heel of his hand.

Charity and the Devil

He would be a good father. At least, he'd try his best. He would never leave his children in the hands of heartless nannies who valued discipline over love, and who had no interest in children whatsoever. They would find him at their side when they were ill or frightened, not forever on the other side of the country without the slightest clue of what was happening in their lives. Most of all, he would never send them away to school to be bullied and made so miserable that they wished they were dead.

Dev forced his feet to carry him back to the cart, plans for his and Charity's future bright behind his eyes. His hopes and dreams were so close he could almost taste them. Everything would be all right. He would make the deal with Blackehart. The fellow was a businessman, if a ruthless one, and the deal Dev would offer him would be so tantalising he'd be a fool not to accept, and Blackehart was no fool. He would make it happen, just as he dreamed it. He had to.

Dev returned to the farm by midday. He warmed the thick soup that Mrs Baxter had left as the day was still damp and chilly and took a bowl up to her irascible husband. Mr Baxter was in a wretched temper, irritated to be confined to bed and frustrated that he was too weak to get out of it. He kept muttering about a crow that had sat on his window sill earlier. It was a bad omen, he reckoned, and made the hairs on Dev's neck prickle by predicting dire consequences for the family. Dev plonked the tray in his lap and escaped as fast as he could with the voice of doom ringing in his ears.

John and Jane had done their usual chores, and John had milked the goats too. To Dev's relief Charity had made time to milk the cow before she left as Dev hadn't the faintest clue how to do that. He prayed Mr Baxter would be well enough to do it in the morning.

As he ladled the soup into bowls and cut bread for the children, he felt oddly domesticated. What on earth would his contemporaries in London think if they saw him now? To his surprise he discovered he didn't give a tinker's cuss what they thought.

Little Jane grinned at him as he placed her soup before her, and his heart lurched in his chest. "Thank you, Mr David."

"Thank you, sir," John said, as he took his bowl from Dev's hand.

John needed guidance that was for certain. He needed a father. Someone who could teach him the things that Dev's father had never taught him. Things he was only now discovering for himself, like what it really meant to be a man worthy of respect.

Dev's own father might have been respected in the House of Lords, he might have done great things for the country, but he had neglected those who had depended on him most. He'd left his wife in the middle of nowhere until the loneliness ate away at her and she turned to opium to ease her pain. He'd ignored his son, never finding time for him and sending him away to school at the age of five when he became too unruly for his staff to manage. After that, Dev only saw his father when he came to reprimand him for his shocking behaviour. He'd never been expelled as his father paid too well for them to keep him. So, no matter what Dev did, nothing ever changed. Nothing he did mattered, for better or for worse.

At Brasted Farm, it mattered.

Here they noticed if he behaved badly, but they also noticed if he tried his best. Charity would tear him off a strip for rudeness and Mrs Baxter wouldn't let him sit idle. Kit would mock him for not having a clue about books and literature, but he admired his horsemanship and had even asked his advice when he'd worried his own horse was lame. John was thrilled if he spent his leisure hours teaching him the finer points of pugilism, and Jane that he was teaching her to ride and was still tending the kittens for her. Mr Baxter could grumble all he liked, but he'd still appreciated Dev's help around the place, and he'd said so too, albeit in a begrudging manner.

His actions had consequences here, and that was new and reassuring.

Though the weather was still unsettled, and so cool that Dev shivered a little working in his shirt sleeves, he spent an enjoyable afternoon. It was strange how squelching about the muddy farm in the drizzling rain made him happy. Tending the animals and ticking off the jobs left him gave him a sense of worth that no amount of fine clothes and gold coins had ever done. It only solidified his belief in the plans he'd made. He was doing the right thing. He was sure of it.

It was almost five in the afternoon when the rain began again. Dev cursed as he looked up. A strange purple colour lit the clouds, and the first strike of lightening juddered across the horizon like a crack in the sky.

"Damn you, Kit, where the devil are you?"

He hurried back to the farm, hopeful that the young man had returned whilst he was in the barn and he'd not noticed. When he got inside, he discovered the children playing with the kittens in front of the fire in the parlour. He'd given them permission to bring them inside, afraid the cold and the damp would be bad for them. Kit, however, was nowhere to be seen.

"John, look after your sister. There's bread and dripping in the kitchen if I'm late back for supper, and make sure you take some to Mr Baxter with a cup of tea."

"Yes, sir," John said, putting the kitten he was holding in his sister's lap. "But where are you going?"

John shrugged into Mr Baxter's oilskin and gave the darkening skies outside an unloving look. *To find your damn fool, brother,* he didn't say, though the desire to curse the young man hovered on the edge of his tongue. "Just to make sure Kit gets home all right," he said, smiling, not wanting to worry them.

John, however, knew of Kit's tenuous health as well as he did.

"He ought not to be out in this weather," he said, clutching at Dev's sleeve, his voice low so that Jane couldn't hear.

Dev placed a hand on the boy's thin shoulder and gave a squeeze. "Don't fret, young fellow-me-lad, I'll have him home and before the fire before you can say knife."

John nodded, still worried but placing his faith in Dev's assurances. "I'm sure you will, sir."

Dev hesitated and then decided to err on the side of caution. "Best make up the fire in his room, John, and put a warming pan in the bed, eh? Just to make sure he gets warm and dry quickly."

"Yes." John nodded, his eyes grave, too full of understanding for a boy of his age. "I'll see to it at once."

"Good lad."

Dev hurried towards the front door, fastening the oilskin as he went. God, it was a filthy night to be out on the moors. Cursing Kit Kendall to Hades, he put up the hood, and headed out into the deluge.

Chapter 14

"Wherein our hero fights fate."

Dev was frantic by the time he saw the sorry image of the bedraggled horse and rider lit up in the bright white glare of the lightening. He had been searching for hours, having ridden all the way into Tillforth, and then back again once the pub's landlord had assured him that Kit had left hours ago. Dev knew how easy it was to miss the path in the dark and frenzy of a storm on Dartmoor. He prayed nothing worse than a good soaking had befallen the young fool though, in his poor health, that could be quite dangerous enough.

"Kit!" he yelled through the din of the storm, urging his tired horse forward.

To his dismay, he found the young man slumped in his saddle with exhaustion.

"David," Kit said, the word barely audible as he gave a wry grin. "Bit foxed," he admitted. "Lost the path. Devil of a thing, never done it before."

Dev clamped his mouth shut against the barrage of angry words clamouring in his head. He needed to get the fool home and in front of a fire. Then he could shout at the blasted scapegrace to his heart's content. It soon became clear that Kit was in no condition to ride, however.

It took all Dev's strength to haul him onto his own horse, and then time he could ill afford chasing Kit's reluctant mount about the moors as he tried to evade being recaptured. Eventually however, horse and rider were firmly in hand and Dev made his weary way back to the farm with as much haste as he dared. The ground was treacherous, and his mount slipped and slid under the extra burden it carried.

By the time they reached the farm, Kit was unconscious. Dev hauled him down from the horse, both men sopping wet. Thankfully he was by far the larger of the two and, though it was a struggle, he hauled Kit over his shoulder and carried him to the house.

"John!" he shouted as he thundered through the front door. The boy ran from the parlour, wide eyed with horror as he saw Dev carrying his big brother. "John, see to the horses. They need rubbing down. I'll look after, Kit, don't worry. Don't come up until you've dried yourself off, understand?"

"Yes, sir," the boy said, his voice faint with worry.

"He'll be all right, John, you've my word," Dev said, praying he wasn't making promises he couldn't keep. "Where's your sister?"

"I put her to bed an hour ago, sir."

"Good lad. Knew I could rely on you," Dev said as he climbed the stairs. He didn't wait to see if John followed his instruction; he knew he would.

For once in his life, Dev felt pity for the valets he'd employed over the years who'd struggled to deal with him in various states of inebriation. Undressing an uncooperative man was no mean feat, especially when that man was soaked to the bone. Just getting his blasted boots off had Dev sweating and cursing. John had been as good as his word and kept the fire blazing, so the bedroom felt like a furnace.

Once Dev had stripped away his sodden clothes, he rubbed him down with a rough cloth to get his blood moving and dry him off. It worked for horses, so Dev saw no reason why it wouldn't be good for Kit, too. Working on the same principle, once Kit had been hauled into bed, Dev hurried down to the kitchen.

The only man who'd ever had any time for Dev as a little boy was an irascible old groom. What that man hadn't known about horses, in Dev's opinion, wasn't worth learning. It had been him who had shown Dev how to make a mustard plaster which had saved a little colt's life. The poor thing had been frozen and only just alive, but the mustard had livened it up right enough.

Dev took a cup of flour and added two large tablespoons of mustard powder, adding just enough water to make a thick and unappetising paste. He snatched up a clean tea cloth before heading back up the stairs.

Kit was awake when he entered the room. His skin was almost translucent, the veins standing out starkly against his unhealthy pallor, though his cheeks were flushed with fever. He turned glittering eyes on Dev as he moved towards the bed.

"How are you feeling?" Dev asked, noting how Kit shivered under the covers.

"Colder than a witch's tit," Kit replied, struggling to get the words out through his chattering teeth.

Dev snorted as Kit wrinkled his nose.

"What the b-bloody hell is t-that st-stench?" he demanded as Dev favoured him with a vengeful grin.

"This is retribution for making me scour the moors on a night unfit for man or beast, you young hell hound." He stripped back the bed covers, making Kit suck in a breath as he sent Dev a look of horror.

"This will put some fire in your blood," Dev said with a wicked grin before slapping a huge dollop of the mustard paste on Kit's chest.

Kit yelled and protested but was too weak to put up any kind of fight. A moment later and the revolting concoction was spread thick over his chest and then covered with the clean tea-towel.

"Bastard," Kit muttered, which Dev took as a good sign.

He fell into an uneasy sleep and Dev sighed, praying he'd done his best for the fool.

Then began the longest few days of Dev's life. His hopes that Kit would sleep and awake recovered were dashed a few hours later as he woke coughing and coughing, unable to catch his breath. The noise awoke John, who brought him the medicine that had been prescribed for him. It seemed to do little good, but eventually Kit slept again from sheer exhaustion.

Dev was rattled now. The young man was burning with fever, and he didn't dare leave him alone.

The days became a blur, terror lurking in Dev's heart as Kit alternately thrashed and sweated with fever and shivered with cold. Dev opened the windows when he burned, wiping him down with cold water straight from the stream, and built up the fire when he shivered, though he hadn't the faintest idea if he was doing the right thing. Mr Baxter was still abed himself, too weak to get out and work yet. That being the case, there was no one to fetch a doctor as Dev didn't dare leave for the half day it would take to fetch one, and John was too young to make the journey over the moors alone. Since the storm, low mists had been rolling the countryside and it would be all too easy to lose the path as Kit had.

So, Dev and John coped the best they could, keeping the farm in order and taking turns watching Kit, though Dev worked like three men to keep the worst of the responsibility from the boy.

It was the hardest thing to watch Kit fight for breath. He wondered how Charity had suffered when her parents died. She'd watched them both waste away from this dreadful disease, and he would not allow her brother to follow the same fate.

He forced soup down Kit's throat, though he protested and complained when he was lucid enough to do so, but Dev was not about to let him lose what little strength he had. The coughing racked his body so hard that Dev wondered how he could possibly survive.

The third night was the worst of Dev's life. As each minute ticked past he became increasingly terrified he would have to face Charity and tell her Kit had died in her absence. The fear of it sat in his chest like a lead weight as he watched her twin struggle for each, rasping breath.

He'd not slept for more than five minutes at a time since bringing Kit home and exhaustion tugged at his eyelids, but nothing on God's green earth would let him fall asleep. He forced medicine and water down Kit's throat whenever he could, keeping him cool as the fever mounted to impossible heights. In a last-ditch attempt to cool him, Dev took a blanket down to the stream and soaked it. The water was icy cold and the sodden blanket cumbersome as he carried it dripping back through the house.

He laid the blanket over Kit and opened every window upstairs, leaving the bedroom door open so that the wind flowed through. Mr Baxter yelled that they'd all catch bloody pneumonia at this rate, but Dev ignored him. He had to do *something*. At least the weather had turned for the better and the night air was no longer as damp as it had been.

Just as the first rays of daylight lightened the skies outside, Kit cracked open his eyes.

Dev sat up, reaching over to put his palm against his forehead.

"Thank God," he muttered, meaning it for once in his life. Though he was still hotter than he ought to be, the fever that had been raging out of control had broken, and Kit seemed to breathe a little easier this morning.

Charity's twin turned his head on the pillow, his feverish eyes finding Dev as a rueful smile curved over his handsome face.

"Should have come home with you, I suppose."

"*You suppose?*" Dev said, relief and anger and terror tumbling around in his chest. "If I hadn't just spent the last three nights praying you'd live, I'd bloody well wring your neck!"

Kit gave a weak nod. "Sorry. Don't tell Charity."

Dev opened and shut his mouth, gritting his teeth. "I'll not tell her anything. You can explain."

"Good man," Kit replied, closing his eyes once more.

Dev sucked in a deep breath, wondering if his heart might consider the possibility of beating again now. He felt as if he'd been holding his breath for days.

"I'll fetch some soup," he said, knowing he sounded grumpy as hell but quite unable to forgive Kit for scaring him so. Not yet, at least. He went to get up when a slender, elegant hand grasped his wrist.

"Thank you," Kit said, his voice full of sincerity.

Dev snorted with amusement and gave the young man an impatient look though there was no heat in it. "I didn't do it for you, wretch."

A smile flickered around Kit's mouth and he dropped his hand. "I know that," he muttered, sounding a little sheepish. "But thank you anyway."

With a sigh Dev nodded, praying he never had to endure such a thing again. "You're welcome."

***

Charity listened to old Mr Jones wittering away about the damage the storm had done to his barn and wanted to scream with impatience. His ancient mare was picking her way along the path at a steady snail's pace and Charity wanted to jump down and hitch up her skirts, running for all she was worth. It had been the morning after the arrival at her Uncle's house in Bristol when the terrible sensation that something was wrong hit her with the force of a lightning strike.

At first, she'd thought her anxiety was from the situation, from being away from home, from fears of the future, Mr Ogden…

Charity and the Devil

David. David wasn't David at all, of course, just to add to her troubles. The Lord knew she had enough to worry about, so at first, she hadn't recognised what was wrong.

Kit.

As twins they knew each other inside out. Charity instinctively knew Kit's mood without him even opening his mouth, as attuned as they were each to the other. So, when dread had hit her square in the chest in the early hours of the morning, she had insisted they leave at once. It had taken time to arrange their return, partly because her uncle thought she was being a hysterical female, overwrought by the loss of her home. Charity had become exasperated and truly hysterical at his lack of understanding, and only Mrs Baxter's calm assurance that if Miss Kendall said something was amiss, it was, made her uncle make the necessary arrangements.

They'd made it back to Tillforth but had no means of making it to the farm. Thank heavens old Mr Jones had taken pity on them and agreed to take them in his cart, but he was taking his own sweet time about it. Charity didn't dare hurry him any more than she had. He was a sweet man and doing them a favour by taking them home, but as her terror for Kit grew it was all she could do to sit still and not grab the reins.

When their familiar, beloved farm came into sight, Charity could stand no more. She leapt down from the cart while it was still moving, yelling a hasty thank you while hiking up her skirts and running full tilt down the muddy track.

By the time she reached the yard she could hardly breathe for terror, but then the scent of frying bacon assaulted her senses. Surely nothing bad could have happened if they were making breakfast? Yet her heart did not believe it and she thundered through the back door, uncaring of the mud and dirt she tracked in, to find John spreading butter on uneven slices of bread as the bacon sizzled behind him.

"Charity!" he cried, dropping the knife and throwing himself into her arms. "Oh, Charity, Charity, it's been awful without you."

"Oh, John," she sobbed, hugging him close before crouching down and staring into her little brother's eyes. "Kit?" she asked, not sure she wanted to hear the answer.

John's lip trembled, and she prepared herself for the worst. "He was so sick, Charity," he whispered, wiping his eyes with the back of his hand as he struggled for composure. "I've never seen him so ill before but... but Mr David was wonderful. He went out in the middle of a terrible storm and wouldn't stop till he found him and... and he's been taking care of him. The poor man hasn't slept, nor eaten, that's why...."

He gestured to the bacon behind him and Charity blinked back the hot tears that were stinging her eyes.

"And Kit?" she prompted, her voice thick.

"He's awake," John said, his voice a little somewhere between a sob and laughter. "The fever broke last night. I... I think he'll be all right now."

Charity let out a broken exclamation as her knees gave out. She sat on the floor, hand to her heart, crying and laughing as John hugged her again and almost knocked her flat. They embraced each other and wept as Mrs Baxter bustled in the room, and burst into tears on seeing them, fearing the worst. By the time she had been reassured she was dabbing at her eyes and demanding to know why her kitchen was full of smoke.

They looked up, noticing the rather acrid burning smell filling the room

"The bacon!" John shouted.

By the time Charity had relayed John's news and Mrs Baxter thrown out the blackened bacon, they had all calmed down a little.

"I must go to him," Charity said, heading for the stairs.

"Be quiet, Charity," John warned her as she left the room. "David was sleeping when I left."

Charity nodded, wondering at what John had told her.

As she crept into Kit's room she could see evidence of everything John had said. Her brother lay back on his bed, propped up with pillows. He looked heartbreakingly beautiful, with the flush of fever still visible against his porcelain skin. He stirred as she entered the room, large, dark eyes flashing as he saw his twin.

"Knew you'd come," he said, the words low as he held out his arms to her. Charity fell into them sobbing and Kit soothed her. "Hush now, David's out for the count. Don't wake the poor fellow with your carry on."

Charity looked up, only now noticing David asleep in a chair in the corner. He looked exhausted: unshaven and unkempt, his head lolling back at an awkward angle. She'd never seen him look more wonderful.

"He took care of you?" she asked, still rather shaken by the news.

Kit nodded solemnly, though a trace of frustration lingered in his expression, and told her just how much he must hate owing the man a debt.

"He did. Reckon I'd be in a box by now if not for him. But... to be honest, it was my own stupid fault. He tried to make me come home. Told me there was a storm coming, only... only...." A proud grin curved over his face, pushing the maudlin frown away. "See, I'm going to be published, Charity! A whole book of my work!"

"Oh, Kit, that's wonderful!" she exclaimed, though she kept her voice low so as not to disturb David. Then her face fell as she realised what the sequence of events had likely been. "You were inebriated," she said, folding her arms and glowering at her twin in anger. "You were drunk as a lord and got caught in the storm."

He at least had the grace to look rather mortified.

"Now, Charity...," he began, and started to cough.

Charity cursed, glowering at him as she helped him sit up a little and held a glass of water to his lips.

"Rest now," she said, through gritted teeth as Kit shot her an anxious glance. "You must get well," she added, straightening the bed sheets and tucking them in with rather more force than was necessary. "Because the moment you are, I'm going to ruddy well kill you."

Kit returned a crooked grin, laying his head back on the pillow. "Get in line, sis," he muttered, jerking his head towards the sleeping figure in the chair. "He said much the same thing."

Charity rolled her eyes at him and cursed the stupidity of men before leaning down and kissing her brother's cheek. "Don't ever do that again, Kit," she whispered. "I was so frightened."

Kit took her hand and gave it a squeeze. "I'll try my best. I promise."

Chapter 15

"Wherein a meddlesome suitor sends our hero's plans awry."

Dev awoke with a crick in his neck, backache, and a raging headache. His mouth felt like something had died in it and his stomach was clamouring for food. Other than that, it was a wonderful day to be alive.

He yawned, groaned as it made his head pound harder, and staggered to his feet, stretching out his aching limbs. A satisfying crack sounded as he stretched his joints. The sun glared at him through the bedroom window and he blinked, wincing a little before he realised he was being watched.

Kit was sitting up in bed, looking remarkably sanguine for a man whom Dev had been certain was about to breathe his last just hours earlier. True, he looked pale and exhausted, but Dev knew the sight of him would have many a tender-hearted woman falling into a swoon. Nothing more likely to do so than a beautiful dying poet in his experience.

"Charity is back," Kit said, a considering look in his eyes as he watched Dev try to straighten his shirt and flatten his hair back down. "I wouldn't bother; she saw you sprawled in the chair already."

Dev glowered a little at him and went to leave the room.

"I owe you a debt, David," Kit said, the words low as Dev put his hand on the door. "If that really is your name."

Dev turned back a little but didn't look at Kit, feeling that the young man saw a deal more than he let on.

"I won't ever forget it, but I need you to know I still don't trust you. I may be dead on my feet now, but hurt Charity and I'll make you wish you were never born."

The words hung between them and Dev couldn't blame him for his caution.

"I wouldn't expect anything less, Kit," he said.

The sound of a horse approaching had them both curious and Dev walked back to the window, then ducked back again as Mr Ogden appeared at the front of the house. Ogden swung down from his horse as Charity walked outside.

If things had gone according to plan, Ogden would tell her the sale had been stopped and Charity could breathe again. Dev waited for her exclamation of joy and frowned when nothing came. With as much stealth as possible, he cracked the window open a little more until their words were audible.

"Have you considered my offer any further?" Ogden was saying.

To Dev's intense relief, Charity looked rather irritated by his demand.

"I requested that you give me some time, Mr Ogden," she said sharply. "That time is not yet up."

"No, no, of course not," the man hurried on. "You must forgive me for being impatient, my love. I am left on tenterhooks here."

Dev cursed the man, clenching his fists against the fury of hearing his steward address Charity as his "love." At least she looked as annoyed by his presumption as Dev felt. Why hadn't he told her about the sale, though?

The conversation carried on, covering mundane issues, but when Mr Ogden asked if they had begun to pack up their belongings yet, the terrible truth dawned on Dev. Ogden wouldn't halt the sale. He'd pretend not to have received the letter. For, if he halted the sale, Charity would have no reason to wed him, and Dev damn well knew it. He must believe that Dev lay dead in a ditch somewhere for he'd surely not dare if he doubted it?

Rage welled in his chest, the desire to knock Ogden down and beat him until he screamed for mercy almost too much to bear. As it was, he endured, watching the disloyal, wretched man as he dared to kiss Charity's hand before bidding her farewell and riding away.

Dev turned away from the window, his chest locked in a vice. He had to stop that bloody sale and he had to do it now. He looked up to find Kit's eyes on him, full of curiosity.

"Eavesdropping is a dangerous habit," he remarked, looking ever more suspicious.

Dev snorted. He was too angry and he had too little time to explain.

"You're damn right it is," he muttered, his tone low and angry. "You never know what you might discover."

With no further explanation, he left and hurried towards his room, hoping to clean up before seeing Charity and making his goodbyes, and almost ploughing into her as he turned the corner.

"David! I was coming to see you." She let out a breath, a flush at her cheeks. "I... I feel odd calling you that now."

"I know," he said, regret and guilt burning in his chest. A name seemed such a simple thing, yet his was the cause of such misery. He wondered if he'd ever hear his real name again without feeling the weight of blame upon his shoulders. "I'm sorry."

He truly was, yet the honesty in those words was the only thing he could give her for the moment.

"Thank you so much—"

"I've got to leave—"

They both spoke at once, blurting the words out and then laughing, the atmosphere between them tense and awkward. Dev rubbed the back of his neck, uncomfortable with the gratitude in her eyes.

"He'd have died, if not for you," she said, the words simple but heartfelt.

Dev shrugged, not sure what to do. He stood in the brightness of her thanks, feeling at once illuminated and on display, his pleasure at her gratitude dissipating under the guilt of the harm he'd done. He could not enjoy her thanks, not until she knew the extent of his duplicity. If she was still grateful after that, after he'd confessed the whole, he'd lap it up like a cat with a saucer of cream.

Until then, he was merely trying to even the balance of debt between them.

"I have no words for you," she said, moving closer and taking his hands.

There was scarce a finger's span between them and the desire to close the gap was maddening, an ache beneath his skin he knew would never leave him if she was never to be his. Yet he made no move. He couldn't touch her again until she could call him by his name, his real name, and he could hear something that wasn't disgust in the sound of it upon her lips. She looked up at him and he lowered his head to rest against hers.

"I'm so happy I was here to help, Charity. That in some way I could repay you for everything, for every kindness, every moment of being here. You'll never know what it's meant."

She snorted, giving him a wry look. "I was rude and hateful to you, and you well know it."

Dev grinned, touching her cheek with his fingertip and fighting the desire to do more as her warm skin lit up his senses. "I loved every moment. You are a remarkable woman, Charity

Kendall. You're bright and funny and clever and beautiful, and you have the worst temper of anyone I've ever known save myself."

Charity blushed and then huffed, and Dev laughed.

"We were made for each other," he whispered, hearing the way her breath caught. He cupped her face in his hand. "Wait for me. Please. I won't let you down. Just don't accept Mr Ogden's offer. I will make everything right if you let me."

Looking into his eyes she made a strangled sound, somewhere between a sob and a laugh. "I must be out of my mind. I want so much to trust you, and yet I don't even know who you are."

Dev smiled, though regret made his expression taut and unnatural. "You'll know everything soon enough, my love, and then... and then perhaps you will allow me to court you properly, as you deserve."

"Perhaps," she said, looking up at him, such hope and such fear shining in her eyes. "But please hurry. There is so little time."

He nodded and dipped his head to steal a kiss, the barest touch of his lips against hers, as much as he dared, or he'd not leave the house as he needed to do.

"I must get ready to leave now. Remember what I said?"

She nodded, her smile tentative as he released her hands, and hurried away.

***

Dev turned his horse, taking one last look at the farm, lit up in the late afternoon sun. A curl of smoke twisted from the chimney in the kitchen and Dev knew Mrs Baxter was there, preparing the dinner. Boiled ham tonight, with some of her best preserves, and buttered new potatoes. There had been carrots too, and runner beans sliced thin, their pink beans glittering like jewels. The longing to return, to immerse himself in the warmth of their messy, noisy, loving family caught at his throat, making it ache. It took a deal of effort to swallow it down and turn his back on the place.

If he didn't do this, if he didn't put things right, then it wouldn't be just him that lost that life. They all would.

By contrast, when Devlin Hall came into view, its grandeur shouting out the pride and wealth of the Devlin name, he felt nothing. The only memories he had of this place were of isolation, of bone deep loneliness that could eat away at your soul and deaden your heart until you cared for nothing and no one. That had been him, he realised now. Dead inside: a creature barely alive, and certainly not living, not until Charity and her fire and fury had breathed life into him. It was like being reborn, the knowledge that there was goodness and hope and love to be had in the world, even for a man so lost in the dark as he'd been.

There was still hope.

His voice echoed around the vast entrance hall as Dev stalked in, ignoring the horrified look upon Jennings' face at the sight of his master dressed like a common labourer. The shocked butler blinked, but said nothing.

"Ogden!" Dev shouted, clenching his fists with rage as he received no answer.

"Mr Ogden is not here at present," Jennings volunteered, though with some trepidation, knowing all too well his master's tempers were to be treated with caution. "I believe he had gone into town. He said had some things to arrange."

Dev cursed and fought the desire to smash something in his fury. "I'll bet he has, the blackguard, and what, pray tell, is he doing about the fact I have been missing for some weeks?"

Jennings opened and closed his mouth and Dev stalked a little closer.

"Well?" he demanded.

"Mr Ogden told us you had stayed a little longer with your friend than you'd anticipated as you did not arrive in London as expected," he said, the words as careful as the look in his eyes.

"We assumed you had written and informed him, we never ..." Jennings trailed off, a dawning look of horror in his eyes.

Dev snorted, only now realising the depths of Ogden's duplicity. If he cared to investigate the books, he wondered if things were really in as dire straits as he had been led to believe, or had Ogden been creaming a little off the top all these years?

"Please inform Mr Ogden on his return that I am anxious to speak with him. Ensure he does not leave my property again until he has done so. I also want someone sent to the post office in Tillforth. They will enquire about a letter that was posted there on the twenty third of July, sent to this address and for Mr Ogden's immediate attention. I want to know *exactly* what happened to that letter."

"Very good, my lord," Jennings intoned, a glitter of curiosity in his eyes.

He suspected that the dismissal of his steward would be a source of great entertainment and discussion when the rest of the staff discovered it.

"I suppose my valet still awaits me in London?" Dev asked, unable to keep the impatience from his voice.

He could have been dead, and they'd not have raised an eyebrow. Yet this was his doing. If he'd been a better master, a man they'd respected, perhaps they'd have worried at the possibility he was lying in some undiscovered ditch. If he'd been kinder, they'd have investigated, rather than doing nothing when Mr Ogden gave them no reason for alarm at his unexplained absence.

"Send me someone capable of taking a letter and sending it immediately to my man of business; a footman who knows his way around a cravat and can pack a valise, and have a hamper prepared for a long journey. I leave for London. My carriage must be ready to leave within the hour."

Jennings acknowledged his orders and, within moments, the house was a flurry of activity. Little over an hour later, Dev had shaved and dressed, and appeared to be the Viscount Devlin once more. With his heart and his hopes held tight, he began his voyage to London, to face Lord Luther Blackehart.

***

The club was busy as ever, the shouts of triumph and disappointment melding with the thick fog of cigar smoke. Dev followed one of Blackehart's men through the melee and out the back of the club to his office. That he'd come here of his own volition was something he couldn't quite believe, but there you had it. He only hoped he'd leave again with all limbs intact, and not in a box as the look he'd been given by the hired thugs who patrolled the place might suggest.

Lord Blackehart was not a lord at all. Not in the real sense. It was a title given through fear and respect. He was lord and master in this manor, and no one forgot it, though there was not a drop of noble blood in the man's body. He'd been born in the workhouse and fought his way out of the filth via a life of crime. They said he couldn't die, that the devil wouldn't take him, and that he was untouchable. He'd been shot, stabbed, and even hanged. He'd survived both the shooting and stabbing, and by some miracle the rope had broken when they'd hanged him. Not right away, though, he had the scars about his neck by all accounts and hid them beneath a cravat. Dev had never cared to ask about the veracity of the rumours. Blackehart wasn't a man you questioned.

Dev entered the man's domain with his heart thudding so hard his lungs felt tight. He was doing this for Charity, he reminded himself as anxiety had sweat prickling down his back. It was for her, for Kit and for John and Jane, and even Mr and Mrs Baxter, for all the worry and hurt he'd caused them. This was his penance. He prayed his offer would meet Blackehart's approval, because if not… he was already dead.

Charity and the Devil

Dev had always considered himself a large man, tall and well built. Blackehart, however, was more mountain than man. He was perhaps thirty, a huge bear-like figure that dominated the room. His eyes were as black as his name, his hair dark too, and an ugly, jagged scar lined the right side of his face. It tugged a little at his eye, drawing it down and giving him a look of permanent anger. Not that he needed the help.

"My Lord Devlin," he said, as he watched Dev enter. His voice filled the room, deep and rumbling, coarse with an accent born of the gutter. "Well, well. You've got balls coming here, I'll give you that."

Dev inclined his head and gave a taut smile. "I owe you an apology, Blackehart, and I determined to do it in person. I had an unfortunate accident and was indisposed for some considerable time, but I owe you a debt and I mean to settle it in full."

Blackehart leaned against the edge of a massive oak desk, and Dev still wondered at its ability to hold his weight. He gave Dev a cool smile, raising one dark eyebrow.

"Some might reckon the time for making deals is long past, my lord," he said, an edge to his voice Dev could not mistake. "We had a deal, and you reneged. Men die for less."

Dev sucked in a breath, holding his composure, aware he could be spirited away, his body dumped in the Thames, and no one ever the wiser. "I think a man like you always has time for a deal which is in his interests. Just hear me out, and I think you'll like what I have in mind. You'll never get another offer like it."

A spark of interest lit the man's eyes now and Dev held his breath, knowing he was curious at least.

"Very well," Blackehart said, moving to sit back down behind his desk and gesturing for Dev to take a seat. "You have my attention. Now tell me… what exactly is it you're offering?"

Chapter 16

"Wherein our hero lives to fight another day ... and fight he must."

Dev returned home, still rather astonished that not only was he alive, but his offer had been accepted. The enormity of what he'd done still stunned him. His father would be turning in his grave. That thought alone made a smile curve over his lips.

For once it had not been about revenge, however. That his father would have howled with rage was merely the icing on the cake, not his motivation. For once, he had his future in mind; a future in which he would build the foundations for a new life, one where the Devlin name was once again respected, but respected most of all by the people who mattered the most... his family.

The Kendall family were not his, he knew that, yet they had crawled under his skin and made him long for their acceptance. He wanted to see John grow into a young man and help guide him in a way his own father had never done for him. He wanted to see Jane turn into a bright and vivacious woman like her sister, yet without the cares and worries that had blighted Charity's life. Kit he would see fit and healthy, and a successful poet. Such things were much easier when you knew the right people. Mr and Mrs Baxter would be safe too, and a crucial part of their lives as always. More than anything though, he would see Charity by his side, always. He would protect her and those she loved from storms and fears and anything that threatened her happiness, he would fight with her and make her furious and love her so thoroughly that she need never regret putting her trust in him.

By the time the carriage rolled to a halt before Devlin Hall, Dev was exhausted. He'd been on the move for almost six days, only stopping when there was no other choice. He'd dozed on and off as the carriage lurched and pitched him all the way home, but his mind was too full of hope and anxiety to let him rest for long.

The same question was circling around and around his brain with no clear answer. What would Charity say when she discovered that he was the man she hated with such passion? What would she do when she realised the villain who had upended her peaceful existence and caused her family such distress was the man they had cared for and sheltered for so many weeks? When she realised the depths of his betrayal, the extent of his lies? Fear of it made his chest grow tight. The all too real possibility that she might never forgive him stole his breath, as the fear of being without her again prowled in his heart.

If she could not forgive him, he would be worse than lost. He'd been lost and alone his whole life and endured it as he'd known no other way of living. Now, however, he'd seen what was possible, what had been within his grasp all along, if only he'd been honest and kind. God, how he wished he'd been kind. Yet he hadn't known how. He'd needed to be taught what it meant to give with no expectation of receiving anything in return. Charity had taught him that. They all had.

He stepped down from the carriage, his limbs protesting after so much time confined in a small space. The ground beneath him felt odd, as if it still moved with the sway of the carriage. Moving forward and hurrying up the stairs he rubbed a hand over his face to wake himself up. He needed to wash and change and get back to the farm as fast as he could. Though he felt sick with anxiety and fear for Charity's reaction, he was impatient to tell her everything. He'd get down on his knees and beg for her forgiveness if he had to. At least he hoped his actions would speak for his intentions; that they would show her how much he'd changed, and just how far he would go to make her happy.

He burst through the doors of the great house, casting hat and gloves at Jennings as he went, and was about to run up the stairs when Mr Ogden appeared.

Dev stopped in his tracks, rage chasing any sense of fatigue from his bones as his blood surged in his veins, the desire to do the man harm prickling over his skin.

"Mr Ogden," he said, fighting the desire to just knock the man down without a word. Not yet.

He watched as Ogden gave him the taut, supercilious smile he always reserved for Dev. The one that implied he knew he was the better man, and it was only the vagaries of fate that had given Dev money and power.

"My lord."

Strange, how he'd never noted quite how insolent his tone was before. Or perhaps that was new, now he had another job to go to.

"Why have you not stopped the sale of Brasted Farm as I instructed?"

"My lord?" Ogden replied, his eyebrows raising in surprise. "But why would I? Your instructions on leaving were clear. I was to ensure the sale of the property proceeded without a hitch."

Dev turned to face Jennings who was watching proceedings with avid interest. "Did you send someone to the post office as I instructed?"

"I did, my lord," the butler replied, his face a mask, though there was a glint of satisfaction in his eyes.

"And?" Dev demanded, folding his arms. "What did they tell you?"

"The post was collected as usual, my lord. Only one letter that particular day. I spoke to the staff and the second footman confirmed that he put the letter into Mr Ogden's hand as soon as he received it."

Both men turned to stare at Ogden, who looked a little less sanguine than he had a moment before. In fact, he looked rather pale.

"Nothing to say, sir?" Dev said, his tone brittle as he took a step towards Ogden.

Mr Ogden swallowed and took a step back.

"I-I can't account for it, my lord. I must have misplaced it and can only apologise. There h-has been so much happening in your absence, the sale and... and...."

"Ah yes, back to the sale," Dev said, interrupting his stuttering explanation. "Tell me, Ogden," he said, advancing on the man as he spoke. "Why did you suggest Brasted Farm ought to be sold?"

He kept his voice light, but he had no doubt Ogden could see the anger blazing in his eyes.

"B-But I didn't.... I—"

"Yes, you did," Dev growled, remembering the meeting with clarity.

He'd spent a deal of time mulling it over, remembering the regretful look on Ogden's face as he suggested it might meet Dev's need to sell something. It had been him who had reminded Dev of Thompson's interest in the land and the farm.

"I took the liberty of studying the ledgers and maps pertaining to my property," Dev said, growing angrier as he spoke. "Something I fully admit I ought to have done many years ago. I also read all the correspondence between you and Squire Thompson. Brasted Farm was one of two properties he was interested in buying. The other is empty as the tenants died but has hundreds of acres of good grazing land, which is what he's after. His interest in it was marked and his offer for it more than generous. Better, in fact, than the offer for Miss Kendall's farm."

Ogden had turned a sickly shade of alabaster with just a hint of green, though two high spots of colour blazed on his cheeks.

"Are you quite well, Mr Ogden?" Dev demanded, folding his arms as the man stared at him in horror. "You look rather ill. But then I suppose putting Miss Kendall in a position where she had no choice but to marry you to save her family would make a fellow feel rather nauseated." He was all but snarling now as Ogden sweated before him. "I know it makes me sick to my stomach."

"You didn't care!" Ogden snapped, his temper rising now he'd been cornered like the rat he was. "I told you all about her, all about her family's troubles. You could have stopped it, but you didn't give a damn. You were only interested in saving your own worthless skin, so you could carry on destroying your father's legacy."

"I know exactly what I'm guilty of, you miserable little prig," Dev shouted, advancing on him. The punch landed with a satisfying crunch and Dev hoped he'd broken the bastard's nose. It had certainly been his intention. Ogden flailed backwards, arms wind milling as he slipped on the polished marble floor. He landed in an undignified heap, blood pouring from his nose as he sought to find his feet and only slipped down again. Dev stood over him, daring the man to stand. He was only too willing to knock him down again.

"My part in this despicable affair is a cross I must bear," he said, as Ogden stared up at him in terror. "And one I will do my utmost to make amends for. You, however, will leave my employment as of this moment, and I will be studying my finances over the past years with the greatest of interest. If I find so much as a farthing more than was your due has found its way into your pocket, you can be assured I will be informing your new employer to be on his guard." Dev took a step back, his fists clenched as his desire to make the man suffer further demanded retribution. "Now get out," he said, knowing if he had to look at the wretched man any longer his temper would get the better of him. "You may send someone to collect your belongings on your behalf, but I want you gone. *Now!*"

Ogden didn't need telling twice. He scrambled to his feet and ran for the door.

Dev stood in the great hall and tried to calm himself. After the stress, anxiety, and lack of sleep of the past days he felt raw, unable to think. He could not see Charity in this state. He needed time to clear his head. Perhaps a cool bath and something to eat would settle him down? Though he didn't want to waste any time, he didn't want to run to Charity unprepared for what he knew would be an emotional confrontation. He wasn't fool enough to think he wouldn't face her wrath. His hopes hinged on his ability to make her see he'd changed. A clear head would be required for that though.

As he crossed the hall and put a foot on the staircase a feminine exclamation of surprise reached him from outside the doors of his home.

What the devil?

He reached the doors just as Jennings opened them. Charity looked up, a battered Mr Ogden at her side, and Dev's heart clenched with fear as recognition dawned on her face.

For a moment she just stared at him.

She'd been standing on the steps that led to the front doors and Ogden's hand rested on her arm. No doubt she'd been on her way to tear him off a strip for his mistreatment of his steward.

Now she stumbled backwards, the shock raw as she tried to breathe.

"Charity," Dev said, his worst fears realised.

He moved forward but she held out her hand, shaking her head, her eyes filling with tears.

"No. No. Don't."

She walked away, and he could hear her breath catch with the effort not to cry.

"Charity!" he said, rushing after her now. He took the steps two at a time and found herself at his side, taking her arm, forcing her to look at him.

Charity yanked her hand free, wrenching away from him like he was the devil himself trying to drag her down to hell.

"Don't touch me!" she cried, the words near hysterical. "Don't you dare!"

Dev dropped his hand as she put more distance between them.

"You're him. You're Lord Devlin."

It wasn't a question and Dev could do nothing but give her his answer.

"Yes," he said. His heart raced in his chest, and he knew that he stood on a knife edge. Of all the worst ways to discover who he was... this had to be the most brutal. "Please, love, let me explain."

She gave a laugh, though it was a terrible sound, raw and tinged with panic.

"Explain?" she repeated, looking dazed and pale, and like she might faint with the shock of it at any moment. Except Charity would never do something as weak as faint. She was far too strong for that. "Yes please, *my lord*, could you explain why you decided to turn us out of our home? Oh, and why, when we cared for you, took you into the home you would steal from us and made you welcome, why you never told us *the truth?* Can you explain that, *David*?" She was shouting now, though her voice quavered as tears tracked down her face. "My God," she said, paling further, her voice dropping to a whisper. "And I... I.... actually thought we might have a future, that you really cared."

She sobbed and turned away, running to the cart where Mr Baxter sat. The old man staring at him in astonishment.

"Charity, wait, please. I'm begging you." Dev ran after her, snatching at her hand, which she pulled from his grasp as she fled from him.

"Leave me alone!" she shouted, her rage incandescent. "Don't you come near me! Don't you come near me or my family ever again!"

Mr Baxter stood, whip in hand and gave him a hard look. "I'd do as Miss Kendall says, my lord," he said, his tone hard and cold. "I don't want no trouble with you."

Dev stood still, chest heaving, knowing it was useless to remonstrate with her when her temper was up. She'd not listen to him in this state. Not that he could blame her for her rage after all he'd done. He'd have to let her go, allow her to calm herself a little. Perhaps then he could reason with her.

"Charity," he said, watching helplessly as she clambered into the cart and stared straight ahead, tears falling down her cheeks unchecked. "Charity, I love you."

Mr Baxter sent him a dark look and snapped the reins, urging the horse to take them away as fast as possible.

Watching Mr Baxter leave with Charity was the hardest thing he'd ever done, but he bore it. He would give her time to breathe, time for her anger to dissipate, and then... then he would try to explain.

Chapter 17

"Wherein hopes are swept away by the storm, but not entirely extinguished."

Dev waited three days.

Three days of utter misery.

He couldn't eat, couldn't sleep, could not even settle to go over his accounts and see if things were as black as Ogden had led him to believe.

Three days of watching the horizon, praying he would see her coming up the drive, even if it was only to tell him what a despicable human being he was.

He was ready to agree with her.

He could only hope three days was enough to have calmed her a little. Enough so she might see him, at least. Yet he knew what fiery, stubborn creatures the Kendall family were. It was their strength and their weakness, and he was by no means optimistic at what his reception would be.

Dev dressed with care, choosing to look his best but avoiding anything that would highlight the differences in their station any more than he had to. They all knew people would think he'd married far beneath him if Charity ever consented to be his wife. Such a thing would only stick in her throat, proud and independent creature that she was. Even if she deigned to forgive him—something of which he had no great expectation—he didn't expect her to fall into his arms. He'd have to fight for her.

For the first time in his life, though, he had something to fight for.

Charity and the Devil

He'd never cared for the title, not beyond the fact it could get him what he wanted when he wanted it. What people thought about him was something he'd never lost any sleep over, and he wasn't about to start now. He'd marry Charity if it was the last thing he did. If it took him years of begging for forgiveness. Anyone with an opinion on the matter could go to the devil for all he cared.

When he crested the brow of the hill and saw Brasted Farm glowering at him in the morning light, the ache in his chest only intensified. They'd all be up by now. The milking would have been done by this time, the animals fed, and eggs collected. Mr Baxter would be sweeping the yard, Charity heading out to gather whatever was ready in the garden. In half an hour or so, they'd all return to the kitchen for breakfast.

The longing to join them struck at his heart.

He'd realised now, he'd been lonely his whole life, but never had it hurt this much. It had been normal, something he'd learned to endure, never aware how debilitating the pain was as he'd never known any different. Now, he understood how hollow it made him, as if his heart had been carved out until it rang like a bell, tolling his emptiness to the world. He'd not known how different life could be then but now he did, and the loss of it clawed at his throat.

"Courage, man," he muttered, gathering up the reins and urging his horse on.

When he saw Mrs Baxter, John, and Jane sitting on a stile waiting for him a good mile from the house, he knew he'd not see her. Not today. His heart dropped but he mustered a cautious smile, wondering what reception awaited him.

They stood as he drew nearer, and he saw Jane take Mrs Baxter's hand. The worry in the little girl's eyes only made his heart ache harder.

"Lord Devlin," Mrs Baxter said, her tone so formal he wanted to howl.

"Please, don't call me that, Batty," he said, wondering how he got the words past the tightness in his throat.

She snorted and gave him a hard look. "And what am I to call you then?"

Dev shrugged, not knowing how to reply. "My friends call me Dev."

Mrs Baxter raised an eyebrow at him and he swallowed. He dismounted and walked towards them.

"Hello, Jane," he said, wondering if she hated him too now.

"Hello, Mr Da—" she began, and then blushed, hiding against Mrs Baxter's skirts.

"Hello, John."

John stared at him, his jaw rigid, his expression one of contained misery.

"She'll not see you," Mrs Baxter said, her tone weary now. "I saw you riding up and... well, I came to tell you to steer clear. Kit's fit to be tied. The temper he's in right now I wouldn't put it past him to shoot you. I've never seen him so angry in all my days, and that's the truth."

Dev nodded, unable to speak. There was something clogging his throat and anything he might have said, any message he might have asked her to convey, would remain unspoken as he dared not open his mouth. Instead he reached into his pocket and took out the letter he'd stowed there. In fact, it wasn't a letter at all, but he'd hoped it might mean more to Charity than anything he could say. He'd also hoped to put it in her hands but... At least Mrs Baxter would see she got it.

She took it from him and nodded. Dev turned back to his horse, needing to go before his composure crumbled before them.

He was reaching for the reins when John ran up to him and threw his arms around his waist. Dev got to his knees, holding the boy tight as Jane joined him, her little arms thrown about his neck as she cried. He hugged them both to him, wondering how his heart could stand it, how he could survive the guilt of the damage he'd wrought.

"I'm sorry, I'm so terribly sorry," Dev said, unable to stop his own tears spilling over in the face of the hurt he'd caused.

"I told them you weren't a bad man," Jane said through her tears. "I told them, but they said I was too little, that I didn't understand, but *I do.*" She stamped her foot and Dev could only feel humbled by her defence of him. He certainly didn't deserve it. "You're not a bad man." She looked up, trepidation in dark eyes so like her sister's. "Are you?"

Dev wondered how in God's name he could answer that with any truth. He glanced up at Mrs Baxter, who was watching him, her expression intent.

"I've done some bad things, Jane," he said, his voice thick. "Things that have hurt your family very much but... but I'm trying my best to make amends. I... I want to change, more than anything." He looked up at Mrs Baxter as he spoke. "I'd do anything to put things right. It's the only thing I want. The only thing that matters."

Mrs Baxter nodded her understanding and he hoped perhaps she realised he meant it with all his heart.

"Come along, children," she said, her voice soft. "Lord Devlin must go now, and I have to get the breakfast done."

Jane kissed his cheek and let go of him with reluctance. "Will we ever see you again?" she asked, her voice trembling as Dev's throat threatened to close completely it ached so much.

"I hope so, Jane," he said, forcing the words out. "More than anything."

She gave a forlorn nod and moved to take the hand Mrs Baxter held out to her.

Only John remained at his side, white faced with the effort not to cry.

"Chin up, John," he said, trying to take his own advice. "Down but not out, eh, lad?"

John gave a taut nod and held his hand out to him. Dev shook it, knowing he wanted to behave like a young man, but his own emotions were too raw, too close to the surface and he pulled him back for a hug.

"Look after your sister for me," he said, before letting the boy go, pretending he didn't see the tears that were staining his cheeks.

"Run back to the house now," Mrs Baxter urged them. "I'll be along in just a moment."

She waited until they were out of earshot before turning back to him, giving Dev a moment to compose himself before he faced her again.

"You love her," she said, watching his face, looking at him as though she could ferret out his darkest secrets if she only stared hard enough.

Dev nodded. "I do, with all my heart."

Mrs Baxter sucked in a breath and then let it out, shaking her head. "What a tangled web we weave," she muttered giving him a dark look.

He returned a weak smile, at a loss for anything further to say.

"You'd marry her?" she demanded, folding her arms, eyes narrowed as she continued to scrutinise him.

"In a heartbeat. If she'd have me."

He watched as she pursed her lips and then gave a decisive nod. "Right you are, then."

She turned to walk away, and Dev felt his heart kick in his chest.

"What do you mean?" he demanded, striding after her.

She turned back to him and gave him a tut of impatience. "I'll do what I can, is what I mean," she said, warmth in her eyes despite the tartness of her words.

"You will?" Dev replied, stunned and incredulous that she would take his side.

He held his breath as she reached out and patted his cheek. "I always did have a soft spot for a rogue," she said, smiling at him with something that looked almost like fondness in her expression. "But don't hold your breath," she warned, her words severe now. "There was never a more stubborn family to walk the earth than the Kendalls, I tell you now. I'll talk her around if it takes me till my dying breath, but I don't say it won't."

Dev gave a startled laugh and before he could think about it he put his arms around her and hugged her. "Thank you. Thank you so much."

He received a brief hug in return and let her go to see the astonishing sight of Mrs Baxter blushing. "Hmph," she said, fussing with her apron and giving him a haughty sniff. "Don't thank me yet, you devil. But don't give up either, eh?"

Dev nodded, more grateful to her than to anyone in his life before.

"Never," he said, meaning it.

Mrs Baxter smiled at him and made a shooing motion, so he mounted up and rode away, pausing for one last look at the farm before he turned his back and headed back to the hall.

***

Charity sighed, staring at the rain pattering against the kitchen window. The weather had turned as though her misery had chased the sun from the skies and would never shine again.

It was almost a month since her discovery of *David's* identity.

Her jaw clenched, though her anger had long since dissipated. Her pride still smarted and her heart… she could not begin to speak of her heart. Suffice to say it was raw and bloody, cowering in a dark corner like a wounded creature, snarling at anyone who got close.

"Are you going to shell those beans or try to frighten them out of their pods?" Mrs Baxter demanded as Charity looked up.

She rearranged her features, realising she had indeed been scowling at them and hadn't moved an inch for the last twenty minutes.

"You read that letter of his yet?" Mrs Baxter asked, a shrewd look in her eyes as she brought a basket of potatoes to the table and sat down opposite her.

Charity ignored the question. They both knew the answer. What Mrs Baxter didn't know was that she stared at the damn thing every night before she went to bed for at least an hour. The truth was she was frightened to open it, frightened to discover what it was he'd said to her. What would it change? If he begged for her forgiveness and told her he loved her it wouldn't change a thing, because no matter what his feelings, he was a viscount.

Viscounts did not marry women with hands like a navvy and a temper hot enough to scorch the sun. They might keep such a woman as a mistress, but not a wife.

If the letter he'd given Mrs Baxter so much as hinted that was something he hoped for… her heart could not endure that too.

A tempting little voice in her ear asked, *what if he wants to marry you?,* but even that was hopeless. As much as she wanted to trust in the loving expression she remembered in his eyes, as much as she wanted to forgive him for the lies and the deceit and all the harm he'd done… it was a ridiculous idea.

She imagined herself as the Viscountess Devlin and the flush crept up her neck as she imagined next what his friends would say of her. He'd be a laughingstock. He'd grow to hate and resent her as he was cut from society for having had the audacity to flout convention.

So, it really didn't matter what his letter said. He could be every bit the scoundrel she had accused him of being at the height of her fury, or he could be the kind and loving man she suspected might linger beneath that cool exterior. Either way, there was no future for them.

Better she held onto her hurt and learned to hate him again. At least then she could protect what remained of her heart for, if she knew that he loved her as she had loved him, the knowledge would eat away at her for the rest of her days.

She sighed again, jumping as Mrs Baxter cursed and threw down the knife she was peeling the spuds with.

"That's it!" the woman said, wiping her hands on her apron. "I can't take another day of this."

She hurried out of the kitchen and Charity watched, open mouthed as she headed for the stairs.

"What... what are you doing?" she demanded, getting to her feet so fast she almost knocked her chair over. She righted it and hurried to the hallway, looking up to see Mrs Baxter as she opened Charity's bedroom door.

"Oh!" Charity cried in horror, snatching at her skirts and running up the stairs two at a time. "Batty! Batty, don't you dare!" she screeched, heart pounding as she rounded the corner. She almost knocked Kit flat as he emerged from his room, hair awry as it often was when he was writing.

"What the bloody hell is going on?" he shouted, infuriated. "I'm *trying* to work!"

"Oh, do mind out, Kit!" she snapped, pushing him from her path and running to her own room as her brother swore and stomped after her.

She got to the door just as Mrs Baxter tore the seal open on the envelope.

"That's private!" she cried, disbelieving that the woman would go so far.

That she'd taken David's... Devlin's... ugh... *his* side, was obvious. She'd been making remarks and dropping less than subtle hints for weeks, all of which Charity had ignored.

"I don't care," Mrs Baxter threw back at her. "I can't watch you throw away a fine man like that because you're too pig-headed to even see what he wrote to you!"

"Batty, please," Charity begged, unable to find the words to explain that it wasn't stubbornness on her part, not this time. It was self-preservation.

It was too late though.

Batty's eyes scanned the paper and she gasped, sitting down on the edge of Charity's bed with her hand over her heart.

"What?" Charity demanded, sick to her stomach with apprehension.

Mrs Baxter seemed shocked so... what the hell had he said? She snatched the paper from her hands, knowing she would have to read it now.

She was trembling so hard she couldn't hold the paper still and it took her several attempts to understand what she was reading. Her breath snagged in her throat and she covered her mouth at the sob that threatened to escape.

"What the devil did the wretch say to you now?" Kit demanded, his eyes alight with fury. "If that bastard has upset you again, I swear to God—"

"Language, Kit!" Mrs Baxter snapped.

Kit glared at her but held his tongue. "Will *someone* be so kind as to tell me what the bloo—what on earth is going on?"

Charity and the Devil

"He's given it to me, Kit," Charity said, her voice faint as she looked up at her twin. "The farm, the land... all of it. It isn't a letter, it's the deed to Brasted Farm, in my name."

Kit stared at her, opening and closing his mouth as her words sunk in.

"Oh," he said, sitting down beside Batty as his anger leached away. "Well, that is... unexpected."

They'd known Lord Devlin had stopped the sale, having heard Squire Thompson had agreed to buy the old Sampson farm instead, some ten miles from Brasted. As Kit had said, though, it was the least the devil could do. The relief of not being made homeless had been negated by their hurt and fury at the way he had deceived them.

And yet now....

Charity stared at the deed in her hand and swallowed, emotions pushing at her throat, demanding release.

"Well then, Miss," Mrs Baxter said, folding her arms and fixing her with a rather piercing expression. "What now?"

"I... I don't know," Charity said, and burst into tears.

Chapter 18

"Wherein a dismal world envelops our hero, and our heroine suffers a greater shock."

It had been a month. A month that felt like an eternity.

Dev stared at the rain falling outside his window. London was grey. Grey clouds, grey weather, dirty, dingy, devoid of any colour. It was as though losing Charity had sucked the vibrancy from the entire world, not just his life.

He'd tried to keep hope alive, remembering that Mrs Baxter was on his side. Yet he knew the passion with which Charity hated Viscount Devlin. He'd been there when she'd raged against his dissolute lifestyle, against his selfishness and his cruel lack of regard for anyone but himself. He still had the letters she'd sent him. The ones where she had done such a thorough job of revealing how low an opinion she held of him. He'd read them several times now, as if he sought penance for his past sins in their pages. Every time he read her words his hopes diminished as he saw the truth of the man he'd been, the one she'd seen him to be. How could she ever forgive him when he could not forgive himself?

He'd allowed his hatred for his father—his hurt at his father's rejection and his mother's neglect—to colour every aspect of his life. He'd allowed that taint to spread so far he'd ruined every hope of ever being anything different than them, anything better.

Since he'd returned to his London home, he'd tried to act as Charity would have wanted him to. He was polite to his staff; he learned their names and enquired after their families. That, at least, had brought rewards. Mistrust had been their first reaction, perhaps suspecting a trap, but little by little they accepted the changes in their devilish master. Now he was greeted with smiles that appeared genuine, if a little cautious. It was… nice.

His life had changed beyond recognition because of her.

Dev no longer socialised, staying out until all hours and awaking in strange beds. He didn't want that life back. Although he'd known it was shallow and contemptuous when he'd lived it, he'd felt there was no alternative for him, no other way. He'd believed he deserved no better, hadn't even known what better looked like. Now, however he'd lived for a brief time in a life so utterly different from his own it had been like being reborn, only to have it taken away from him.

Now he couldn't sleep because he dreamed of her. He couldn't eat because he longed for simple wholesome fare that tasted real and fresh. There was something satisfying in eating produce you'd picked with your own hands. It was such a modest pleasure his old self would have sneered and had a scathing remark to make, but now it seemed important to him.

Tonight, he felt his hopes were little more than a flickering light, burning with defiance in the dark of a raging storm. He wouldn't give up. He would return to Brasted Farm and try again… once he had mustered the courage to face her.

For the moment he was drowning his sorrows.

It had been awhile since he'd drunk with such single-minded determination, but it appeared he hadn't lost the knack. The decanter at his elbow emptied as the skies darkened, the streets below evacuating as everyone hurried home to get out of the filthy weather.

Dev closed his eyes and remembered the sun upon his face, the sound of John and Jane laughing as they played with the kittens. In his mind he heard Kit cursing everyone and yelling for quiet and inhaled the smell of dinner drifting from the kitchens as he rubbed down the horses, their contented whickering a soft sound in the cool of the barn.

Most of all he remembered Charity, her sun-browned face and the little scattering of freckles over her nose. He saw the warmth in her eyes, and the fire when she was cross with him. He remembered with too much clarity the feel of her in his arms when he'd held her close, and how willing she'd been to give him everything… before she'd known the truth.

Dev rubbed at the ache in his chest, knowing it would never leave him.

Not until he got her back.

***

Charity watched the imposing sight of Devlin Hall as it got closer, her heart beating so hard she felt it might break free of her ribs.

She didn't know what she was doing here, what she would say, but she had to say something, to thank him at least for… for giving her the farm.

She didn't know if she ought to tell him he was forgiven.

If what he'd said to her was true, if he really wanted to court her, then if she forgave him he might repeat the offer, and she could never live the life he would need her to. She had no notion of how a fine lady behaved, or what would be expected of her, and—what was more—she didn't want to learn. She belonged here, in the wild expanses of Dartmoor, where the wind felt like it would wipe every living thing from the face of the earth and everything clung on, determined for survival. Spending half the year in town and going to parties and the theatre and endless dinners….

Her throat grew tight, panic closing in on her at the thought. It seemed such a narrow world, so confining, stealing her breath and making her feel trapped.

Charity sucked in a deep breath, her fingers tightening on the simple cotton of her best day dress. There was no need for fancy silks and muslins and fine fabrics that would only get torn and dragged in the mud or end up snagged and tangled in a bramble. That was not her world. This was.

She stared around her at a landscape that rolled as far as the eye could see. A man could walk into that wilderness and disappear, never to be seen again. It appeared barren and yet teemed with life; it was rugged and harsh and dangerous… beautiful, and where she belonged.

With all her heart, she wanted him back. She wanted him to be David, to come and live in her world and fit back into the part of her life that was now empty. There was a gaping, ragged hole where he had made a space for himself, forcing apart that tender spot under her ribs and making a void only he could fill.

But he was the Viscount Devlin, not David, and she wasn't foolish enough not to know that made them an impossibility. Their lives did not fit together, could not intertwine, and trying would only make them both miserable.

Mr Baxter eased the cart to a halt and Charity frowned, exchanging glances with him as they looked at the activity around the vast building. There were rows of covered wagons, and staff hurrying in and out of the building, removing furniture, carrying endless chests and containers.

Charity got down from the cart, moving through the melee and wondering what on earth was going on, though it was clear enough.

He was leaving.

Her breath hitched and she ran for the stairs, hiking her skirts and running as she ignored the curious looks from the men who worked around her.

The snooty butler was nowhere to be seen and Charity's heart crashed against her ribs harder than before. He couldn't have left already, surely? She had to at least say goodbye.

With panic tightening her chest and making her breathless it was hard to get the words out, but she grabbed at each man in turn as they passed her and lugged paintings or carpets, or heavy boxes of Lord knew what.

"Where is Lord Devlin? Is he here? Please, could you tell me—"

"Lord Devlin no longer owns this building."

A deep, rumbling voice filled the now echoing entrance hall, as though the house was already hollowed out without its master in residence. Charity turned and then gasped at the sight of the man before her, if he *was* a man. He seemed more a giant, some hulking monster from a child's story.

"W-What do you mean?" she asked, a cold sensation creeping under her skin. "This is Devlin Hall, it's been their seat for generations, he…." Charity stopped in her tracks as a terrible truth occurred to her. David, Devlin… whoever the hell he really was, had been selling their farm and the land to raise money to pay a debt to a Mr Blackehart. A ruthless man who would likely not take kindly to not being paid.

A dangerous man.

The man who stood in front of her would certainly fit that description.

She swallowed, taking an involuntary step away, though the man had made no move towards her.

"Lord Devlin sold the hall to me," he said, watching her, a curious look in his dark eyes. He had a rough voice, a harsh accent that spoke of back alleys and low company in a big city.

"You're Mr Blackehart?"

He nodded, the faintest trace of a smile at his lips. A scar ran the right side of his face, pulling his eye down and she suppressed a shudder. A dangerous man indeed.

Charity and the Devil

Charity reached out, grasping the newel post as the ground seemed to lurch beneath her feet.

"Are you quite well, Miss?"

To her surprise he crossed towards her and then hesitated, as if he would steady her but was aware his nearness would frighten her. She sank down to sit on the stairs, uncaring that she was making a show of herself, too shocked to worry for it.

"You, there. Bring me some brandy."

Charity watched as Mr Blackehart barked out an order, still too dazed to point out that there would be unlikely to be such a thing in the house as it was being packed up and taken away. From the authoritative tone of the man's voice and the terror in the eyes of the one he'd addressed, however, brandy would be found from somewhere.

"You didn't know he'd gone?" Blackehart demanded, a considering look in his eyes.

Charity shook her head, still trying to come to terms with the enormity of what David—he would have to be David for now—of what he'd done, for them, for her. He'd sold his inheritance, his history, the home of generations of Devlins before him, just to save a small farm that scrabbled for survival in a rough environment.

She frowned, remembering that Squire Thompson was buying another farm, so why ...

Casting a glance up at Mr Blackehart who was still watching her, his dark eyes full of interest, she knew he was not a man to wait for what he wanted. Had it been the only way David could get out from under his grasp alive?

Charity shivered, forcing herself to stand as a beleaguered looking servant hurried up with a tray bearing a bottle of brandy and two glasses. Blackehart poured a small measure and handed it to her.

"Drink it."

Her instincts bristled, unused to being ordered about and disliking it. Bravery seemed in short supply as the man towered over her though and she did as she was bid, she needed it too much to protest. As the liquor pooled in her belly, creating a warm glow that eased through her, calming her shattered nerves, she knew she had to see David again. She had to know why... why had he done it? Had it been for her?

"Thank you, sir," she said, replacing the glass and turning to leave.

"He has a house in London."

She paused, eyeing the man with distrust.

"I didn't leave the poor bugger destitute, if that's what's got you in such a pucker."

The man folded his huge arms and Charity pitied his tailor as she saw the way the fabric strained over his biceps. It must be like clothing an oak tree. He might dress like a gentleman, but no amount of fine tailoring could hide the fact he certainly wasn't one. What the locals would make of Devlin Hall going to a man of his ilk she couldn't fathom. There'd be uproar.

"You'll find him on Harley Street, if you care to look. All arms and legs intact last I saw."

There was a devilish glint of amusement in his eyes at that comment and Charity gritted her teeth.

"Thank you for the information, sir," she said, her tone brittle as she glowered back at him. "I will bid you a good day."

***

Charity stared up at the grand house on Harley Street and gripped her umbrella tighter as the wind threatened to snatch it from her grasp. Certainly not destitute, then.

This had been a ridiculous idea.

Charity and the Devil

It had taken a deal of persuasion to get Kit to accompany her to London. Getting out of their lodgings before he'd woken and without arousing the notice of the busybody of a house keeper had been worse. She'd been careful not to share David's precise address with him, so he wouldn't know where to look for her.

Now she'd done it, she rather wished she hadn't.

If Kit had been here David could not say things that would stir up her heart and her hopes and fears. He could not give her hope, nor shatter her forbidden dreams. It would simply be a polite visit in which they expressed their gratitude and he told them it was really nothing... selling his family's inheritance meant nothing at all. What nonsense.

She'd not hear polite nothings. Charity had never been a coward and she'd not start now. She'd have the truth and face it and... and she didn't have the slightest idea what came next.

Telling herself she was made of sterner stuff than this, she marched up the stairs and knocked on the door. She turned and watched the carriages roll past as she waited, glimpsing a fashionable lady with an extraordinary hat plumed with huge feathers in one. Her bored expression flickered over Charity, a look of contempt on her face as she turned away.

Charity flushed, aware that her best dress marked her out as a country mouse, a poor relation, perhaps, and an embarrassing one at that. She didn't belong here. It wasn't as if she hadn't known it, but everything she'd seen in the short time she'd been in London made her realise her instincts had been right. The gulf between those wealthy creatures that David must call his friends and her was even more marked than she'd realised.

The sensation only intensified as the door opened and a scandalised looking butler took in the sight of her, *alone* on the front step. Oh, Lord. She ought to have brought Kit. Charity put up her chin, looking the man in the eye.

"Miss Kendall, to see Lord Devlin, please."

The butler looked over the top of her head and intoned in a bored voice: "His lordship is not at home."

The snooty devil went to shut the door but hadn't banked on Charity's temper. Furious at being dismissed in such a manner after the God-awful journey she'd endured to get here, she stuck her umbrella in the gap before the door slammed in her face and levered it open again, slipping through the space she'd created.

"Tell his lordship that Miss Kendall is here," she said, thrusting her sodden umbrella into the startled butler's grasp and giving him a hard stare. "I promise you, he will wish to see me. What's more he'll likely throw you out on your ear if he discovers I've been turned out and you didn't inform him."

The man was obviously unused to such hoydenish behaviour and just gaped at her for a moment, too stunned to react as her umbrella dripped all over his shiny shoes.

"Oh, for heaven's sake," Charity muttered, folding her arms. "Where is he?"

"Miss…!" The butler spluttered, coming back to his senses as Charity took matters into her own hands and began to open doors, looking inside for any trace of Dev. "This is outrageous! I must insist that—"

"Lord Devlin!" Charity shouted at the top of her lungs, as none of the doors downstairs revealed the man she was looking for. She hoped to God he was here and not away from home as the butler had suggested. If he wasn't, she might have to lock herself in somewhere to stop from being ejected. She squealed as the butler made a lunge for her, and hurried towards the stairs. Ejection appeared to be more imminent than she had hoped. Not stopping to look behind and see if he was following, she ran, praying she would find what she was looking for.

Chapter 19

"Wherein ... a reunion."

Dev sighed, trying to grasp hold of the dream, to stay within the comfort of its embrace, no matter that it wasn't real. Reality was too hard, too painful. He'd had a belly full of reality and he wasn't ready to face another day of it.

Next week he would smarten himself up and return to Dartmoor, face the inevitable confrontation with Charity, and do everything and anything to get her to give him a chance. If she hadn't calmed down by then she never would, and there was no point in fooling himself that it was otherwise.

For now, however, he would wallow in his own misery and drink himself insensible. As plans went, it was simple but comprehensive.

Dev reached for the glass on the bedside table and swallowed a mouthful of brandy with a grimace. That was breakfast sorted, then. He turned on his side again, allowing sleep to tug at his mind, hoping the dream would return to him. He conjured Charity's face, traced the outline of her lips with his fingertips, sighing as the longing for her made the hollow bell of his heart ring out with sorrow. Her voice was low, intimate as she asked him for a kiss and he moved closer, about to press his mouth to hers... and then jolted as she shouted at him.

What?

Reality and dreams collided, and he forced his eyes open, blinking in shock.

"Lord Devlin! *David!* Or whatever the bloody hell you're calling yourself these days!"

A furious voice rang through his house. Strident and utterly enraged... it was the most wonderful sound he'd ever heard in his life.

Dev sprung from the bed and then wished he hadn't as his head throbbed and the room spun. Still unsure he was awake, he scrabbled for his silk banyan, pulling it on and tying it shut as he ran for the door. A feminine shriek echoed through the lofty hall as he threw the door open and Charity barrelled into him.

The two of them stared at each other, Charity breathing hard, her bonnet askew, dark curls escaping as she clutched at his arms for support.

"My lord, forgive me," called Meekins, the town butler as he puffed to the top of the stairs. "I could not stop this dreadful creature from forcing her way into the house."

Dev's mouth curved into a hopeless smile, his heart lifting for the first time since he'd said goodbye to Mrs Baxter and the children.

"I know," he said, his voice soft, never taking his eyes from hers. "She has a habit of barging into places she has no business in going."

His smile grew as Charity narrowed her eyes at him and tried to step out of his embrace.

"Oh no you don't," he said, holding her tighter. "You're not going anywhere."

"Should I call for a runner, my lord, or a magistrate perhaps?" the butler demanded as Dev tried to convince himself it was real, she wasn't a dream. She was flesh and blood, warm in his arms, and none too pleased about it, from the flicker of irritation in her eyes.

"No, thank you, that won't be necessary. Leave us, please, Meekins."

"But... my lord...?"

Charity and the Devil

Dev scowled, tearing his gaze away from Charity to glare at the wretched fellow.

"Go. Away!"

The tone was familiar to anyone who had worked for him for any length of time, no matter his recent good intentions. It suggested his words be obeyed at once, and without question, or the consequences would not be pretty.

Meekins had been with him for many years and hurried back down the stairs.

"You're here," Dev said, unable to keep the wonder from his voice. "I thought I dreamed you."

Charity looked up at him, her expression hard to read. She was stiff in his arms, as though she would bolt at any moment, yet there was a shy look in her eyes which was unfamiliar. A tinge of colour touched her cheeks and made him hope it wasn't the desire to rage at him that had brought her here.

She moved away from him and this time he let her go, though with reluctance. He watched as she adjusted her bonnet and returned a more familiar rather wry look.

"Hardly the stuff of dreams," she muttered, gesturing to the muddy hem of her skirts, a victim of the foul weather outside.

"I hate to contradict you, love, but you've never been more wrong."

The flush deepened and his smile grew.

"I've missed you," he said, hopelessly lost, desperate for her forgiveness. "I missed you every second of every day."

"Don't. David, I...."

She scowled and threw up her hands, and fear licked at his heart. He hadn't won this, not yet.

"My friends call me Dev," he offered, wondering how she should address him.

She wrinkled her nose at that and he found himself unsurprised. Any reference to Devlin would not sit well with her.

"Come," he said, holding out his hand. "We can't talk about this in the hallway."

Charity folded her arms, looking a little scandalised. "I'm not going into your bedroom!"

He laughed and then adjusted his face as he realised this wasn't the right tack to take. "No," he said, hurrying on and leading her to the sitting room instead. "Of course not."

Dev saw her eyes widen as she walked into the grand and opulent room. His father had enjoyed showing off his wealth. Thank God she'd never set foot inside Devlin Hall. He could almost see her shrink into herself a little, faced with the lavishness of what his life had always been: the gilding and fine furniture, paintings and carpets. the like of which she'd never have seen in her life before.

"Luke," he said, as he closed the door behind them, wanting to take her attention from her surrounding, from things he didn't care about enough to let her give up on him.

Charity turned and stared at him, perplexed.

"My name," he added, wretched that she was only learning this now. "Luke Linton."

Her eyebrows rose, her mouth forming a little 'o' of surprise.

"Luke," she repeated, as Dev rubbed the back of his neck.

The corners of her mouth kicked up a little, and he felt it was an unwilling smile, but she couldn't help herself.

He shrugged awkwardly. "No one ever uses my name, I've always been Dev or at school I was Linton."

"I rather like it," she said, her tone softer now.

She turned away from him and moved to the window. Dev watched her, unsure of what to do or say now. He had the distinct feeling he was holding his breath, his chest growing tight. If he made a wrong move, said the wrong thing, she would run from him.

"Why have you come?" he asked, not yet daring to believe his hopes and prayers had been answered and she'd come to tell him she missed him, she loved him, and she could not stay away. There was too much tension in her for that. He could see the way she held herself, contained, wanting to keep him at arm's length. That needed to stop.

She turned back to look at him. "You've sold Devlin Hall."

Dev nodded, fighting the desire to cross the distance and just take her in his arms. It was like trying to get closer to an injured bird; if he moved too fast she would take flight and injure herself further to escape, although his intentions were never to hurt her again. She no longer trusted him, and he could not blame her for that.

"Why?" she demanded, clutching her arms about herself as if she was cold.

"You know why."

Charity shook her head, tears sparkling in her eyes as she turned away from him to hide her agitation. "Don't say that. You can't have!"

Her voice was harder now, angry on the surface yet he was no longer fooled, he could hear the despair she was hiding.

"That was your legacy, your history, the inheritance you would leave to those who come after you! How could you be so foolish? Do you care for nothing at all?"

"Yes," he replied, moving closer to her now despite fears she would flee from him. "I care. I care a great deal, more than you will ever know, but not for Devlin Hall. That place means nothing but misery and loneliness, and I've had my fill of those."

"What do you mean?" she asked, holding his gaze as he drew nearer.

Her expression showed she was puzzled by his words, but he wouldn't tell her of his wretched past yet. He needed to hold her, to show her the truth of how much he cared, not dwell in the mire of days long gone.

"I love you," he said, slipping his arms around her, even as she shook her head though she didn't move away from him. "I do," he said, holding her tighter, needing to find the words that would make her believe him. "You can deny it all you like but it won't change anything. I love you, with my whole heart, with everything I am, so help you, for you know how dreadful a confession that is."

"Stop it," she said, crying now, clutching at the silken gown that covered him as if she would push him away and hold tight at the same time. "Dav— oh, *Luke*! Can't you see how impossible it is? I don't even know who you are!"

"Yes, you do," he said, cupping her face with one hand, forcing her to look up at him. "You told me once you knew exactly who I was. You said I wasn't as black-hearted as you'd believed, or even as I'd believed myself." He stroked her cheek with his thumb, savouring the warmth and softness and needing so much more. "You were almost right. I was every bit as despicable as you believed me to be, but I've discovered that I can be more than that. You taught me that. I *want* to be more than that, for you. Please, love, I've changed. Won't you believe me?"

She held his gaze and nodded, a tear rolling down her cheek as she smiled at him.

"Yes," she said, as his heart seemed to skip in his chest. "I believe you."

He made a startled sound, his breath catching as she laughed in return and he muffled the surprise of it by pressing his mouth to hers, unable to hold back a moment longer. There was a moment of tension as she started in shock and he prayed she would not push him away. She didn't, softening in his arms, pliant as she reached one hand up to touch the back of his neck, tentative at first as the other hand still clutched at the silk of his dressing gown.

Desire, need, the desperate misery of the past weeks, all conspired to strip his control away from him as he slanted his mouth over hers and deepened the kiss. He'd wanted to do this right, to court her, to ask her to marry him and have her consent. The kiss swept away all his plans and hopes in the simple joy of the moment, of having her here, in his arms, after so many nights alone and fearing he would never hold her again.

He would make her his so she could never deny that she belonged to him. The words that were always so hard to find, the explanations that never seemed to illustrate what he had in his heart were so easy to misinterpret, to forget or misremember, but this… this there could be no mistaking. She would never forget how he loved her, the tenderness with which he showed her his love for her, and then when she knew, when she really understood, she would forgive what had gone before. They could begin again.

***

Charity knew she was trembling, but she couldn't make herself stop. Being here, in his arms, it was all too much and yet nowhere near enough. Longing filled her heart, no matter how she tried to stop it, no matter that she knew this had to be goodbye. There was no place in his life for her. If she hadn't known it before, the simple act of walking into this room had illustrated the impossibility of any future together. He might as well have been a prince and she a pauper for all the difference it would make. The gulf between them yawned wide, threatening to swallow them both whole, and yet she could not walk away from him, not yet.

She had offered herself to him twice now and he'd refused her, proving he was not the heartless wretch she'd believed him to be. Not heartless at all, but loving and giving, wanting so much to give her everything. He would offer her marriage if she gave him the chance, a life with him in his world, and her heart ached with the longing for it to be possible. But he was being foolish, ignoring reality and hoping to bend the world to his will. Perhaps that was what came of being a viscount and always getting your own way. In this, however, he would have a rude awakening. He would find himself shunned, ostracised and cut off from his own kind, and Charity would not be the cause of that. Yet neither could she deny her feelings, deny that she loved him and wanted him with all her heart, or that she wanted him to know the truth of it.

Before this day she'd wanted to give herself to him because she'd known it was her only chance. It would only happen once, because she'd known he would leave and she would return to her world. She would raise John and Jane and care for Kit until he had a wife to do so for him, and then… and then she would continue to work on the farm, finding contentment living in the place she loved and belonged, until there were nieces and nephews to love too. That had always been her fate and she'd known it since her parents died. If once she had resented that fact, those days were gone. Until *he'd* come into her life, at least.

Now she wanted to rage against fate but there was no point. Fate was not a man you could shout at, a tangible presence you could fight, hoping to wear it away. Fate was an enemy that would grind you down and would put up a fight you could never win.

So, she would do as she had intended all those weeks ago. She would give herself to him, completely, irrevocably, so he would know he held her heart and always would, but instead of him leaving and returning to his world as she'd believed he would, it would be her who left and ran back to the land she belonged in.

She gave herself up to his kiss, finding he tasted of brandy as she committed each detail, every touch, to memory. His body blazed through the silk that covered him, even the fabric screaming wealth and status as her work-roughened fingers revelled in its luxury. They were as disparate as oil and water, and no matter how they shook the world to fit their desires they could never join for more than a fleeting moment.

That moment was here and now, and Charity would not let it slip from her grasp again. So, when he broke the kiss, his gaze intent and an unspoken question in his eyes, she smiled and nodded, and followed where he led.

Chapter 20

"Wherein joy is overwhelming, and all too fleeting."

Dev was once again afraid he was dreaming but found he was too nervous to voice his doubts as he took Charity's hand and led her back to his bedroom. That she came willingly was at once wonderful and unnerving.

She had forgiven him.

The truth of it was astonishing. Hopes that had been all but snuffed out now blazed to light once more, the light so brilliant it whited out his sight. The glare lit up the dark corners where every problem and obstacle lingering in his heart had lurked, shining so brightly that he could no longer see them at all. If she had forgiven him, she could love him. Perhaps she already did? The look in her eyes had made him believe it possible. He had expected to have to fight for her, to meet every argument she threw at him with one of his own, to wear her arguments away until she saw it was futile to resist him.

The ease with which she'd fallen into his arms was unsettling. Yet he was certain he'd seen love in her eyes, surely he had, and if she loved him they could do anything, start again….

Anything was possible.

He allowed her a moment, watching as she tugged at the ribbons of her bonnet, her fingers trembling. She placed it on his dressing table, taking time to touch a finger to the fine silver backed brush it sat beside before turning her attention to her pelisse. Her hands were shaking so hard now she fumbled the buttons and Dev moved closer.

He covered her hands with his own.

"Don't be frightened. I would never hurt you."

She let out a breath, huffing a little. "I know that. I … I don't know why I'm being such a silly goose about it."

"Because it matters," he said, frowning as he pulled her closer. "It isn't silly at all, only I don't want you to be afraid or to regret it. We can wait if—"

"No."

He raised his eyebrows at the vehemence in her tone. Was there something wrong? Was that sadness in her eyes where there ought to have been joy?

She reached up, pulling his mouth down to hers and kissing him, pressing against him and then tugging at the silken belt that held the banyan closed. All at once it slid open and she pushed it from his shoulders. He heard her intake of breath as she moved back to look at him and any doubts of what she was feeling fled at the desire he saw in her eyes as she looked at him. He dropped his arms, allowing the silk to slither to the floor in one, fluid movement.

The colour at her cheeks blazed but she did not look away or pretend anything other than interest in the sight of him naked before her. She raised her hand tentatively, and Dev's breath snagged in his throat as her fingers touched his skin. He couldn't think, could do nothing but watch as her fingers trailed over him, igniting an inferno he feared would consume him if he couldn't touch her in return.

"You're wearing too many clothes," he said, aware of the husky sound of his voice as she looked up at him.

"That must be why I'm so hot," she said, a glimmer of mischief in her eyes.

Dev laughed, delighted at her as his hands reached for her buttons. "Get this blasted coat off before I rip it to shreds," he commanded, pleased that she laughed and squealed as he at turns undid a button and tickled her, hoping to put her more at ease. At last the buttons were undone, the coat thrown in a heap on the floor and the glittering light in her eyes told him she was amused and no longer in afraid of him or what would happen between them.

He paused as he wondered where her brother was, and what the devil she was doing here alone in London?

"Where's Kit?" he asked, wondering if his door was likely to be pounded to dust by her irate twin at any moment.

"Still in bed, I expect," she said, a rather naughty grin tugging at her mouth. "I ran away from the lodgings we were staying in and neglected to give him your full address. He can scour London for all he's worth, he'll not find me."

Dev sighed, torn between scolding her for her recklessness and delight in her determination to see him alone. "You must never do such a thing again. This is not Dartmoor. London is dangerous, and in a far different way than your beloved moors. You must learn a new set of rules here."

For a moment the smile at her lips faltered but she returned her attention to her exploration of his person, and any further discussion of the matter was halted.

"Turn around," he said, alarmed to find his own hands were shaking as she did as he asked and he untied the fastenings of her dress. Gone was the practised lover he'd become over the past years, fled in the light of something that was new and outside his experience, something that mattered. He bent his head to press a kiss to her shoulder as the dress slid away, pleased by the shiver that travelled over her skin. He dispensed with the rest of the layers as fast as his trembling fingers could manage, until she stood before him in just garters and stockings.

Dev trailed one finger from her shoulder down her arm, noting the change from porcelain white to tan, as that skin always hidden from the light was revealed to his heated gaze. He turned her back towards him, his heart expanding in his chest as he looked his fill.

"Mine," he said, meaning to smile at her but finding the word was every bit as possessive as it sounded. He pulled her closer, revelling in the feel of her skin against his, the gasp of shock she made as his harder body pressed against her softness. His hands travelled over her, her skin a finer silk than any material he could buy, no matter the cost. Dev cupped her face in his hands, pressing his mouth to hers. "Mine," he said again, not caring if he sounded like a damned caveman, it was how he felt in this moment. "You're mine now, mine alone. You know that don't you?"

Her hands covered his, her eyes guileless as she stared back at him.

"Yes," she said, her voice quiet. "I know it. I've known it since the first."

"Thank God for that," he growled and pulled her into his arms.

***

Charity could not argue with him. For all that she knew they had no future, it didn't make the truth any less true. She was his, had been his since the first, when she'd seen him bloody and unconscious and her heart had gone out to him. He'd seemed so alone, hurt, and abandoned to the cruelty of the moors. She never had been able to resist trying to mend something broken. Kit had been right all along. She couldn't help herself.

For once though she would take something for herself, even if she had to give herself to have it. A memory she could keep to warm her when the winter nights were coldest, and Brasted Farm seemed to be the loneliest place in the world. She would remember him then, she would remember this, a shining moment of happiness in a world that would not allow them more than that.

His hands moved over her and her heart picked up, her skin alive with sensation. Such large hands, so warm, and rough now too. She smiled as she remembered how soft they'd been at first.

"What?" he asked, noting her smile and returning it.

She took his hand and raised it to her mouth, kissing his palm and the calluses on his fingers. "You had such soft hands," she said, shaking her head and sighing, a mournful tone to her voice.

He snorted, knowing she was teasing him. "Oh, I will show you what these hands can do, my lovely hellion," he said, smirking now and then laughing aloud as he lifted her with ease and she gave a yelp of surprise.

She gasped as he tumbled her onto the bed and then prowled over the mattress towards her. Charity stared, still not able to believe what she was doing. Goodness, but what would Mrs Baxter say if she knew? Thinking about it, Mrs Baxter would probably encourage her, so long as she got a ring on her finger.

She pushed away that thought at once. There was no point in dwelling on what was to come, what could never be. She would not spoil the moment worrying about what she couldn't have. Instead she reached for him, smiling as he sighed under her touch. The press of his body against hers was astonishing and her breathing hitched even as she welcomed him, coiling herself around him. His body was at once so much larger and harder than hers, yet soft too, his skin satin beneath her fingertips and so warm.

Charity lost herself in kisses that dazed her and made her blood surge. Kit had once brought them a bottle of Champagne and she remembered the fizz and tickle of the fine liquor. She felt as if the bubbles existed beneath her skin now and, as Dev lowered his head to her breast and took her into his mouth, they threatened to spill over. She arched beneath him, helpless with surprise and pleasure as he cupped her breasts in his hands and lavished equal care between them.

"Luke," she said, his name breathless as he raised his head, a startled look of pleasure in his eyes.

"No one ever calls me that," he said, his voice full of wonder. "But I like it when you say it."

"Then you shall be Luke for me alone," she said, running her hands down his back, feeling the heavy muscles shift as he moved, and wishing it wasn't for such a short time.

"Yes," he agreed, covering her lips with his own as his body pressed closer. "Oh, yes."

His hand slid between them and Charity held her breath, knowing what he sought. She closed her eyes as he found the source of her pleasure, sliding his fingers through the curls, touching her where only she had ever touched herself before.

"So beautiful, love," he said, the sincerity in his voice tearing at her heart. "I want you so much."

"Yes," she said, the word impatient now as he stoked a fire that had been lit weeks ago, one that had burned for him and longed for him and would not allow her to walk away. He soothed her with hands and lips as she moved, restless beneath him and then all at once he was there, where she needed him.

Charity felt her heart as it raced, aware that there was no going back now. She had made her decision, sealed her fate, though in fact she'd made that decision a long time ago. He nudged forward, pressing into her as she held her breath, not knowing whether to breathe, to keep still, or urge him on.

"I love you," he said, tearing her attention from her anxious wondering, bringing her eyes to his and the honesty that shone from them, the love and desire that made her heart hurt and her body clamour for him.

"You too," she managed as he eased inside her, making her breath catch as she clutched at his shoulders. "I love you too."

It seemed all the reassurance he'd needed, and he surged inside her, thrusting forward in one fluid movement that made her cry out, but more with the shock of the intimate invasion than from any sense of pain.

From that moment on she was lost, caught in the tide of pleasure he swept her up in. His hands touched her like she was the most precious thing in the world to him, his lips upon her skin as though he needed her to breathe, overwhelming her senses and filling her poor heart until the enormity of what she'd done crashed down upon her.

It was only as she cried out, holding on to him as his body held her close and he called her name, that she realised she had tasted what her life could be like if she'd been born into his world. It was only as the waves of pleasure receded and she clung to him that she realised she should never have tasted the gift that loving him would have given her.

For now, she had to walk away, knowing everything she could never have, and she knew she would never be whole again.

***

Easing out of his embrace was the hardest thing Charity had ever done.

Luke.

She found she liked thinking of him so, using the name that no one ever called him, even though it was strange to give him yet another name. He stirred in his sleep and she paused, leaning in to kiss him, smiling at the stubble that prickled beneath her lips. She would have liked to have shaved him again, but she didn't dare stay any longer.

If she stayed, he would voice the proposal she had seen in his eyes and it would force her to refuse him, and to explain her reasons. He was so damn stubborn that she knew he would argue, would keep on and on until he wore her down and persuaded her that black was white, when she knew damn well it was dark as pitch and just as unforgiving. She could not ask him to give up his world and live in hers, and the world would never allow her to inhabit his, even if she'd dared make the attempt. They would end up betwixt and between, neither fish nor fowl, belonging nowhere, welcomed by no one. She couldn't do it to him.

So, she swallowed down the sobs that tore at her throat, afraid to cry in case he heard her, though the tears fell thick and fast in the silence of the room as she dressed. Every rustle of clothing seemed to roar in her ears, every sound loud enough to wake him, yet he slept still, a contented smile at his lips. Her heart ached at the sight, but she tied the ribbons of her bonnet all the same, finding her hands shook harder now than when she'd untied them. When all was done and there was nothing left to keep her she reached inside her reticule for the letter she had written last night.

She had thought to put it into his hands if things had become too heated and her explanations jumbled in her distress. She had written it when she'd been cool-headed, the future clear to her. At least it ought to illustrate all the difficulties he'd been so obstinately ignoring.

She wondered if he'd be angry and hoped for his sake he was. Anger was so much easier to bear than heartache; that much she had learned to her cost.

Charity moved to the bed, staring at his sleeping figure with her heart so full of regret and longing that the pain was like a knife wound. The desire to bend down and steal a last kiss was tantalising, but she dared not risk waking him. So, she put the letter on the pillow beside him and turned away, creeping from the room like a thief.

***

Dev stirred, finding a smile at his lips as he remembered. Charity. Charity was here.

He turned, reaching for her, only to find the bed cold and empty. His heart lurched, terrified that it had been a dream after all, though his body refused to believe it. She had been here—her scent lingered on his skin, the taste of her upon his lips—and then he saw the letter.

No.

No, please God....

He snatched it up, praying it said only that she'd gone to see Kit, to tell him not to worry, that they were to be married... even as he knew in his heart it was nothing of the sort. He broke the wafer that sealed the sheet, sending it shattering into crumbs over the bed. His trembling hands almost tore the paper in his haste to read her words, his heart stuttering as his worst fears were realised.

He crumpled the letter with a shout of distress, casting it across the room in fury. When had she left? Moments ago? Hours? Had he still time to catch her?

Dev flung back the covers, intending to shout for his valet but something stopped him. He sat on the edge of his bed, chest heaving as though he'd run for miles, the pain beneath his ribs so fierce he couldn't breathe, and yet the truth was clear to him. If he went after her, she wouldn't listen to him, stubborn, pig-headed creature that she was.

He took a breath, allowing his lungs to unlock, pushing his terror and misery away as determination took their place. She loved him. He knew the truth of it now, the truth of her. She couldn't take the words back or pretend them unsaid. He'd seen it in her eyes, known it with every fibre of his being. He didn't doubt that she'd been crying when she'd left, and his heart ached for her too, for that she still didn't realise what he was prepared to do to have her in his life.

Charity believed he would have to give everything up to be with her, make a sacrifice he would regret for the rest of his days. He'd been so swept up in the joy of finding her here, in his desire for her, that he had not troubled to explain, not shown her the truth of his existence before he found her. Selling Devlin Hall had been like cutting a cancer from his life. It had been liberating, setting him free from a world he'd been born to, and yet despised. But if he tried to explain this *now* she would think he was just countering her argument with one of his own.

So, he wouldn't argue with her. He wouldn't discuss it at all. He would act. He would show her they were meant to be together, and nothing on God's green earth would keep them apart. Not if he had a say in the matter.

Dev may have sold his ancestral home for far less than its value, but that hardly made him a pauper and he was still a viscount. Charity was about to find out just what it meant to have power and money, and the ability to move heaven and earth for the woman you loved.

Chapter 21

"Wherein broken hearts, schemes, and breaking ground."

"Where the bloody hell have you been?"

As she'd expected, Kit was incandescent with rage by the time she made it back to their lodgings. His fury fell away in a moment however, when he saw she was pale and miserable and close to tears.

"Charity? Charity, what happened? Are you hurt?" He pulled her into a fierce hug and any remaining grasp on her emotions fell away. She clutched at his jacket and sobbed, knowing it would only make him frantic but unable to stop herself.

"Damn it, Charity, tell me what's wrong! Did something happen?"

There was terror in his voice now, real fear in his eyes and she tried to look at him, to shake her head and reassure him, but they were twins and he'd always seen more than she cared to show him.

"You saw him and he… he…? By God, I'll kill him."

"No!" Charity shouted and grasped hold of his arm as he turned from her. "No, Kit! No! He's done nothing wrong, nothing at all. He asked me to marry him."

Kit spun around, staring at her, his confusion clear, "He did?"

Charity nodded, tears rolling down her cheeks. She wasn't about to tell Kit that he'd never actually said the words. The words had been in his eyes, in everything he'd said and done. If she'd stayed to watch him wake, she knew they'd have been the first words on his lips.

She sat down and Kit crouched before her and took her hands. "I don't understand. You're in love with him, Charity. It's so obvious it's painful. If he wants to marry you, why—"

"Why do you think?" Charity demanded, snatching her hands away, incredulous that her brother couldn't see the obstacles before them, but then he was the romantic one. For Kit, love was everything. The practicalities of where a body would eat and sleep were nothing compared to *living* the emotion. He felt the experience should encompass you heart and soul and that nothing and no one should hinder it, no matter the who, what, or where. She was the practical one. She was the one who read his poems and pointed out that a night on the moors would be cold and damp and far from romantic, no matter how beautifully he wrote of two star-crossed lovers spending the night there. They'd more likely end up with wet feet and a nasty cold rather than a night of passion.

Kit shrugged, clearly at a loss, and Charity gave an exasperated laugh, shaking her head.

"Oh, Kit, he's a viscount. They marry noblemen's daughters and spend half the year in town, going to parties and the theatre and who knows what else people like that do. Look at me." She waved an arm to encompass her sun-browned face, her well-worn clothes, and her hands already rough from work, which would become red and chapped in the winter. "I'm not made for that world, Kit. I don't belong in it and… and I don't want to belong. Can you imagine me spending half my life here?"

Kit sat back, frowning at her as he crossed his legs. "You'd not last a month," he said, the words full of understanding. "It would be like caging a bird."

Charity smiled and gave a little huff. "Well, nothing half so romantic, but yes. But if that was the only reason then I would try, Kit. For him, I would try." She reached out her hand and he took it, the pity in his eyes making her heart ache. "They would never accept me. You know how cruel people can be, Kit. They would cut him, ridicule him, and if that happened he would come to resent me. Even if he didn't, I… I would know everything he'd lost on my account and I couldn't bear it."

Charity burst into tears and Kit got to his knees, hugging her.

"I'm so sorry," he whispered, holding her tight. "Damn it, this is all my fault. I saw the way it was between you, I saw the way you looked at him from the start. I should have made him leave before this began."

There was anguish in his voice and Charity looked up at him, astonished.

"How can *you*, of all people, say that to me?" she demanded, pushing at his shoulder and staring down at him. "I love him, Kit. I love him with all my heart, so much that the pain of it is tearing me apart, but I'll leave him *because* I love him. I'll let him go because it is better for him if I do. Isn't this what your poems are all about?" she said, becoming strident now as Kit's eyes glittered with emotion. "Isn't this the great love that people die for? The all-consuming emotion you've longed for? I found it, Kit. *Me*! Charity Kendall, who never set foot farther than Tillforth." Charity let out a breath, a tremulous smile at her lips. "You should celebrate for me, you know."

Kit laughed, though she knew his heart was bleeding for her. She could see the pain in his eyes, and perhaps a little envy at having found what he'd been seeking.

"Charity," he said, his voice low, "did he know you would say no before…?"

"Before he took me to bed?" she asked, making him sigh at her plain speaking. "No. I didn't give him an answer, I just—" She avoided Kit's eye, knowing he could tell when she was lying. "—prevaricated, and then I left while he was still sleeping."

Kit cursed and rubbed a hand over his face. She knew his desire to break her lover's nose warred with his own beliefs about love and life. It was clearly harder to enforce such rules when they applied to one's sister.

"Tell me he was careful, at least," he said, his voice a growl as he glanced up at her.

Charity opened her mouth and then felt the blush that scalded her cheeks.

Oh.

She'd been so caught up in the moment she'd not even considered…. So much for being the practical one.

"Oh, for the love of God!" Kit exclaimed, throwing up his hands now. "*Charity!*"

Charity opened and closed her mouth, too appalled herself to reply.

"I'll kill him," Kit said, getting to his feet, his mouth thinning into a hard line that sat ill on his beautiful face.

"No, you won't," Charity said, standing and clutching at his hand. "He wasn't to know I'd refuse to marry him, or that I'd run away from him. This was my doing, Kit. My choice, not his. I wanted to be with him, just once before… before…." Her voice quavered, and Kit's face softened, understanding in his eyes.

"Oh, Charity." He pulled her close and stroked her hair. "My heart is breaking for you, truly, but what if you're with child? That would change everything. It would have to."

Charity shrugged, knowing if she was carrying his baby, Luke would move heaven and earth. He'd stop at nothing before she agreed to marry him. Yet she could raise a child alone if it came to it. She kept such thoughts to herself, knowing Kit would not be so sympathetic if a baby was involved.

"Well, I'll cross that bridge when I come to it," she said, giving him a crooked smile before letting go of what remained of her control and crying her heart out.

It would be the only time she showed such weakness, she promised herself. From now on, she would be strong, determined. She would need to be, for she knew he'd be on her doorstep soon enough, demanding that they marry. This was only the beginning of her fight, and one she must be strong enough to win, for both their sakes.

***

Kit escorted her home to Brasted Farm and saw her settled before returning himself to London a week later. Charity worried for him, for the strain of the journey on his health, and the fact he'd be alone in London with no one to check he was looking after himself. His publishing house had requested him to attend a meeting, though, and Kit was full of excitement, and yet afraid to leave her alone. It was his big chance to be a real success, a famous poet, and Charity knew he couldn't miss out on it, no matter the cost.

"*Go!*" she said, exasperated, as Kit dithered on the doorstep.

"But…" he began, aware that she'd cried herself to sleep every night since they'd left London. "I can stay. You might need me if—"

"Kit!" she said, a warning note in her voice now. "This is your big moment, and I might remind you that we need the money you bring in. Don't you dare spoil it now." She leaned closer and kissed his cheek. "Go. I will be here when you return and none the worse for your absence, I promise you. You'll be famous, Kit, I know you will, and I'll be so proud of you. So, run along now, and make sure you take care of yourself. No walking in the rain or going to sleep in damp sheets, make sure your bed is aired and keep that chest of yours warm."

Kit groaned and rolled his eyes as she knew he would.

"Fine," he grumbled, before raising a finger to point at her, narrowing his eyes. "But you stop crying now, you hear me?"

Charity nodded, her expression solemn, though it was a promise she would be unlikely to keep. "I will."

She watched him ride away, sitting on the low stone wall surrounding the farm as his figure grew smaller and smaller and finally disappeared. The rain had stopped at least, and it was warmer, if damp. The clouds hung low in the sky, promising that the sun was not to be seen again for some time, and that more rain would come soon enough. She prayed Kit would make his journey without getting wet. The damp was terrible for his chest and she knew damn well he'd not heed her words and take care of himself.

At least the weather was good for the garden, she assured herself. For her own part she was relieved that the sun had stopped shining. It would be all too easy to remember Luke here, working in the sunshine, stopping what he was doing to smile at her, or give her a cheeky wink.

If she was honest it surprised her that he hadn't turned up yet. No. Not surprised, shocked. She'd assumed he'd come here directly after her having left him in such a way. So far, however, there had been no sign of him. Not even a letter.

Perhaps he was angry with her. Perhaps he was so angry he no longer wanted to marry her. Perhaps, a spiteful voice murmured, perhaps he'd not wanted to marry her at all and was no longer interested now he'd had what he'd wanted.

No.

She'd not believe that. It was easy enough to believe he was angry though, so angry he didn't want to see her again. For if not, why wasn't he here? Why hadn't he come to demand to know why she'd left?

Why wasn't he putting up a fight?

Charity frowned, not understanding it. Not that it mattered. If he didn't come, it made her life easier. If he didn't come, she'd not have to persuade him of all the reasons they couldn't marry. She could avoid the emotional scene she'd been dreading. That should put her mind at ease… and yet, it did not.

***

Dev smiled at the serving girl and refused a second helping of stew. His appetite had deserted him the moment he'd awoken to an empty bed. The first helping he'd forced down was sitting in his stomach like lead as it was. He stared out of the window, a tankard of ale in his hand. Charity was an hour's ride in that direction. If he made haste, he could be there before it got dark.

With a heavy sigh he lifted the tankard and drained it. There was no point in seeing her yet. He knew it, but it didn't stop the longing for it turning his chest inside out.

Tomorrow he had meetings all day again, and at least that kept his mind busy. His plans were becoming reality, albeit gradually. *Slowly, slowly catchy monkey*, he reminded himself, and then grinned as he imagined Charity's indignation at being compared to such a creature. Damn, but he missed her.

Soon enough, he promised himself, soon enough she would see that there was no denying him. She could dig her heels in and provide as many reasons they could not marry as she cared to, but his reasoning would win out. He loved her, she loved him. The world could go to hell in a handcart for all he cared. Yet, if *she* cared what the world thought, as from her letter appeared to be the case, then he would build the world anew with his bare hands, and if she didn't believe him… she could just watch.

Luke. His real name on her lips was something that haunted him at odd moments of the day and night. He'd stopped on the moors today, convinced he'd heard it on the wind, yet there had been nothing and no one around him. He'd always hated being called Devlin; it had been his father's name. So, his friends, such as they were, had called him Dev. His father had hated it, which had been good enough reason for him.

During his time on the farm he'd realised he hadn't missed those friends with whom he'd spent his leisure hours at all. Once he'd returned to London he'd grasped a sad fact: not one of them had asked after him during his disappearance. They'd not wondered where he was, or shown any concern. Oh, the invitations had begun again once they knew he was back in town, but not one of them had called to enquire as to his absence, or if he was well.

It had been his own fault, he reasoned, once he'd given the matter some thought. He let no one close enough to be a real friend, and he'd shared nothing of himself. Not until he'd pretended to be someone he wasn't. How ironic, that it had taken lying about his identity to discover who he really was. Still, no matter how it had happened, it *had* happened, and he wouldn't ignore the truth of what he'd discovered. He wouldn't go back to being that man, living that life.

He couldn't.

With that decided in his mind, he got to his feet and headed upstairs to the room he'd booked for the duration of his stay. The landlord had been beside himself to get such a lengthy booking, and from him of all men. The countryside was abuzz with the news he'd sold Devlin Hall, and he knew many people thought he was bankrupt. He'd paid the landlord in advance to stop the fellow worrying about it. The idea amused him. Perhaps if Charity believed he had pockets to let she'd marry him immediately? He'd toyed with the idea but refused to begin their married life on a lie, and besides, the thought of her marrying him out of pity rankled. No. She'd marry him because she loved him, and because she knew they'd be happy together. He would make her see it if it was the last thing he did.

The next morning, Dev looked over the plans that his surveyor had brought him.

"You're sure?" he asked, excitement making his heart thunder in his chest.

"All the results of my investigations have been conclusive, my lord. This is the place."

Dev grinned at him and slapped the man on the back. "Then why are you still standing here?" he demanded, though he was laughing. "Begin! Begin at once, the sooner the better."

The surveyor, a Mr Appledore, who was a middle-aged man with a wide girth and a twinkle in his eyes, had gained Dev's approval by being the only man who hadn't kowtowed to him. He had told Dev what was what without so much as a glimmer of apology, thoroughly unimpressed by Dev's title or his bank balance.

His finances had in fact been something Mr Appledore had forced Dev to prove, much to his chagrin, but tales of his bankruptcy and spendthrift ways were rife. Appledore was a local man who knew gossip, but he also knew the land and knew what it was that Dev was after, and it appeared as if he'd found it.

It was close to Plymouth, but still on the edge of Charity's beloved moors.

"If it's all the same to you, my lord, I'd have you sign your approval in writing before I hand things over and set the wheels in motion."

"Yes, yes," Dev said, shaking his head and signing the proffered papers. "There, now will you get on with it, blast you?"

Mr Appledore sighed, and gave Dev a reproachful look. "Aye, my lord, now I'll get a move on. May I ask when the happy event is due?"

Dev raised his eyebrows in enquiry.

"In my experience," Mr Appledore replied, his tone dry, "when there is this much pressure to begin works, there is either an impatient wife or a frustrated bridegroom in the equation and seeing as you're not married...."

Chuckling, Dev passed the man back his signed documents. "Quite right, Mr Appledore. Not married *yet*."

Chapter 22

"Wherein Kit makes a discovery."

Charity sat on the wall and watched the horizon. Autumn was in the air; she could smell it. It was faint yet, but the air was cooler, crisper, though the sun still warmed her back. The scent of September drifted across the moors, something ripe and fecund as the earth gave the last of her bounty before the winter left her barren once more.

She'd spent the morning picking blackberries with John and Jane, trying to allow their cheerful chattering to gladden her heart, just as their constant demands to know when they'd see David again tore it into smaller pieces. Charity sighed and rubbed her sore hands on her dress. Her fingers were stained red and stung where the prickles had stabbed her. Scratches covered her arms and she'd torn her dress on a particularly vicious thorn, another job for her to do this evening. Why was it that the sweetest, most tempting fruits were always just out of reach? She always had to get her hands on them, some stubborn sense of determination refusing to be thwarted no matter how the thorns dug into her flesh.

She sighed, wishing the tear in her heart could be mended as easily as the one in her gown. Except that it was more shattered than torn.

There had been no letter. No emotional visit begging her to change her mind.

Nothing.

Days had turned to weeks and had forced Charity to accept that either her actions had hurt Luke so deeply he couldn't forgive her, or that she'd been wrong about him.

She wasn't wrong about him. The truth of his feelings, the knowledge he loved her—or *had* loved her—was something she would not allow herself to doubt, which meant that he was too angry and too hurt to forgive her. The thought made her shrivel inside. It made her want to curl up into a little ball and hide away, wallowing in her misery. Wallowing was not in her nature. There were animals to feed, the garden to see to, John needed new shoes… she would have to go into Tillforth at the weekend, and little Jane was growing like a weed too. So, there was no time for wallowing, or for regrets and doubts and what might have beens.

Yet when she lay in bed at night and the world was dark and quiet, she remembered what it had been to lie in his arms, what it had felt like to be loved by him… and her soul wept for everything she'd given up.

At least Kit would be back today. His last letter had been full of his triumph and excitement and she longed to see him. At least she could share in his wonderful news and hope that his good humour would rub off on her and force her from the gloom that enveloped her, sapping her energy.

A figure appeared on the horizon and Charity jumped off the wall, getting to her feet and waving. The figure waved back, and she grinned, running along the path to meet her brother.

"Where have you been?" she called as he got close enough to hear her. "I expected you hours ago. Batty will scold you."

"Nothing new there," he said, grinning at her and getting down from his horse to give her a hug.

"Let me look at you." Charity held him by the arms and looked him over. "You look well," she said, her tone cautious as he laughed at her.

"I am!" he said, rolling his eyes at her. "Fit as a flea, so stop clucking about me."

She smiled, relieved as she let him go.

"I have news," he said, his eyes bright with it as Charity laughed at him.

"Well I know that," she said, linking her arm through his as they walked the path back to the farm. "That's why we're so impatient to see you. There's roast pork for dinner and Batty's made a summer pudding for you. See how the prodigal is greeted on his return," she teased.

Kit stopped, turning to her. "I don't mean that," he said, shaking his head. "I mean, news you are not aware of." There was something in his expression, he was bursting to tell her something, but was unsure of how she would take it. He looked anxious.

"Oh?" Charity stilled. There was a strange, prickling sensation running down her spine that she could not account for.

"I stopped in Tillforth for a bite to eat at *The Nag's Head*," he said, his tone nonchalant.

Charity snorted, relieved it was just local gossip after all. "A pint, or two or three, and an earful of chatter with your friends, you mean," she said, tutting at him and pretending to be cross.

"Well, of course," he said, waving that away as being obvious. "But the village is alive with talk."

"Oh, do get on and tell me, Kit," she said, laughing at him now. "I can't stand the suspense!"

"He's here." Kit stared at her, watching for her reaction.

Charity stiffened, knowing instantly who *he* was. She stared out at the moors for a moment, telling her heart to stop being so foolish and settle down.

Charity and the Devil

"Well, what of it?" she said, turning away from him and shrugging in as casual a manner as she could manage. "It's a free country. He was born here, after all."

"*You're* here, Charity," Kit said, his expression impatient now. "And I don't think for one minute he's forgotten about you, or that he's angry, or he's given up. Well," he added, his tone thoughtful. "He might be angry. I know I damned well would be if my beloved had pulled such a trick with me," he added with asperity.

Charity shot him an impatient glare, sorry now that she'd confided her fears in her letters to him. Except there was no one else to talk to. She'd refused to discuss it with Mrs Baxter, simply saying she had thanked Lord Devlin and they'd parted as friends. Batty had given her a look that said she didn't believe a word but had at least held her tongue.

"Just because he's back here… it means nothing, Kit." She shook her head, able to think of many reasons he might have returned, none of which had anything to do with her, though her heart was hammering in her chest all the same. "If he's here for me, why not come and see me? Why not get in touch?"

Kit snorted and threw up his hands. "Because you won't listen to him," he said, frustrated. "You're a pig-headed, stubborn, wilful—"

"Yes, thank you, Kit," she retorted, the words tart as she pursed her lips at him. "Any one of those insults could perfectly describe you and you know it."

"Of course," he said, shrugging, before turning and winking at her. "You're my twin."

He reached over and tugged her hair and she couldn't help but smile at him.

"Seriously, Kit. Please, don't make anything of it," she said, her voice low now, a pleading note to the words she hoped he would heed. "I'm sure it's nothing to do with me. That part of my life is over." She smoothed a hand over her flat stomach. Her courses had begun again, much to her relief. Why that relief had made her weep as though her heart was breaking all over again she couldn't say. "I must get on with things here, now we know we are staying. It's not as if there isn't plenty to keep me busy, is it? I was thinking about the roof of the smaller barn," she said, determined to move the conversation to safer ground. "It's about time—"

"He's building a house."

Charity stopped in her tracks, staring at her brother.

"Oh." She breathed. None of her affair. It was none of her affair. "Well, good for him."

"It's between here and Plymouth."

Suddenly her heart was beating in her throat.

"What?" she demanded, her voice at once squeaky and alarmed.

Kit nodded, his eyes gleaming. "Less than an hour's ride from here, I reckon. Good farming land he's bought, by all accounts. I heard he had his surveyor working all hours. He instructed the man to find good farmland and a suitable site for a grand house, but it had to be within an hour's ride of a certain spot."

She couldn't breathe. Her chest had pulled tight and the knack of her lungs expanding as she inhaled seemed to have escaped her.

"Want to know what spot?" Kit demanded, waggling his eyebrows at her.

Charity shook her head. No. He couldn't. He couldn't do this. She couldn't see him every day, couldn't face him every single day and keep saying no to him. Damn the man. He knew she was in love with him, why did he have to go and make such a grand gesture. He'd come to hate her for it when she'd never asked it of him. She knew he would.

"We'll have to sell the farm," she said, panic surging through her blood, as she gasped for air.

"What?" Kit said, his eyebrows hitting his hairline. "Don't be ridiculous! You love it here, your heart and soul is here, same as mine is. Where would we go? Besides, it's ridiculous, Charity. You fought to be here, and now, he's fighting for you."

Charity paused, shaking her head. She was trembling, and she didn't know why. Was this trembling anger at him turning her life upside down again fear because she believed *he* was angry and punishing her, or excitement and hope because… because he wasn't giving up?

He wouldn't give up on her.

She took a deep breath and then hitched up her skirts. "Help me up, Kit," she said, lifting her foot to the stirrup.

"What?" he said, his eyes widening as he realised her intention. "No! Lord, Charity. I'll take you over there tomorrow, first thing."

"No." Charity replied, shaking her head, dizzy with anticipation. "I'll go mad if have to wait that long. I must see him. Now. I need to know what he's doing, what his plans are. I… I have to."

"But it's a man's saddle. You'll have to ride astride," Kit said, scandalised despite often declaring himself the most open minded of men.

"So be it." Charity glared at him. "Help me up, damn it."

Kit did, knowing all too well that Charity in this mood could not be reasoned with.

"But you don't even know if he's there. The place will be alive with workmen. It's no place for a lady, Charity."

"I'm not a lady, Kit," Charity shot back at him, shaking her head. "That's the whole point."

"Damn it, Charity, I'm going to the farm and getting Goliath and then I'm following you, hear me?"

"If you must," she said, gathering the reins. "Now, where will I find this building site?"

"You know the old shepherd's hut where we used to picnic as children?"

Charity nodded, remembering the spot well.

"About three miles after that, as if you were heading towards Plymouth. Stick to the track and if you get lost go back to the hut, I'll find you."

She didn't wait to hear any further instructions, her heart and her emotions too jittery to stand still another moment. Kit's horse seemed to pick up on her urgency and allowed her to ride hard. At least Kit hadn't come far today, and the horse was fresh and eager to stretch its legs.

The shepherd's hut came into sight about forty minutes later and Charity paused to get her bearings. What was she doing? If he was here for her, why hadn't he come to her? Why hadn't he said anything?

Because you're pig-headed and stubborn and wilful.

She gave a little laugh, hearing the truth in Kit's words and torn between terror and hope. Yet she didn't know what she would say to him, or what she was hoping for when she knew there *was* no hope but see him she must. She couldn't bear another day of not knowing. So, gathering her courage, she urged the horse on.

Chapter 23

"Wherein confessions are made ... and a proposal."

Dev stared at the hundreds of men at work on his land. Carts moved back and forth, the horses weary now after a day of shifting tons of earth. The workmen sweated although the heat had left the sun and a cool breeze stirred the grass at his feet.

It was happening. His vision for the future set in motion, the foundations being laid not only for a new home, but a new beginning. He only hoped it would not become a monument to his foolishness, to hopes and dreams built on sand when he'd thought there was rock beneath his feet. Dev let out a breath, wishing he knew Charity would believe in him, take a chance on him, and—as if he'd conjured her with the thought—he noticed a figure riding towards him.

He knew it was her even before she was close enough to be certain of whether it was a man or a woman. She was riding astride, galloping across the expanse of flat land the surveyor had chosen for the building site. Her hair flew out behind her, her body in perfect accord with the huge horse thundering towards him. He should have known she would ride like that, without fear, with absolute control.

Dev watched as she eased the horse back into a canter and then stopped right in front of him. Both horse and rider were breathing hard, the horse blowing, nostrils flaring, excitement still shining in its dark eyes. Charity's chest rose and fell as she stared at him, her cheeks flushed with exertion, exhilaration, and something in her eyes that he could not read.

He stared at her, all the words he'd hoped to say when she eventually came tangled and snared up, caught in his throat.

"What are you doing?" she asked, not taking her eyes from his.

"Building us a house," he said, at a loss for anything less direct.

Charity took a deep breath and stared around at the work already done. Carts of stone were being hauled in now, the foundations beginning in the morning.

"But... I left you," she said, and he saw the tears glittering despite the way she held her jaw taut, trying to keep her composure. He heard too, the anguish in her voice. "It's not possible," she said, the quaver behind the words audible now. "I explained this, you must see—"

"Charity," he said, and his voice was harder now. He wouldn't let her throw him over a second time. "You've had your say. Would you be so kind as to let me have mine now?"

She bristled a little at the autocratic tone of his voice but gave a stiff nod as he held his hand out to her. He helped her dismount, longing hitting him hard and fast as his hands rested on her waist, memories of the last time he'd touched her all too easy to remember. The blush tinting her cheeks told him she remembered it too and he smiled, taking her hand.

Once he'd given her horse into the care of one of his men, he guided her away to a rocky outcrop where they could sit and talk undisturbed. They sat side by side, silent, as Dev's heart beat in his throat. She wouldn't make this easy for him, he knew that, so he would be blunt. He would make her see how everything she'd said and assumed was wrong.

"You hurt me, leaving as you did." The words were raw, exposing his heart to her and he didn't try to soften them. They were too true.

She darted a look at him, her expression appalled before she turned away again, hiding her face from him.

"No more than I hurt myself," she said, and he knew that was true too. "But there was nothing else to be done, nothing else to say." He knew she'd intended those words to sound hard, fatalistic, but he wasn't fooled. She longed for a way forward just as he did.

"Oh, there's plenty more to say, my love." He reached out and put his hand to her cheek, turning her face to his. As he'd suspected, her tears had already begun. He sighed, hoping she would listen to what he ought to have said when she came to London, if he hadn't been so blinded by desire. "You made a great many assumptions about my life, about what I'd be forced to give up if I married you. So now I'd like to tell you the truth, and then you can tell me if you still believe I'm about to make some heroic sacrifice at the altar of our love." He quirked an eyebrow at her and she frowned but nodded, wiping her eyes on her sleeve.

"My father was a great man, I think you know that?" he said, watching her nod before he carried on. "He did a great deal of good for the country, fighting for the welfare of those less fortunate than ourselves. He was not so supportive of his own family. I now think all the good he did was incidental if you want the hard truth, and yes, I am aware how bitter and selfish that sounds. Yet I know it's true, he did it for the adulation, because he loved to hear what a good and kind and big-hearted man he was, when in fact he had no heart whatsoever."

Dev rubbed a hand over his face. He had never spoken of such things, not to anyone, and it was hard to keep his anger at bay.

"My mother was a society beauty. She lived to be seen, to go to parties and be admired. From everything I now know of her she was vivacious, funny and full of life. Father married her and buried her here in the back of beyond. She hated it here, but he was jealous of everyone and so he kept her isolated and she saw no one. I think she rebelled against him and her behaviour became erratic and so...." Dev swallowed hard, the bile and bitterness of his emotion flooding him. "I cannot prove it, but I suspect my father gave her laudanum, in a hope to control her. However it began, she became addicted. My only real memory of her is one of her screaming because her room was filled with spiders. I must have been four I think. She died the following year."

"Oh, Luke." Charity was watching him now, her eyes filled with compassion as she threaded her fingers through his. "I'm so sorry."

He smiled at her. "I feel like someone new when you call me that," he said, squeezing her hand. "Like I can begin again and be someone worth loving, worth fighting for." She bit her lip and he looked away, the desire to kiss her so strong he had to fight to keep talking, but she must hear this. All of it. He wouldn't allow her to distract him again.

"Father didn't know what to do with me. He was too busy, too important to have time for his son. He didn't believe in spoiling children, by which I mean he wanted absolute control over me. I was not to be hugged or shown affection, which would make me weak. I was to be beaten if I was naughty or disobeyed an order."

Dev kept his gaze on the ground, trying to tell her without letting the truth of his words get under his skin, to overwhelm his emotions. He'd spent long enough wasting his life on anger and regret; he'd get this out and over and done, and then she would see she was saving him, not ruining him.

"My behaviour became worse, so he sent me away to school. I was five. At school I was bullied until I learnt to fight back, and I *did* fight back. I was threatened with expulsion at least once a term, but my father would simply pay them more to keep me. I would receive a lecture from him about how disgusted he was with me, what a disappointment I was to him, how I would never amount to anything. I soon realised it didn't matter what I did, nothing would ever change." He swallowed, knowing that this had been the pivotal moment in his life, the only way he'd been able to take back some control. "So, I became the boy the others were afraid of and I learned to use that fear. If I disgusted my father, I decided *that* was the only way to get to him, to hurt him. It was the only power I had, and I used it."

Dev cleared his throat, aware that his hopes of keeping his narration unemotional were failing miserably.

"I became a man worthy of his disgust. I was cruel and selfish and indulged all of my baser instincts." He looked up then, wondering what Charity made of his confession. Did she despise him for being weak? There was only compassion in her eyes, though, such warmth and such love and understanding that a lump rose to his throat. He forced it down, needing to finish this, to ensure she understood. "I didn't realise how much I despised myself, though. I never stopped to wonder what my life might have been if I hadn't been so hell bent on hurting him, on destroying everything his *good* name stood for." He reached out then, touching his hand to her face. "I didn't realise until I met you. Pretending to be someone else, it… it freed me. It let me see I could change, I could be different… *better*. If I just had someone who would give me the chance to be that man."

Charity opened her mouth to speak, but he pressed a finger to her lips.

"Selling Devlin Hall was the first step and it was like cutting a cancer from my soul. I'll never regret it, Charity, not for a moment." The words were hard and full of certainty and he held her gaze now, willing her to acknowledge the truth what he'd told her. "You think I'd be giving up my life, that I'd be losing friends, losing my self-esteem." He gave a laugh, shaking his head at the idea. "I had no life before you. Do you know that no one… *no one* came looking for me when I disappeared? No one cared, and I can't blame them for that. If you married me, you'd not be condemning me to a life I will come to regret, love, you'd be giving me a life. If not for you I'd have drunk myself to death in a year or two or been killed in a duel or some back-alley brawl."

He heard her sob, and she covered her mouth with her hand as he reached for her, grasping her arms and nodding towards the house he was building. "I'm building a future for us here, Charity. The land is good, I had it surveyed. It's rich, and there's healthy grazing land too. This will be a farm, you see, except… except I barely know what a bloody potato looks like and I can't do this without you. I don't *want* to do it without you. Not without you, or John and Jane and Kit and Mr and Mrs Baxter. Please love, say you'll marry me. Don't condemn me to that life again. I won't survive it."

She didn't answer, tears streaking down her face as she stared at him. Dev held his breath, waiting, hoping and praying he'd not just exposed his heart and soul only to have it trampled underfoot.

Charity launched herself at him, throwing her arms around him and unbalancing him so he slid from the rock and landed in an awkward sprawl on the floor. She was laughing and crying and clinging to him and Dev found himself unable to speak, to ask if this was a yes. He tumbled her onto her back, pushing the curls that had fallen over her face away so he could look at her.

"I hope this is a yes, love," he said, the words breathless and anxious. "As you're in a very compromising position now, and quite thoroughly ruined."

She laughed, a slightly hysterical sound as much a sob as amusement.

"Yes," she said, reaching up and tugging at the back of his neck. "Yes, yes, I will, because if you're foolish enough to want to marry such a pig-headed, stubborn, wilful creature, then you only have yourself to blame."

Dev made a sound of triumph that echoed over the land, and if anyone hadn't seen them sprawled on the ground together, they had certainly noticed now. Determined not to give her any grounds for wriggling out of her acceptance, Dev submitted to the pressure on his neck and bent to kiss her.

"Hey!" An angry shout had him looking up, finding Kit's furious countenance above them as he swung down from his horse.

"Get your hands off my sister, you bloody bastard. What the hell are you thinking? Have you no sense of honour, propriety?"

Dev eyed Kit with caution and got to his feet, tugging Charity with him and holding her close. "We're to be married," he said in a rush, not wanting to start life with Charity with her twin enraged with him. "She just said yes."

"Oh." Kit's face cleared, and he grinned at them. "Well, that's all right then. Mind you, she's got a shocking temper."

"Kit!" Charity exclaimed, glaring at her brother, who merely winked at her.

"Too late now, love, he's committed."

Dev laughed and let Charity go for long enough to hold out his hand to her brother. Kit stepped closer, smiling, until he wasn't. The blow came out of nowhere and Dev stumbled backwards, landing on his arse with a thud.

"Kit!" Charity screamed.

"What the…?" Dev touched a tentative hand to his nose, finding it bloody as Charity fell to her knees beside him. "What the hell did you do that for?" he demanded.

"That was for what happened in London," Kit replied, his voice grim. He cleared his throat, rubbing his knuckles with a scowl. "Damn, you've got a hard head," he muttered, before offering Dev a hand up. "It's all right, old chap, I feel much better now."

"I wish I could say the same," Dev remarked, taking his hand with caution. "You've got quite a punch for a poet."

Kit returned a rather feral grin. "Never judge a book by its cover, nor a poet, come to that. Just because I write of love and romance, doesn't mean I can't hold my own in a brawl."

"I believe you," Dev said, staunching the flow with his sleeve.

"Oh, Luke, you're bleeding," Charity cried, fumbling for a handkerchief. "Kit, how could you?"

"Luke?" Kit said, looking confused.

Dev held out his hand once more. "Luke Linton," he said, feeling a little absurd. "I'm a new man," he added with a grin. "I hope I'll be one you'll be happy to have as a brother-in-law. I shall certainly try to be."

Kit snorted and took his hand this time, shaking it and giving him a warm smile. "I reckon we'll rub along well enough," he said, nodding. "If you can endure Charity, I'm easy to get along with. I'm the nicer twin."

Dev laughed as Charity smacked her brother on the arm and Kit cried out like she'd done more than just tap him.

He pulled her away from her twin and into his arms once more, unable to stop touching her. Happiness bubbled up in his chest, the emotion so new and overwhelming he didn't know what to do or say next.

"Come along you two lovebirds, it'll be dark soon," Kit said, gesturing up at the skies which had dimmed already. "Charity, didn't you say something about roast pork and summer pudding?"

Charity nodded, grinning at him. "Batty will be furious with us for spoiling her welcome home meal," she said, giving Dev a look that made his heart turn in his chest. "We'd better hurry."

"Me too?" he asked, not wanting to presume, though she'd seemed to be inviting him.

"Of course, you too," she said, tugging at his hand. "You're part of the family now."

Dev savoured the shock and delight of her words as they rolled over him. He *was* part of the family now. He wouldn't ever have to be alone again. He belonged somewhere, and to someone. People would care for him, about him, and he for them. If he ever got lost on the moors, if he ever failed to come home, there were people who would worry, who would look for him and not stop until he was found. The knowledge swelled in his chest, sinking into his bones and filling his heart until he couldn't breathe with the wonder of it.

He belonged.

"Are you coming then?" Charity said, her voice soft as she looked at him, perhaps now understanding the enormity of what had happened to his life. "I'm not going anywhere without you," she added, moving closer and pressing a kiss to his lips. "Not ever again."

Chapter 24

"Wherein a home coming, and a wedding."

Batty welcomed him with open arms as she came out into the yard to greet him. She hugged him hard as she heard their news, blushing at her own audacity. Dev smiled as she dabbed at eyes with her apron, sniffing. "And about time, I might say," she scolded, shaking her head at Charity, who opened her mouth to protest and then thought better of it. "Honestly, didn't I tell you the Kendalls were the most stubborn creatures on God's earth?"

"That you did," Mrs Baxter," Dev replied, grinning at her. "And you weren't wrong."

Charity elbowed him, pursing her lips with indignation. "We're engaged, that means you're supposed to be nice to me."

"But I'm not a nice man," Dev replied, winking at her. "I told you that from the start. Besides, if I was, you wouldn't have agreed to marry me. Who would you argue with then?"

"True," she replied with a happy sigh, leaning into him.

"Mr David!"

Dev jolted as the high-pitched squeal almost burst his eardrums and Jane wrapped her arms about his legs. "You came back! I knew you would. Charity said you wouldn't, but I *knew* you wouldn't leave us, nor the kittens."

Dev bent down and lifted the little girl up, feeling his heart contract as she clung to him, her arms clutched about his neck. "Of course not, sweetheart. I could never leave you, nor the kittens."

Charity and the Devil

Jane squeezed her skinny arms about his neck and kissed his cheek, giggling. "Are you going to stay this time?" she asked, her voice a little shy.

"Yes, love," he replied, smiling at her even as he hoped his voice wouldn't break as he was perilously close to blubbing. He felt turned inside out, his emotions too near the surface, as though his skin was too frail to contain such fierceness. It was overwhelming. "I'm building a house for us, a new house with lots of land and you're all going to come and live there, if you'd like to?" he added, anxious all at once at the daunted look in the girl's eyes.

"A big house?" she asked, blinking at him.

"Quite big," he replied, cautious now. "Not as big as Devlin Hall, that was too big. You could get lost in it. Just the right size I think. With a lovely bedroom just for you."

Jane's mouth formed a little 'o' shape and Dev cleared his throat. "Is ... is that all right?"

"Yes!" the little girl squealed, clinging to him. "Can we go now?"

"Not now," Charity replied, laughing as she unwound her sister's arms from Dev's neck and made her get down. "It isn't built yet, but we'll show you where it will be tomorrow. We have to get married first."

Another ear-piercing squeal greeted this news as Jane hugged Charity with delight.

Dev turned and realised why Charity had untangled him from her sister. John dithered in the yard, eager to see what the noise was about but looking at Dev with caution, waiting.

"Hello, Lord Devlin," he said, uncertain now.

Dev looked up to see Charity had ushered everyone away into the kitchen, pausing only to give him a smile as she left him with John.

"Hello, John," he said, wondering what he ought to say. It was easy enough once he'd thought about it. The truth. "I'm so glad to see you again, and I'm sorry for all the upset I caused everyone, so sorry for pretending I was someone I'm not but... but I learned a valuable lesson when I was here. One you helped teach me, and I'm more grateful than you'll ever know."

"I-I did?" John replied, frowning.

Dev put his arm around the boy's narrow shoulders. "You did. You remember how you stood up to the gypsy boys?"

"Yes, sir."

"Luke," Dev amended. "My name is Luke, and I should like you to use it."

"Yes, my lord, I... I mean, Luke." John nodded, still looking perplexed, so Dev carried on.

"My father was a bully, John, and I never stood up to him. I tried to punish him in other ways, by being as wicked as I could, by being an embarrassment to him. I never realised that I was only hurting myself by meeting his worst expectations." He turned to face John, holding his gaze, hoping the boy could see it wasn't just words, but that he meant it. "I wasn't as brave as you, standing up for myself and doing my best to be a man instead of a sulky boy. I've changed, though, because of you and Charity and Jane, all of you. So, I hope you'll give me another chance."

John's face cleared, and a tentative smile replaced the frown. "You're really going to marry Charity?"

"I am," Dev said, the happiness bubbling in his chest at that extraordinary statement.

"And you're building a new house for us?" He sounded a little incredulous now, perhaps expecting Dev to take his sister away from them. *"All* of us?"

"All of you," Dev replied, squeezing the lad's shoulder. "It will be a farm, John, and I will need your help."

John's eyes widened, and he laughed at that. "I should say so," he exclaimed. "Charity said you'd never seen a potato that hadn't been roasted before."

Dev's lips twitched, and he returned a rueful expression. "That is true," he admitted, rubbing the back of his neck. "So, you see how much you must teach me?"

"Everything," John replied, nodding gravely. "But that's all right, I'll teach you about farming and you can teach me to box." He frowned, peering at Dev's face. "What happened to your nose?"

"Your brother planted me a facer," Dev said, touching a finger to the bruised article and wincing. "Damn near broke it."

"*Kit*?" John exclaimed, astonished. "*Kit* knocked you down?" He gaped, having trouble swallowing this information. "He never did."

"Oh yes, he did," Dev replied, guiding the young man towards the kitchen as his stomach was growling and the enticing smells of a roast dinner were becoming hard to ignore. "I must tell you he was most ungentlemanly about it too. Took me completely unawares."

John gaped, dumbfounded by this information, and Dev took the opportunity to hurry him inside.

***

They were married in the church in Tillforth. Unbeknownst to Charity, Dev had acquired the licence weeks ago. He'd been carrying it about with him ever since, the paper increasingly dog-eared and burning a hole in his pocket.

The bride wore her best cotton gown and a simple chip bonnet.

Luke Linton, Viscount Devlin, who had prowled the ballrooms of the ton and had his pick of their lush beauties, was tongue-tied, stumbling over his words in front of the vicar and sweating through his shirt. He clutched Charity's hand to stop his own from trembling, his palms damp, his heart filled with the enormity of what he was doing. When, at last, they were pronounced man and wife, he turned to her and was gifted with a joyful smile that stole his breath and made his eyes sting with pride and happiness.

Of course, the story got about and soon everyone in the area knew Charity Kendall was the new Lady Devlin. Dev held his breath the first time she was addressed as such but, aside from a faint blush at her cheeks and a look of surprise, she seemed to accept that this was her now. They both had new names after all, new lives to begin and grow into.

The wedding breakfast was *not* a quiet affair, though there was only Kit, John and Jane, and Mr and Mrs Baxter in attendance with the newlyweds.

Everyone was in high spirits. Mrs Baxter had outdone herself and provided a spread that could have fed an army on the march for several days. The children laughed and giggled, overexcited and full of cheek. Kit indulged in the Champagne that Dev had provided and topped up Mrs Baxter's glass whenever she wasn't looking.

This resulted in some surprisingly bawdy jokes and an enthusiastic rendition of a song she'd learned in her youth that made Charity blush and send the children out to fetch a jug of water.

The celebrations went on until late, no one being in any hurry to go to bed… except for Dev, and—he hoped—his new wife. However, it was such a blessing to be included in this warm and vibrant family, to feel so welcomed and such a sense of belonging. So, Dev decided he could wait a little longer to be alone with his bride. Not much, but a little.

Kit put John and Jane to bed, as Mrs Baxter had fallen asleep at the table. With surprising deftness Mr Baxter had removed her half-eaten slice of cake moments before she'd used it as a pillow.

"She's always loved a good knees-up," he remarked, smiling with fondness at his wife, whose soft snores now filled the room. "I'll see to the animals and then come back and wake her." He got to his feet, giving them both a sly grin. "I wish you both very happy," he said, and they both held their breath as they waited for his inevitable prediction of doom. "You'll neither of you like to give the other the last word, but... I reckon you'll do." He winked at them and ambled out of the room, whistling a jaunty tune.

"My," Charity said, eyes wide as he left them alone. "That was almost...."

"Optimistic?" Dev supplied for her.

Her lips quirked as she realised he'd supplied the last word for her.

"Quite," she added, her tone tart though her eyes danced with laughter.

There was a crash and Charity gasped as a voice from the hallway called out, "I'm all right!"

A moment later, Kit stumbled into the room.

"Fell down the stairs" he said, beaming at them, a little worse for wear by now. Charity shook her head at him.

"You're foxed," she said, laughing.

"Not at all." Kit gave a dignified sniff. "Missed my footing is all." He spoiled his retort by almost sitting on the floor instead of a chair and Dev snorted with amusement.

"Oh, by the way, Batty made up the master bedroom for you," he said, snagging the remnants of a bottle Champagne and filling his glass.

"Oh," Charity said, surprised.

Dev turned to her, knowing neither she nor her brother had liked to take the room for themselves before, but Kit held up a hand before she could object.

"Do a fellow a favour, Charity. Your bedroom is next to mine, the master bedroom on the other side of the house. I don't intend to spend the time it takes to build your house sleeping in the study."

Charity blushed scarlet as Dev smothered his mouth with his hand. He cleared his throat and got to his feet, tugging Charity with him. Dev held his hand out to Kit.

"Good to be part of the family, Kit. You may be sure I'll take good care of them... of all of you," he amended, remembering the doctor he'd contacted in London.

Kit looked a little disgusted. "You're marrying my sister, not me. I don't need looking after."

Charity rolled her eyes and muttered something contrary to that statement behind Dev's back.

"Still," Kit said, magnanimous now. "I appreciate the sentiment." He shook Dev's hand and then waved them away. "Run along now, my children. I'm nicely stewed and my muse is calling."

Charity gave him a pitying look but bent to kiss the top of his head. "Goodnight, fool," she said with affection.

"Goodnight, harridan," he replied, equally jovial.

Dev climbed the stairs, Charity's hand in his and feeling suddenly nervous, which seemed absurd but to his chagrin was true. He opened the door to the master bedroom but before Charity could step over the threshold, he swung her up into his arms.

"Can't buck tradition, can we?" he said, grinning at her as she clutched at his neck in surprise.

"I think we already did," she murmured, blushing a little as he carried her into the room and kicked the door shut. "I feel rather a fraud."

Dev frowned, shaking his head. "Don't say that, love. It makes me feel you regret it."

"Oh, no, never that," she said in a rush as he put her down again. "How could I?"

"I'm glad." He pulled her closer, one hand moving to cradle her head. "You're still a little innocent, you know," he said, his voice low and amused now. "And I will show you just how much you've yet to learn."

"Oh?" she replied, her eyes widening, her voice a little squeaky now.

"Mm-hm," he said, bending his head to kiss her neck. "I'll be very instructive."

He backed her towards the bed until her knees met the mattress and she sat down with something of a thud.

He looked down, pleased at the rapid rise and fall of her breasts as they pushed against the demure neckline of her gown. Dev got to his knees before her, taking her hands.

"You really are mine now," he said, still feeling a peculiar rush of shock and delight run over him as the truth of it sank into his bones.

Charity laughed at him, squeezing his fingers. "I always was, silly. Though I wasn't always sure if I wanted to slap you or kiss you."

"Perhaps both?" he suggested, grinning at her.

She nodded, her face grave. "Oh, certainly."

"Perhaps just kiss me tonight, break me in gently."

There was a teasing note to his voice and Charity pursed her lips, considering the idea.

"Well," she said, sounding somewhat reluctant. "Just for tonight, but I make no promises for the future."

"Fair enough," he murmured against her lips.

He slanted his mouth over hers, his heart and body alive and taut with love and desire as she opened to him, welcoming him. Her hands slid into his hair as he pulled her closer and Dev wondered at all the meaningless encounters he'd experienced in the years before Charity had entered his life. He'd never understood how different things could be with someone who held your heart.

Dev pulled away from her with one last, gentle press of his mouth to hers. Giving her a wicked look designed to make her wonder what came next, he sat back and took her foot in his hand, removing her shoe. He caressed the arch of her foot and she sighed, a blissful sound that made him smile as he removed her other shoe and did the same.

"Lay back," he instructed her.

She gave him a dubious look but did as he asked, and Dev slid his hands up her ankles, sliding his palms around her legs, curving around her calves before finding the soft skin of her thighs at the top of her stockings. He paused, pushing her skirts higher, hearing her breath catch.

"No drawers, love," he said, pleased to see the fashion for such things had not yet caught on in Dartmoor.

She lifted herself on her elbows, looking down at him and looking as haughty as a duchess, never mind a viscountess.

"Certainly not," she said, scandalised. "They're not at all proper."

Dev chuckled, enjoying the shiver that ran over her as his breath feathered over her skin. "I quite agree," he murmured, reaching to untie her garters. He slid first one stocking from her leg, then the other, his hands smoothing over her skin as he did so before pressing a kiss to the silky skin of her inner thigh.

Her breathing hitched, and Dev looked up, seeing his wife's eyes widen as her shock only grew. "W-What is it you are doing?" she asked, the words tremulous and a little daunted.

Dev held her gaze and pushed her knees a little further apart. "If I told you... it would spoil the surprise," he said, failing to keep the amusement from his voice. "You can stop me at any time," he added, before kissing her a little further up her leg. He doubted she missed the confident tone in his voice, the one that suspected she wouldn't be stopping him anytime soon.

To his pleasure she proved him correct and lay back again, her breathing becoming erratic as he inched closer to the apex of her thighs and the little nest of curls that hid the spot he sought. As he ran his tongue over the crease between her hip and thigh, she gave a startled gasp and his own desire surged in his blood. All at once he was as impatient as a green boy. It took a great force of will not to stop and sink himself into the heat of her welcoming body as he remembered the pleasures to be found there. Instead he took a moment to steady himself, smiling as even the touch of his breath made her body tighten.

Dev slid his hands up to her hips and tugged her a little closer to the edge of the mattress. He caught her gaze as she raised her head to look down at him and didn't look away as he lowered his mouth to her. The look of dazed shock, the glittering desire in her darkening eyes as his tongue ran over her, was something he knew would be ingrained in his memory for all time. Her head fell back as she clutched at the sheets beneath her, arching helplessly as he teased and caressed her with mouth and hands and tongue. The sound she made moments later, as pleasure overwhelmed her, was almost enough to take him over the edge in her wake.

She lay dazed, panting and breathless as he stripped off clothes that were suddenly too small, too tight, chafing his skin and suffocating him. He snatched at his cravat, throwing everything down in an untidy heap as an amused smile curved over his wife's lovely mouth.

"In a hurry?" she asked, her voice a tantalising mix of innocence and the husky tone that remained from the pleasure he'd just brought her.

"You could say that," Dev managed, throwing first one boot and then a second to the floor in a manner that would have made his valet weep. Charity gave a squeal of laughter as he decided against removing his trousers and merely pushed them down before landing on the bed with such a thud they both bounced on the mattress.

"I think it was a wise decision to take this room after all," Charity said, laughter in her voice as Dev cursed, pushing too many skirts and petticoats out of his way in frustration. He grinned at her and leaned down for another kiss.

"I intend to show you just how wise," he said, joining them with one swift movement that had her arching and crying out beneath him. She clutched at his back, staring up at him.

"I believe you," she whispered.

There were no more words for a long time after that, at least nothing more than whispered murmurs of love and pleasure.

Later, with his new bride sleeping in his arms, Dev lay awake, listening to the soft sound of her breathing, and to the lonely cry of a fox hunting on the moors. He felt a helpless smile at his mouth. All the anger, all the dark rage and regret he'd harboured towards his parents dissipated in the light of his happiness. Those feelings were still there, and he suspected they'd never leave him completely, but they no longer had any power over him. He no longer felt the need to destroy what his father had created, nor grind their good name into the dust.

Perhaps this Viscount Devlin would not be known throughout the land for his zeal for reformation and change, but he would be known as a good man who loved his family above all else, and who could be relied upon by everyone he cared for, friends, neighbours, and tenants alike. His world might be smaller than his father's, but it would be fuller and happier, and perhaps, in his own way, he might do some good in the world.

Dev turned his head, pressing a kiss to Charity's forehead, and went to sleep.

Epilogue

"Wherein a new house, new baby, new beginnings."

"He's here, he's here!" Jane screamed, leaping down from her position at the window and running from the room.

Charity hurried to her feet, though it was a relative sort of hurrying as the bulk of the child she carried weighed her down.

"Calm down, love," Dev said, crossing the room to help her up as she sat back down again with a heavy thud. "He's staying all summer, there's no rush."

Charity huffed with impatience and Dev pulled her into a hug as she found her footing.

"Are you going to tell him how proud you are of him?" he asked, watching her face with amusement. "Or merely tear him off a strip for all the scandals he's been involved in?"

His wife gave a dignified sniff and returned an imperious look. "I haven't decided yet," she retorted, before waddling out of the room.

Not that Dev was about to tell her she waddled. The baby was due any time now and her temper was fraying as she became tired and frustrated at her own inactivity. He was no fool and he didn't have a death wish, so he kept such observations to himself.

Her twin had become something of a public figure over the past year. A famous poet sought by society and welcomed into the higher echelons of the ton. On seconds thoughts, infamous was perhaps more accurate. As Dev had predicted on first meeting him, Kit's rather ethereal beauty, the knowledge that his health was somewhat uncertain, and the fact he was a poet... well, women fell at his feet left, right, and centre.

The smug devil was having a ball.

Not that Dev envied him. He wondered just how long it would take before such a life lost its glitter and proved to be gilt rather than gold. Not long, he suspected. Kit was far cleverer than he'd ever claim to be and, he suspected, rather more self-aware.

He got to the entrance hall to find Charity clinging to her twin, whom she'd not seen for many months and had missed more than she cared to admit.

"Damn it, Charity, when did you get so fat?" Kit demanded as Dev groaned. He couldn't have waited until after dinner, at least? She was always in better spirits after dinner.

Dev held his breath as Charity glared at her brother and let out a huff. "I'm too tired and too pleased to see you to let you goad me into an argument yet, you wretch," she said, linking her arm through his. "And it's cruel to mock the afflicted. This is your nephew or niece I carry, remember. I'd think you might be nice to me for five minutes at least."

Kit grinned and leaned over, kissing her cheek. "Quite right, old girl. Forgive me. I just missed you so much I couldn't resist."

Charity looked up at him and then flapped her hands as her eyes brimmed. Dev fumbled in his pocket for his handkerchief and thrust it at her as Kit looked up, appalled.

"Don't worry," Dev replied, pulling Charity into a hug as she sobbed. "She does this a lot now. Quite frankly you're better off being rude to her, the results are less alarming."

"Shut up," Charity sniffled, blowing her nose on his hanky. "I *am* here," she said, glaring at her husband though there was no real heat in it. "Now come along, Kit. Batty is dying to see you."

"Dying to ring a peal over me, you mean," Kit muttered his tone dry as he lifted Jane into his arms. "My, you've grown a foot too. When did you get so big?"

"Still not as big as John," his little sister said with a frustrated sigh.

Dev smiled as he watched John follow his big brother down to the kitchen with a look of pure admiration. John had shot up in the last six months. He had the gangly look of a lad teetering on the brink between boyhood and manhood and was growing up to be a fine young fellow. Dev felt a glow of pride in him. They'd both been as good as their word and Dev had taught him to box, and to fence, and if he was less appreciative of his Latin and Greek tutors, he had the grace not to say so. In return, both John and the rest of the family had taught Dev about the running of a farm, though he'd also employed a manager as his estate was far larger than Brasted Farm.

The old farm, Charity had gifted to Kit, a place for him to return to once the glitter and glare of London had dimmed and he wanted to come home and write in peace and familiar surroundings. That she hoped he would soon return with a wife and settle down was obvious, but Kit was showing no signs of doing anything of the sort for a while yet.

The house they had built for themselves—for Dev had discovered that Charity had some strong ideas on the design—was exactly what they'd hoped it would be. Large and elegant and spacious, it was still warm and cosy and a family home where everyone was assured of a whole-hearted welcome. They had many friends in the area, local farmers and landowners delighted to discover that the viscount did not stand on ceremony. If they now thought the rumours of his dissipation and cruelty had been falsely reported, Dev did nothing to correct their assumptions. That part of his life was over, but remained something he would always feel a flush of shame for.

They sat down to dinner in the kitchen today, at Dev's request, and if the new staff required for a large house thought it odd that the viscount and his wife dined with Mr and Mrs Baxter in such a fashion, then so be it.

The table groaned under the weight of a huge chicken and ham pie, a massive gammon bejewelled with cloves, and a platter laden with cold sliced meat. Jars of Mrs Baxter's chutneys and pickled onions jostled for space with buttered new potatoes adorned with sprigs of mint, and bright bowls of fresh green peas and sliced beans.

Dev's stomach growled in anticipation. Of all the dinners Mrs Baxter served up, this was his favourite. That he had spent the afternoon with her shelling peas and gossiping about the latest *on-dits* from London was quite true, but something he would deny fervently to anyone who asked. Not that it mattered. He had already gained a reputation as something of an eccentric and found that much about him hadn't changed. He still didn't care a fig what anyone thought.

"What's all this about you and a Mrs Dashton?"

Kit choked on his ale at this rather blunt enquiry from Mrs Baxter. At least she'd waited, sending John and Jane for the apple pie and cream before asking him.

Kit sent him an appealing, somewhat panicked look, to which Dev just shrugged. He knew Mrs Dashton, or *Dasher,* as she was known in certain circles. A beautiful Cytherean, she courted scandal and adored beautiful young men. Kit would have been just the fellow to catch her eye. There was a story making the rounds that someone had discovered Kit with her in the Duke of Ware's garden at a party, and in a rather compromising position.

"She sounds no better than she ought to be, you ask me," Batty grumbled, folding her arms over her capacious bosom and narrowing her eyes at Kit, who blushed, much to his twin's amusement. "Not the sort of woman you ought to be associating with. Still, said my piece now," she muttered, thinning her lips with disapproval. "So, I'll say no more."

"Thank God for that," Kit muttered, just loud enough for Dev to hear as Charity smothered her laughter. Mrs Baxter got up and bustled about, serving the apple pie with a healthy dollop of clotted cream.

To everyone's astonishment Charity refused her share and struggled to stand up. "I'm sorry," she said, eyeing the dessert with obvious regret. "I'm feeling rather out of sorts. Would you excuse me? I think I'd like a lie down."

Dev leapt to his feet, putting his arm about her. "Is anything wrong?" he asked, fear licking down his spine. The only thing that spoilt his peace of mind of late was anxiety for her, and fear for their child. He knew as well as anyone how dangerous childbirth was, and the terror of losing either of them had given him many sleepless nights of late.

"I'm fine," she said, patting his hand in an indulgent manner. "Just a little tired." She kissed his cheek and then leaned down to embrace Kit. "I can't tell you how glad I am to have you home, Kit. I missed you."

Kit hugged her and kissed her cheek in return. "And I you. Now run along and look after yourself and my niece or nephew. I'm not going anywhere."

"I'll come with you," Dev said, moving to escort her upstairs.

"No!" Charity laughed, shaking her head. "Finish your pudding. I'm quite well and am just going for a nap. I'll see you all later." Dev hesitated, still unsure as she rolled her eyes at him. "Sit down," she commanded, though her eyes were full of gratitude for his concern.

Dev did as she told him, knowing better than to argue at the moment. He sat scowling at his dessert bowl until Mrs Baxter moved around the table to lay a hand on his arm.

Charity and the Devil

"She's fine. Stop fretting. Her time's close is all. Reckon you'll have a son or daughter in your arms before the weekend."

Dev gaped at her and went to get to his feet and rush after his wife, but Mrs Baxter pushed him back down. "Stay!" she instructed. "You've been told once. Let her have her nap in peace. She'll shout if she needs us."

"Saw two magpies this morning," said Mr Baxter, his voice rolling over the table like a prophecy as Dev and Kit held their breath. "Saw three this afternoon too." He took a deep a sip of ale before sitting back in his chair with a smile. "One for sorrow, *two* for joy... three for a girl."

Both men let out a breath and Kit smacked him on the back, grinning now. "Like a little wager on it. Five guineas it's a girl."

Dev tutted at him and shook his head. "Not likely," he said, nodding at Mr Baxter. "You've got inside information. What do you take me for?"

The rest of the meal passed with good company and conversation, and all the while an air of expectation hung over the house.

***

Lucinda Felicity Linton was born two days later.

Charity sighed, exhausted but elated as Dev gazed down at his daughter. He was enchanted, and as the baby wrapped her tiny hand about his finger, he knew Lucy could reverse the situation in no time at all. She would wrap her devoted papa about her own little finger before she could talk, and he wouldn't even put up a fight.

A quiet knock on the door had them both looking up as Charity called for whoever it was to come in.

Kit stood there, smiling, Jane clutching at his hand while John dithered behind him, trying not to look too eager to see his niece.

Dev smiled as eager faces crowded around him to see the new arrival.

"Give me a cuddle then," Kit said, holding out his arms. Dev scowled a little, not quite ready to give her over yet, but her uncle looked so delighted to greet her he could hardly refuse.

"She's beautiful, Charity," Kit said, glancing over at her with such pleasure in his eyes he saw Charity sigh. She was certain that Kit would be a wonderful father if only he'd stop burning the candle at both ends as he appeared to be doing. Dev knew she wanted him to talk to Kit, to stop him raising hell and advise him to settle down before his health gave out. Dev had to admit, her brother looked pale and tired to his eye and he knew how Charity worried for him.

Kit took the babe to the window his voice low as he spoke. "A thing of beauty is a joy for ever. Its loveliness increases. It will never pass into nothingness, but still will keep a bower quiet for us, and a sleep full of sweet dreams, and health, and quiet breathing."

"Oh, Kit," Charity exclaimed, blinking back tears. "That's so beautiful. Did you write it?"

"No," Kit replied with chagrin as he gazed upon his niece. "Sadly not. A rival of mine. Terribly gauche to recite one's own work at such a moment, but still. I *will* have to write something now, just for Lucinda. Something exquisite to remind her that her old uncle was terribly proud of her long after he's gone."

"Oh, Kit, don't speak so," Charity replied, cross with him now as she snatched up a hanky and blew her nose.

"What?" Kit demanded, looking up. "Oh, Charity," he exclaimed, laughing at her. "I don't mean to turn up my toes just yet. I mean when she's grown up with children of her own."

"Hmph," she said, still glowering a little but mollified for now.

Charity and the Devil

Kit moved back to Dev and gave Lucy back to him. "Congratulations," he said, his voice quiet, and for a moment Dev thought he saw longing in his eyes.

Dev carried the baby back to the bed and sat down beside Charity, placing Lucy in her arms with care, and then putting his arm around his wife and holding her tight. Jane clambered onto the bed and snuggled up to Charity on her other side. John sat close too, leaning over to stroke the downy hair on his niece's head.

All at once Dev felt his eyes burn as happiness overwhelmed him. This was his family, his to care for and protect, and he would do it. They would none of them ever have anything to worry for or cry over if he could help it. Dev glanced up at Kit, standing at the end of the bed, too pale and slender for his own good. He would talk to him as Charity had asked him to, and he would ensure that Kit took heed of his words too. Dev knew what it was to waste the life you were given, to throw away the gifts that loving and belonging to a family could bring you. Kit would know it too. If not for his own sake, then for Charity's.

Little Jane sighed, beaming up at him and reaching over to grasp his hand.

"I'm so happy I feel like I could burst," she exclaimed, grinning at him.

John snorted, his tone dry as he retorted as only an older brother can. "I think you'll find that's your third helping of lemon meringue pie speaking."

The room erupted into laughter and Dev could only echo her sentiment, and he was sure that in his case, it certainly wasn't the pie.

For a look at the next instalment in the Rogues and Gentlemen series out October 19, 2018 – keep reading.

A Slight Indiscretion

Rogues & Gentlemen Book 12

When his older brother and father die in quick succession, Fitzwilliam 'Will' Lancaster finds himself Marquess of Henshaw. It is a role he has secretly coveted and spent his entire life preparing for. Unlike his predecessors, he has determined that his name be one worthy of respect, one with no shameful shadow, not even the faintest hint of anything scandalous.

And then Miss Selina Darling crashes into his life.

Miss Darling mixes in artistic circles, her friends are poets and painters and writers, and glamorous characters who are not entirely respectable. Miss Darling also has the unfortunate habit of saying exactly what she thinks, without thinking about what she's saying. The only man in her life who adores her without reservation is her scandalous father, Mr 'Bertie' Darling, beloved of opera singers and pretty bits of muslin throughout London.

When the Marquess does the gentlemanly thing and rescues Selina from a tricky situation, things go quickly awry. The only way to avoid being the scandal of the century is to marry the wretched creature though it's the last thing he wants. Before he knows what's hit him, Will discovers himself married to a girl without an ounce of propriety and a penchant for embarrassing him in public with her dreadful friend.

Try as she might, Selina cannot stay out of trouble nor find any way of pleasing her dour and determined, joyless husband. Yet she's sure there is another man hiding beneath his impeccably tailored clothes, just itching to get out … if only she could reach him.

Chapter 1

"Wherein we meet the players, each of whom dream of entirely different characters."

It was March, and a cold damp night pressed against the windows of the handsome house on Cheyne Walk. At four am it might have been supposed that every soul in Chelsea was asleep, quiet as it was. Yet at number sixteen, some hardy creatures were awake still, despite a convivial evening of society, wine, music and lively discussion. In secluded corners sleepier and more philosophical conversations still drifted, but even here the sound of soft breathing, and the occasional snore was all that disturbed the darkness.

Miss Selina Darling, whose father owned number sixteen, looked around the place with a sigh. It had been a wonderful party. The ever-popular Bertie Darling's parties generally were, but this one had been especially entertaining. Clearing up afterwards was not so much fun but then you couldn't have one without the other.

With a fond smile she looked down at the twin sofas in their elegant sitting room. On one side Kit Kendall sprawled. He was an emerging poet of increasing renown though he looked rakish and rather dissolute from this angle. His eyes were closed, and Selina admired the sweep of long dark eyelashes against his pale skin. A beautiful man by anyone's standards. Beside him, the painter, Jack Mills snored, his head pillowed on his arms. He'd spent most of the evening arguing with Kit about the true nature of art and trying to persuade the man to sit for him.

On the opposite sofa three more artists. Rupert Drake was catching flies, his head in his sister Lizzie's lap. She made a lovely picture in repose, her dark hair spilling out over the blue velvet of

A Slight Indiscretion

the settee. Beside her, and bearing Rupert's feet in his lap, Erasmus Ponsonby was one of the few still awake, his nose buried in a book. A big blond chap of perhaps thirty-five with the ruddy complexion of a man who enjoyed being out of doors, he was a handsome, friendly giant. He glanced up and gave Selina a weary smile.

"Fabulous party, darling," he said, setting down his book and stretching out his long limbs. Erasmus was a large man and Selina suppressed her anxiety at seeing him and the Drake siblings on the elegant settee. The slender legs of the piece seemed unlikely to support Erasmus's bulk. "Did your father enjoy it?"

Selina gave a snort. "He disappeared around midnight, so I think we can assume so," she replied, her tone dry. She bent and picked up a rather lovely green satin slipper, looking around for its partner to no avail. Who had come wearing green? She couldn't remember now. So many glamourous ladies had passed through the house last night.

"Is Dasher still here?"

Selina reached for a candle and got to her knees, craning her neck to look under first one settee, then the other. "No," she said, her voice a little muffled. She sighed as no slipper revealed itself and sat upright. "She went an hour or so ago."

"And left Kit here?" Erasmus said, a considering tone to his voice.

She smiled at him and got to her feet. "That one will never go the way you want it to, Ras, darling. They like each other very much, but Kit is looking for his one true love, and I'm not sure Dolly will ever settle down forever. No matter how much you wish she would."

Erasmus sighed, and Selina cast him a look of sympathy. The fellow had a romantic heart and wanted to see everyone happily paired off. He never missed an opportunity to matchmake.

"And what of you, lovely Luna?" he asked, using her pet name. Her father also called her Luna, or moon, as that was the meaning of her name. "No handsome prince to sweep you off your feet tonight?"

"Alas, no," she replied, shaking her head as she got to her feet. "I fear my requirements are too numerous and complex to be met. I am resigned to be a scandalous lady with a string of handsome young lovers to my name. It seems to suit Mrs Dashton well enough." She said the words lightly. Erasmus knew her well enough to know it was not what she truly wished for, though it seemed to be a fate that grew ever closer. Men were such a disappointment overall.

Erasmus sat forward, intrigued, and Selina cursed herself for saying anything. He was forever casting eligible men before her as it was. "What is it you want then?" he asked. "How does this paragon of masculinity present himself?"

She snorted and went to sit on the arm of the settee beside him before thinking better of it. Instead she bent and pushed a dozen empty wine glasses to one side of the coffee table and perched on that instead. "Let me see," she said, ticking each item off on her fingers. If Erasmus was going to play matchmaker – and there was certainly no stopping him - he may as well have something to go on. "He would need to be open minded and not in any way impede my freedom. I couldn't bear to marry a man who would forever dictate who I would see and where I could go."

"Naturally," Erasmus replied, sitting back in his seat and nodding. "So perhaps a creative sort who would encourage your love of the arts."

"Perhaps," she said, considering the idea with a frown. "I don't care if he has a fortune or not, though being penniless does not appeal, yet he must also be solid and dependable. No feckless painter or poet, no matter how romantic. I have no taste for starving in a gloomy garret. No offense."

"None taken," Erasmus said, his voice grave, though his lips twitched just a little.

Selina nodded and carried on with her list. "I want someone who will also be a friend and companion, not just a lover. Not someone who will spend all our money on paint and canvases without a thought for my feelings or lock himself away for months at a time while he communes with his muse. He must also be utterly faithful," she added, her voice stern as Erasmus's thick blonde eyebrows drew together. "That one is *not* negotiable."

"Quite right, darling."

"I want someone who is strong yet can be soft. Intelligent and sure of himself, with a romantic streak of course. A man who can bend and adapt and enjoy the unexpected but who will always be there when I need him. He must love art and poetry and reading and having fun, oh and be a good father to our children. The type of man who would get down on the floor and play with them without fearing he looked foolish."

"A paragon indeed," Erasmus said, his tone considering.

Selina let out a sigh. "I know it," she replied. "I'm not six and twenty years and still unmarried for no reason, you know." She cast him a wry smile and he held out his hand to her. Selina held her own out and he pressed a soft kiss to her fingers. "I will think on it, lovely Luna. He must exist somewhere. I will not rest until you are happy. To love and be loved is the only goal in life to my mind."

"Big softy," she said, affection for the big man in her words.

He didn't deny it and just squeezed her fingers. "Go to bed, sweet. Forget tidying now. The mess will be here in the morning still."

"That's what I'm afraid of." Selina gave him a rueful smile and he laughed, a good, rich sound that made her smile widen further.

"I'll help you, and Lizzie and Rupert will too. We'll aide you in casting these good-for-nothing creatures out into the cruel morning, I promise."

"And who will cast you out?" she asked, raising her eyebrows at him, an amused tone to her voice.

"Oh," Erasmus replied, pressing a theatrical hand to his chest as though he'd been struck by an arrow. "That hurt, darling."

"Absurd creature," she said, laughing at his dramatics. "Very well, I shall go to bed. Though I have no idea who or what may lurk in the house now. There seem to be bodies everywhere."

"Lock your door," Erasmus said, nodding. He wasn't joking this time and Selina bent to kiss his forehead.

"I will. Goodnight, Ras."

"Goodnight, darling girl. Sweet dreams."

***

Lord Fitzwilliam Lancaster, fifth Marquess of Henshaw, regarded himself in the looking glass with a critical air. It was not vanity that made him inspect his reflection, but rather a need to ensure that he'd done the best he could. His hair was dark and thick and neatly cut. No rakish Brutus style for the marquess. Simplicity, neatness, a lack of fuss and ornamentation, these were ideals for a man who disliked ostentation. Wearing a garish waistcoat or tying his cravat in some complex manner was anathema to Will who preferred to be discreet rather than noticed.

"That will be all, Button, thank you," he said, satisfied that he could make no improvements about his person.

"Very good, my lord."

Button bowed, a little stiffly, and left his master alone. Will suspected the damp air, after a night of heavy rain, was making the fellow's arthritis act up. Not that Button would admit he had arthritis. The cool, wet spring weather, combined with the dizzying number of steps at Castle Hadley in Dorset would be a challenge for a man far younger than he, however.

Will knew he ought to raise the matter of his retirement, but Button gave him a sense of security. The man had been his father's valet for many decades, and though only in Will's service for a matter of months, he seemed to know a great deal about the business of being a marquess and often soothed away Will's doubts with a quiet word of assurance. He always did it with such subtlety it never even sounded like advice. A valet would never dare give opinions to his master of course, yet Button did, in a roundabout way. Will was neither so high in the instep nor so dense that he couldn't see it for it was however, and he was grateful.

The past months had been filled with numerous highs and low, his emotions battered on all sides, leaving him feeling older, greyer and rather less confident than he'd been before.

It had begun with the unexpected death of his older brother Hugh, the Earl of Dreighton. That had been a terrible shock. Hugh was only forty-two, though his years of overindulging had left him fat and florid. Despite his doctor's advice to follow a lowering diet and to avoid over excitement, he had done nothing of the sort. He'd continued to eat and drink as if each meal was his last ... until it was.

His death had shocked Will deeply. Not that they had ever been friends. Hugh was an overbearing bully and had always been his father's son and heir, while he and his younger brother Ben were merely spares. While their sire indulged Hugh at every turn, he ignored them. Ben had distinguished himself by being as scandalous as possible. Before his recent marriage he'd been known as a womaniser and rakehell of the first order, therefore earning his father's pride as a man the old marquess would swear was a chip off the old block.

Will, instinctively feared notoriety. The thought of people talking about him for whatever reason was enough to make him break out in a sweat, a sick sensation roiling in his guts.

So Will had set about earning his father's respect by being the steady one and learning all he could about the running of the estates. His father and brothers may spend money like it was going out of fashion, but Will planned, and economised. He followed the rules of society, never deviating from those rules which made a gentleman, a gentleman. Yet all he had earned himself was a lack of interest from his father who thought him a dull dog, and contempt from his older brother. He and his youngest brother Ben had always rubbed along though he knew Ben thought him a prig all the same.

Perhaps he was right?

So, when Hugh died, for a few brief days, Will had been Earl of Dreighton. His father who had been bedridden for years followed him to the grave in short order, making Will, Marquess of Henshaw.

For as long as Will could remember he had coveted both titles. Unlike many who might admit the same, it was not to give him power or superiority, so he could lord it over those who were not his equal. He simply wanted to do the job as it ought to be done as he *knew* it must to be done. It was a job, in his mind, a responsibility that should be a burden.

It was a burden that both his father and elder brother had shirked their entire lives. Yet thousands of people relied upon the running of his many and vast estates, and he felt the weight of their lives in his hands. He would be everything that a man of his rank should be. Honesty and integrity would be the foundation upon which he built his legacy. There would be no opera singers, no dancing girls, no gambling, whoring, or dissipation. The family name would lose its notoriety, the scandalous stories that his siblings and sire had fed the gossip mills buried under the weight of his reputation as a man of moral strength and unimpeachable honour.

It was his destiny to restore the polish to a name too many years tarnished, and he would allow nothing to divert him.

***

It was mid-afternoon when Will's younger brother's carriage arrived at Castle Hadley. Lord Ben Lancaster jumped down from the carriage sending Will a grin before turning to help his wife down. Dinah was a glamourous creature, far too beautiful for any man's peace of mind to Will's way of thinking though he respected her. At first, it had horrified him to hear of Ben's marriage to a woman who had no family to speak of and was far from *good ton*.

His sensibilities had been further worked upon when his younger brother had become ever more notorious by setting up a gaming hall, of all things! The knowledge had caused Will many sleepless nights. It sat ill with his intentions for the future, but the deaths of his father and elder brother were still fresh in his mind. Ben's life was his own to live, he had decided after days of agonising soul searching, and as Will was genuinely fond of him, he knew cutting him from his life was something he could never do. Besides which part of being the honest and moral man he hoped to be he ought to lead by example rather than censure others for behaviour which he could not control.

Will greeted both with genuine pleasure. He'd not seen Ben since the funerals of Hugh and their father, and he looked forward to a more convivial time getting to know a man he'd seen little of in recent years.

"Dinah, you are looking radiant as ever," Will said, smiling. The words were not flattery either. His brother had confided that Dinah was with child, and the woman seemed to glow with it. That the two of them couldn't be happier was obvious and Will suppressed a surprising pang of jealousy. He had put in a deal of thought into finding himself a wife of late and seeing Ben and Dinah's obvious happiness only made him feel restless.

"Good to see you, Will," Ben said, shaking his hand with warmth. "I must I call you Henshaw now?"

Will snorted and rolled his eyes. "As if you would, even if I demanded it," he retorted as Ben slapped him on the back and laughed.

"Well, I know what a stickler you are for the rules, brother mine."

Ben winked, and Will shook his head. He wouldn't rise to Ben's baiting, he'd been looking forward to seeing him too much, besides, he was a big enough man not be slighted by his brother's teasing. An image of himself as the benevolent head of a large and happy family filled his mind for a moment and pleased him so much that he cast both Ben and his wife a warm smile.

"I'm so glad you both came. I want you to know you are always welcome here whenever you wish to come."

Ben paused and returned his smile with equal warmth. "Thank you, Will. That means a lot, to both of us."

Suffused with a sense of immense well-being, Will led them both into the huge and sprawling building that was Castle Hadley.

Want more Emma?

If you enjoyed this book, please support this indie author and take a moment to leave a few words in a review. *Thank you!*

To be kept informed of special offers and free deals (which I do regularly) follow me on *https://www.bookbub.com/authors/emma-v-leech*

To find out more and to get news and sneak peeks of the first chapter of upcoming works, go to my website and sign up for the newsletter.
http://www.emmavleech.com/

Come and join the fans in my Facebook group for news, info and exciting discussion...

Emmas Book Club

Or Follow me here......

http://viewauthor.at/EmmaVLeechAmazon
Facebook
Instagram
Emma's Twitter page
TikTok

About Me!

I started this incredible journey way back in 2010 with The Key to Erebus but didn't summon the courage to hit publish until October 2012. For anyone who's done it, you'll know publishing your first title is a terribly scary thing! I still get butterflies on the morning a new title releases, but the terror has subsided at least. Now I just live in dread of the day my daughters are old enough to read them.

The horror! (On both sides I suspect.)

2017 marked the year that I made my first foray into Historical Romance and the world of the Regency Romance, and my word what a year! I was delighted by the response to this series and can't wait to add more titles. Paranormal Romance readers need not despair however as there is much more to come there too. Writing has become an addiction and as soon as one book is over I'm hugely excited to start the next so you can expect plenty more in the future.

As many of my works reflect I am greatly influenced by the beautiful French countryside in which I live. I've been here in the

South West for the past twenty years though I was born and raised in England. My three gorgeous girls are all bilingual and the youngest who is only six, is showing signs of following in my footsteps after producing *The Lonely Princess* all by herself.

I'm told book two is coming soon ...

She's keeping me on my toes, so I'd better get cracking!

KEEP READING TO DISCOVER MY OTHER BOOKS!

Other Works by Emma V. Leech

(For those of you who have read The French Fae Legend series, please remember that chronologically The Heart of Arima precedes The Dark Prince)

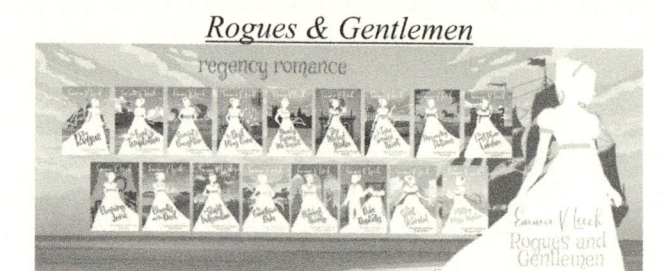

Rogues & Gentlemen

Rogues & Gentlemen Series

Girls Who Dare

Girls Who Dare Series

Daring Daughters

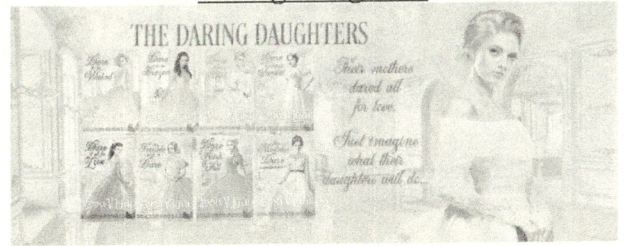

Daring Daughters Series

The Regency Romance Mysteries

The Regency Romance Mysteries Series

The French Vampire Legend

The French Vampire Legend Series

The French Fae Legend

The French Fae Legend Series

Stand Alone
The Book Lover (a paranormal novella)
The Girl is Not for Christmas (Regency Romance)

Audio Books

Don't have time to read but still need your romance fix? The wait is over…

By popular demand, get many of your favourite Emma V Leech Regency Romance books on audio as performed by the incomparable Philip Battley and Gerard Marzilli. Several titles available and more added each month!

Find them at your favourite audiobook retailer!

Girls Who Dare – The exciting new series from Emma V Leech, the multi-award-winning, Amazon Top 10 romance writer behind the Rogues & Gentlemen series.

Inside every wallflower is the beating heart of a lioness, a passionate individual willing to risk all for their dream, if only they can find the courage to begin. When these overlooked girls make a pact to change their lives, anything can happen.

Ten girls – Ten dares in a hat. Who will dare to risk it all?

To Dare a Duke

Girls Who Dare Book 1

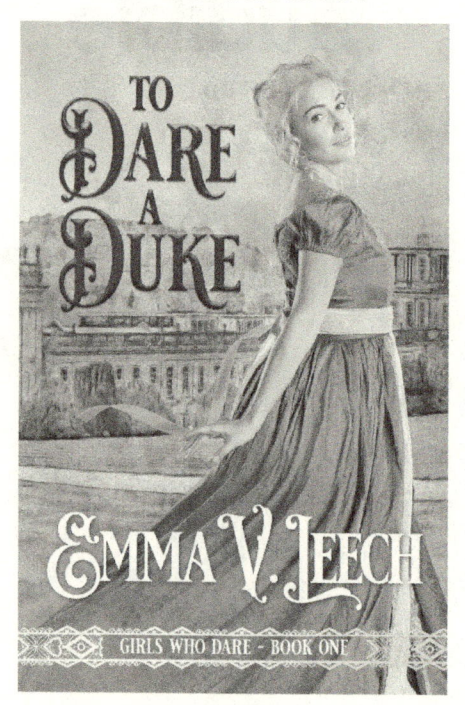

Dreams of true love and happy ever afters

Dreams of love are all well and good, but all Prunella Chuffington-Smythe wants is to publish her novel. Marriage at the price of her independence is something she will not consider. Having tasted success writing under a false name in The Lady's Weekly Review, her alter ego is attaining notoriety and fame and Prue rather likes it.

A Duty that must be endured

Robert Adolphus, The Duke of Bedwin, is in no hurry to marry, he's done it once and repeating that disaster is the last thing he desires. Yet, an heir is a necessary evil for a duke and one he cannot shirk. A dark reputation precedes him though, his first wife may have died young, but the scandals the beautiful, vivacious and spiteful creature supplied the ton have not. A wife must be found. A wife who is neither beautiful or vivacious but sweet and dull, and certain to stay out of trouble.

Dared to do something drastic

The sudden interest of a certain dastardly duke is as bewildering as it is unwelcome. She'll not throw her ambitions aside to marry a scoundrel just as her plans for self-sufficiency and freedom are coming to fruition. Surely showing the man she's not actually the meek little wallflower he is looking for should be enough to put paid to his intentions? When Prue is dared by her friends to do something drastic, it seems the perfect opportunity to kill two birds.

However, Prue cannot help being intrigued by the rogue who has inspired so many of her romances. Ordinarily, he plays the part of handsome rake, set on destroying her plucky heroine. But is he really the villain of the piece this time, or could he be the hero?

Finding out will be dangerous, but it just might inspire her greatest story yet.

[To Dare a Duke](#)

From the author of the bestselling Girls Who Dare Series – An exciting new series featuring the children of the Girls Who Dare...

The stories of the **Peculiar Ladies Book Club** and their hatful of dares has become legend among their children. When the hat is rediscovered, dusty and forlorn, the remaining dares spark a series of events that will echo through all the families... and their

Daring Daughters

Dare to be Wicked
Daring Daughters Book One

Two daring daughters ...

Lady Elizabeth and Lady Charlotte are the daughters of the Duke and Duchess of Bedwin. Raised by an unconventional mother and an indulgent, if overprotective father, they both strain against the rigid morality of the era.

The fashionable image of a meek, weak young lady, prone to swooning at the least provocation, is one that makes them seethe with frustration.

Their handsome childhood friend ...

Cassius Cadogen, Viscount Oakley, is the only child of the Earl and Countess St Clair. Beloved and indulged, he is popular, gloriously handsome, and a talented artist.

Returning from two years of study in France, his friendship with both sisters becomes strained as jealousy raises its head. A situation not helped by the two mysterious Frenchmen who have accompanied him home.

And simmering sibling rivalry ...

Passion, art, and secrets prove to be a combustible combination, and someone will undoubtedly get burned.

Order your copy here Dare to be Wicked

Interested in a Regency Romance with a twist?

Dying for a Duke

The Regency Romance Mysteries Book 1

Straight-laced, imperious and morally rigid, Benedict Rutland - the darkly handsome Earl of Rothay - gained his title too young. Responsible for a large family of younger siblings that his frivolous parents have brought to bankruptcy, his youth was spent clawing back the family fortunes.

Now a man in his prime and financially secure he is betrothed to a strict, sensible and cool-headed woman who will never upset the balance of his life or disturb his emotions ...

But then Miss Skeffington-Fox arrives.

Brought up solely by her rake of a stepfather, Benedict is scandalised by everything about the dashing Miss.

But as family members in line for the dukedom begin to die at an alarming rate, all fingers point at Benedict, and Miss Skeffington-Fox may be the only one who can save him.

FREE to read on Amazon Kindle Unlimited.. Dying for a Duke

Lose yourself in Emma's paranormal world with The French Vampire Legend series.

The Key to Erebus

The French Vampire Legend Book 1

The truth can kill you.

Taken away as a small child, from a life where vampires, the Fae, and other mythical creatures are real and treacherous, the beautiful young witch, Jéhenne Corbeaux is totally unprepared when she returns to rural France to live with her eccentric Grandmother.

Thrown headlong into a world she knows nothing about she seeks to learn the truth about herself, uncovering secrets more shocking than anything she could ever have imagined and finding that she is by no means powerless to protect the ones she loves.

Despite her Gran's dire warnings, she is inexorably drawn to the dark and terrifying figure of Corvus, an ancient vampire and master of the vast Albinus family.

Jéhenne is about to find her answers and discover that, not only is Corvus far more dangerous than she could ever imagine, but that he holds much more than the key to her heart ...

Now available at your favourite retailer

The Key to Erebus

Check out Emma's exciting fantasy series with hailed by Kirkus Reviews as "An enchanting fantasy with a likable heroine, romantic intrigue, and clever narrative flourishes."

The Dark Prince

The French Fae Legend Book 1

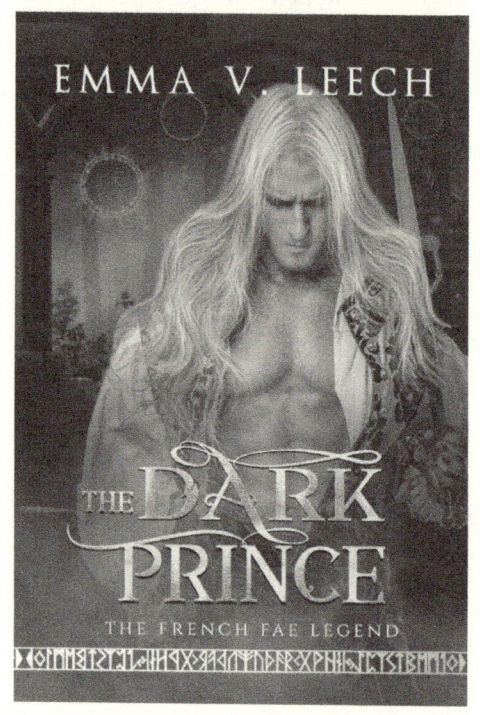

Two Fae Princes
One Human Woman
And a world ready to tear them all apart

Laen Braed is Prince of the Dark fae, with a temper and reputation to match his black eyes, and a heart that despises the human race. When he is sent back through the forbidden gates between realms to retrieve an ancient fae artifact, he returns home with far more than he bargained for.

Corin Albrecht, the most powerful Elven Prince ever born. His golden eyes are rumoured to be a gift from the gods, and destiny is calling him. With a love for the human world that runs deep, his friendship with Laen is being torn apart by his prejudices.

Océane DeBeauvoir is an artist and bookbinder who has always relied on her lively imagination to get her through an unhappy and uneventful life. A jewelled dagger put on display at a nearby museum hits the headlines with speculation of another race, the Fae. But the discovery also inspires Océane to create an extraordinary piece of art that cannot be confined to the pages of a book.

With two powerful men vying for her attention and their friendship stretched to the breaking point, the only question that remains...who is truly The Dark Prince.

The man of your dreams is coming...or is it your nightmares he visits? Find out in Book One of The French Fae Legend.

Available now at your favourite retailer

The Dark Prince

Acknowledgements

Thanks, of course, to my amazing editor.

To Victoria Cooper for all your hard work, amazing artwork and above all your unending patience!!! Thank you so much. You are amazing!

To my BFF, PA, personal cheerleader and bringer of chocolate, Varsi Appel, for moral support, confidence boosting and for reading my work more times than I have. I love you loads!

A huge thank you to all of Emma's Book Club members! You guys are the best!

I'm always so happy to hear from you so do email or message me :)

emmavleech@orange.fr

To my husband Pat and my family ... For always being proud of me.

Can't get your fill of Historical Romance? Do you crave stories with passion and red hot chemistry?

If the answer is yes, have I got the group for you!

Come join myself and other awesome authors in our Facebook group

Historical Harlots

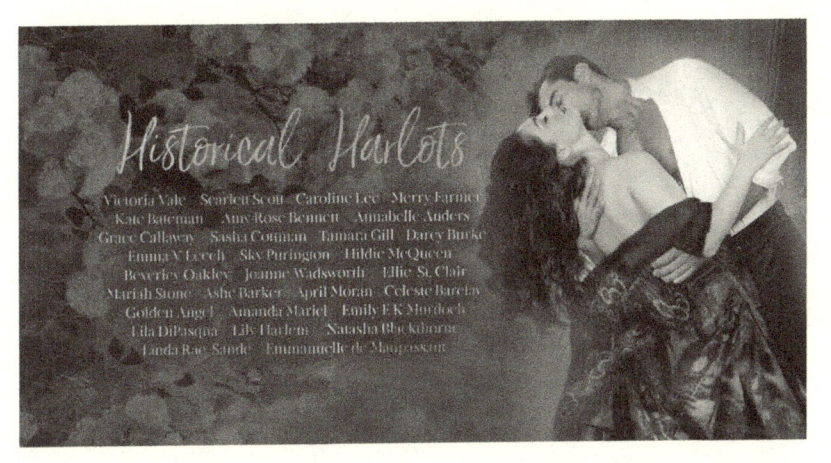

Be the first to know about exclusive giveaways, chat with amazing HistRom authors, lots of raunchy shenanigans and more!

Historical Harlots Facebook Group

Made in United States
Orlando, FL
26 December 2023